AND TROUBLES RISE

a love story

MORRISA TUCK

AND TROUBLES RISE

AND TROUBLES RISE

Copyright© 2021 Morrisa Tuck

Cover & Interior Design: Morrisa Tuck

ISBN-13: 9798529075135

All rights reserved.
No part of this book may be reproduced or transmitted in any form or by any means without express written permission from the author.
This is a work of fiction. Unless otherwise indicated, all the names, characters, businesses, places, events and incidents in this book are either the product of the author's imagination or used in a fictitious manner. Any resemblance to actual persons, living or dead, or actual events is purely coincidental.

{Works by Morrisa Tuck}

TIMES LIKE THESE-Now Available!

Rachel Parker's picture-perfect existence as the first lady of the most prominent African American Church in Oak City, AL is about to be turned upside down. A murdered pastor, his hidden lover, the family left behind and a struggle for power brings his wife, his church, and his community to their knees.

Available on Amazon, www.morrisatuckwrites.com,

For Heaven's Sake Christian Bookstore (Alexander City, AL), Central AL Libraries, Barnes and Noble (online), blackbookstore.com, and more!

PLAYING CHURCH-Coming early 2022!

Southern Missionary Baptist Church receives new Senior Pastor.

Saints and Aints may be difficult to discern.

Please handle with prayer.

***Sequel to TIMES LIKE THESE**

EVERY STORM-Coming 2022!

First Lady Donetta Houston has her priorities straight: God, then everything else. Battle weary from personal health struggles, familial heartbreak, and marital discord, she wears her faith like a badge of honor. But when everything she has worked so hard to achieve comes tumbling down around her, will Donetta cling to her hope in God, or will the storms of life carry her away?

AND TROUBLES RISE

ACKNOWLEDGMENTS

While I live will I praise the Lord. I will sing praises unto my God! None of this, not a single moment of my life, would be possible without God. He is my everything. I am eternally grateful to be called His own. The most important people in my world call me wife and mom. Just when I thought my heart couldn't get any bigger, God stretched it bit by bit for each one of you. To my husband, Jamison, you are my beloved. And I am yours. What a blessing to be able to continue to write our love story in each moment we spend together. Your love is a gift, and I am grateful.

To our young kings, Jared, Caiden, and Jordan, how I adore each one of you. How you fill our home and our hearts with love. I don't know what I could have done to deserve the joy and privilege of being your mother, but I am forever grateful that God blessed us with each of you. To my precious bonus babies, Javoskie, Jammie, Rhylinn, Jaxon, Jai'Ceon, and our sweet goddaughter, Ariah. You are all loved beyond measure! My life is better because God saw fit to make us a family.

My parents always make me feel loved. Mary Fernandez, you beautiful, resilient, anointed woman of God…I love you! Mr. Jimmy Lee, and Mrs. Elaine Tuck, I'm so blessed to be your number eight! Talk about examples of faith and strength for your children, the three of you are that much and more. Each of you is a treasured part of my life. Thank you!

It's always a blessing to have someone in your corner, no matter what. A cheerleader and encourager, a sister and friend, a brainstorming partner and a selfless, generous, beautiful person inside and out. Ashlea, I'm so grateful for our unbreakable bond. Your love and support is without measure. I hope you feel the same from me in return. Thank you.

Pastor Tiffany, you are an inspiration. Your honesty, integrity, your grace, your ability to say what I need to hear exactly when I need to hear it. I'm so thankful for your friendship, your wise counsel, your spiritual guidance, your prayers and unwavering support. So blessed to know you!

In addition to Ashlea and Pastor Tiffany, all of my beta readers and development support team are amazing! Theresa (Tee-forever my dear sister and friend), Joyce, Christale, Angela, and Courtney. You guys are fantastic! Because of each of you, Reese is everybody's favorite friend, church member, colleague, and sister. She's real because you guys are real, and the support each of you has provided is immeasurable. Reese and I appreciate each of you! Thank you!

My siblings are such cool people. Thanks for being supportive of me in so many ways. I'm grateful for you all! We are family, not only by blood, not just because of law, but most definitely because of love. My brothers: Tommy, Chris, Sean, Tyrone, Justin, and Darius. My sisters: Theresa, Ashlea, Melinda, Wendy, Kimberly, Christale, Tiffany, Lauran, and Brittany. Thank you all!

Pastor and Sister Powell, and the entire Elam #2 Church Family, thank you for continuing to pray for me and support my work. I can certainly hear your cheers and feel your prayers. I appreciate each and every single one of you.

Hailey and Rosanna, over the years you both have been such a positive representation of women in the media. I am honored that you shared part of your world with me to better craft Reese's world. For giving me the inside track on all things TV news, for sharing your experiences as women of color in this field, and for being so amazing, I'm sincerely thankful. We Stan! Shine on!

I am so very grateful for everyone who has supported my journey as an author. Some of you invested in my first novel, and here you are, ready to support my work once again. Thank you!

Our character naming contest winner was none other than a cherished friend and mentor, Patricia (Peggy Sue). Thank you for supporting me! It is an honor to name Reese's mother, Mrs. Martha Louise Joseph, after your own mother. Mrs. Martha Louise was a beautiful woman and treasured matriarch of your family. I hope Reese's mother does her memory proud.

Readers, never give up on your dreams. God's will for your life will come to fruition in His time. The setbacks, the disappointments, the mistakes, they help you appreciate the triumphs, the victories, the impossible made possible in Him. Be grateful for the sunshine as well as the rain. Becoming an author has been a dream realized, a dream planted in my heart many years ago. God's not done with me yet, and please believe, He has much more ahead for you, too! Press on!

I've been asked about the inspiration behind AND TROUBLES RISE, and I have to say that this work is simply a tribute to my fellow Proverbs 31 women, my sisters just trying to be the best they can be each day. This one is for the phenomenal women in my life. The strong women. The fierce and fabulous women. The intelligent and the wise women. The married women. The single women. The surviving women. My mother. My mother-in-love. My sisters. My godmother. My aunts. My bonus babies. My beautiful and precious goddaughter. My sweet nieces. My cousins. My friends. My church members. My neighbors. My mentors. My colleagues. The wonderful women God has peppered my life with through the years. May we all see ourselves the way He sees us.

We are beautiful. We are treasured. We are His. We are enough. We are loved.

Always, Morrisa

AND TROUBLES RISE

CHAPTER ONE
Living Single

I'll keep this one short and sweet. I've finally figured out the reason why we call them "blind dates"...because no one can really see the point of them!

Until Next Time-Candy Girl

Saved. Single. Suffering. Officially I'm just two for three, but my friends and family would have you believe that at my age, and without a husband, I must be all three. But I beg to differ. I lead a pretty fulfilled existence: strong faith in God, two loving parents, a knuckleheaded older brother and beloved niece, a thriving career in journalism and two of the best friends a girl could ask for. The way I see it, my life is too full to be worried about adding a man to the mix. And at thirty-two, I'm sick of folks praying for "my change to come". Shoot, if the Lord wants me to have a husband, he'll send one my way. Not because one of my best friends directs him to me.

I know what I bring to the table, so honestly I don't mind eating alone. And yet I find myself in this same predicament once again. I'm not entirely opposed to love, I guess. Just a firm believer that what is meant to be will be. My current situation is a struggle to focus on what my date is saying, and I know I'm fighting a losing battle against boredom and indifference. Typical blind date for me. Maybe Ebony and Tameka will finally give it a rest one day. Hope springs eternal. I am a grown woman, and I take full responsibility for my decisions. When Ebony offered to set me up on yet another blind date, I could have said no. I should have said no. But I said yes. So here we are. At least my shoes are cute…comfortable, too. All the better to make a quick exit with, if need be.

"So Reese, Ebony tells me you're a big sports fan. I for one love the Los Angeles Lakers. And of course anywhere Tom Brady plays. He's the GOAT, amirite or amirite?" My date bellows, his large teeth also resembling a certain farm animal. I smile politely in return. He's a little loud, this one. And more than a little obnoxious, to boot. Focus, Reese. Give the brother a chance. After countless blind dates, my personal pep talk has lost most of its pep, but it's not his fault.

"Last year I was in LA on business and had a chance to catch my boys in the Staples Center. I was so close I could reach out and high-five LeBron if I wanted to. Good times, man, those were some good times. Great game, too." I'm waiting for a volley that I can return, but this one-sided conversation doesn't exactly lend itself to give and take.

"What type of business were you in LA for?" I ask, preparing to enjoy another mouthful of my eggplant parmesan. At least the food is good, but it always is at Angelo's Little Italy. I figure this question should buy me a few more bites, at least.

"An insurance convention. I thought I told you I was in the insurance business. Dang, girl, keep up. Ebony said you were sharp." He ribs, but the joke falls flat. Clearly this one doesn't realize that we haven't reached that level of comfort yet. Not in the first hour of the first date, at least. He won't make it to a second.

"No harm meant, Reese. Loosen up, we're supposed to be having a good time." I guess the look on my face is unmistakable. I've never been good at hiding my emotions. At least not without a camera around.

"If you'll excuse me for a moment, I just need to use the restroom."

"Of course, no problem." He says, but I'm already out of my seat. The bum doesn't even rise with me, instead turning his attention back to his spaghetti Bolognese. I walk past him, down the short path to the restrooms. Lost in thought, I don't even notice the sharply dressed man walking in the opposite direction until it's too late. I stumble towards him before he has a chance to see what's coming.

"I'm so sorry!" I say, feeling the heat in my cheeks rising as I untangle myself from him.

"No problem. My pleasure running into you." He smiles back, clearly unbothered by my clumsiness. I get a better look at him now, and my, oh my this man is fine. If I wasn't already on a date I would strike up a conversation with him. But that would be in poor taste. So for a split second I consider just flirting for a moment before walking to the restroom.

"Maybe we should run into each other again, under different circumstances?" He beams again, flashing two rows of camera-ready, pearly whites. His eyes are bright and inviting. His dimples spell trouble. Have mercy, Lord.

"I think I'd like that." I stammer, suddenly shier than expected. I tug at the hem of my blouse, getting readjusted. An unintentional tapping of my left foot starts up, and I'm feeling a twittering of butterflies from somewhere deep within. And then the inevitable happens.

"Davis, over here." A woman's voice calls out, and we both look over at the same time. A tall, attractive woman is motioning in our direction. Davis must be her man, or her date at the very least. Figures. He holds a finger up, buying another moment. Then he looks at me again, and now his brows are furrowed with worry and regret.

"Hey, I'm sorry, I didn't even introduce myself. I'm…"

"Davis" I say flatly, finishing the thought for him.

"And you are?"

"Unavailable." I respond, already walking towards the bathroom. Ugh, why did I even get my hopes up? Who has time for a womanizer? Not me. And the audacity of trying to flirt while his lady is seats away. At least my date will be promptly deleted from my cell phone as soon as dinner is over. I drown out his voice, asking me to wait, and instead find refuge in the ladies room. After several minutes have passed, I make the decision to get back out there and finish the date, deliberately choosing an alternate route back to my table. I've got some choice words for Ebony, though. My nerves and frustrations are starting to get the best of me, and this feels like a wasted evening. I could've chilled at home and watched Bravo instead, because baby, this date most certainly does not deserve an encore. And just like Davis, and my farce of a companion for the evening, Ebony won't see what's coming, either.

My ice cubes are melting so very slowly. And the seat, the padded seat that seemed so comfortable when I first sat down is now beginning to bother my butt. The couple beside us has their hands intertwined across the table. They're feeding mouthfuls of pasta to one another and seem to be the picture of bliss. I look back over at my date and wonder if his face is fighting a losing battle with the tablecloth over the sauce smeared across his chin. It's hanging on, but not for long. How charming.

Despite being oblivious to generally accepted table etiquette, this man would be almost tolerable if he wasn't such a know-it-all. That trait is never attractive, even if a brother is smart. Leaping from subject to subject without considering if I'm even along for the ride, being more than a little rude towards our server, texting throughout our conversation, it's a wonder this gem hasn't been snatched up already. The cherry on top is how full of himself he is, or is trying his best to convince me he is. It's a struggle to even make it through the rest of the meal with this clown. My mind is elsewhere, nodding robotically on occasion, dare he attempt to check my pulse. Anywhere but here, Lord. Anywhere but here is my simple prayer.

"Chile, everybody needs somebody. If they say they don't they a fool and a liar". Words of wisdom from Ms. Bean, our neighborhood's answer to Yoda, play like a sad soundtrack to my perpetually condemned to singledom existence. Yet she's never given up hope that I will eventually settle down with the right man and make her proud. I guess graduating summa cum laude and landing a job straight out of college wasn't enough for her and my mom. I tend to give my family members (and Ms. Bean is practically family) the benefit of the doubt, rationalizing that they are either 1) old school in their way of thinking, 2) unhappily married themselves (and misery loves company), or 3) lacking some sort of personal fulfillment that causes them to become unnecessarily

invested in my own love life. Or maybe it's just some strange amalgamation of the three.

It feels like she is sitting on my shoulder, mocking me, daring me to accept his invitation for dessert and coffee. And lose another half hour of my life, time I'll never get back? No thank you Ms. Bean and random blind date brother… Clyde? Clint? Craig? Honestly I forgot by the time our server brought the appetizer. I don't want to be rude, but neither one of us is getting any younger here. Reclaiming my time.

"Thank you for the offer, but I have an early morning tomorrow. I should probably head home."

"Don't be like that Reese. I've heard this place has the best tiramisu in the tri-county area." His eyes and mouth plead with me to reconsider.

He's right, they do. But their amaretto cheesecake is better. Not about to tell him that, though.

"I'm not real big on sweets." Lord Jesus, this is a bold lie. Forgive me, Lord.

"C'mon now, girl. Don't be difficult. I'm trying to get to know you better. I'm a catch, okay? Whatever you think I make, add a couple more zeroes to it. You have full access to me tonight. Full. I've cleared my quite busy calendar to spend the evening with you. You should make the most of it. You should be grate…"

"What were you about to say? I should be what?"

"You should be grateful we're here together, that's what I was going to say."

Houston, we have a problem. Hard to please? Yes. Hard up? Never.

"You should be grateful that I'm too much of a lady to throw my lemonade at you. You should be grateful I've stayed as long as I have. You should be grateful that Ebony gave you my number, which you promptly need to lose. And you should be grateful my brother Thad isn't here to kick your trifling behind. I should be grateful, what the what? I should be grateful we drove separately, so you don't have to take me home. Believe me, I am beyond grateful for that. I should be grateful, the nerve of this fool. I should be grateful. I. Should. Be. Grateful. You should be grateful that I'm paying for my share of the meal." I say, already reaching in my purse and placing forty dollars on the table.

"You should be grateful I'm not going to report on this date, because frankly, there's nothing good about it to report. And you should be very grateful to be able to see me walk away, which is the best view you will have of the night."

I gently blot the corners of my mouth with the cloth napkin, folding it and carefully placing it on the table. He sits there, completely and utterly stunned, speechless for the first time this evening, as I find my purse strap and pull it over my shoulder, rising from my seat and dusting my skirt off. I should be grateful, he says. I consider pouring my water goblet on him, just for a moment, but I know better. Report the news, don't be the news, I hear my college mentor, Sherry Healey, say in my head. So I cross my arms, giving him the most piercing frown I can muster, and I leave. Relieved that my dignity is intact, I walk with my head held high, not looking back until I've reached the comfort of the supple leather driver's seat of my Toyota Avalon.

    I should be grateful that I won't settle for less.

CHAPTER TWO
Thanks for Playing

Matchmaker, matchmaker, make me a match...on second thought, Matchmaker, can you stay out of my business? Can you stay in your glass house, Matchmaker? Can you tend to your husband, or fiancé, or boyfriend, Matchmaker? Can the one God means for me find me, Matchmaker? You know what the hardest part is about your friends playing matchmaker? Meeting their gaze to tell them that it didn't work out. Because of course, it didn't work out. I'm not some algorithm that can be used to code the perfect guy (on second thought, that doesn't sound half bad). Suddenly I'm six years old in an intense game of Go Fish. The stakes couldn't be higher to find my match. But I'm over thirty now, so I don't have much use for playing games.

Always-Candy Girl

AND TROUBLES RISE

I should have known something was up when Ebony called me at work around 7:30 this morning to invite me to lunch. Not that we don't go to lunch together, we do at least once a week. The main differences are that Ebony knows she'll see me later at the station and more importantly, she knows I had just experienced another disaster date with her friend , the latest victim of "Find Reese a Husband", the horrible reality show my life has become.

None too eagerly, I agreed to meet her at Mimi's, a local bistro and bakery that has sandwiches to die for. I arrive before she does, which isn't a good sign. And I order the usual for both of us: an apple-pecan chicken salad on spinach for me, and a roasted vegetable hummus plate for her, with lemonades for us both. Mimi's has the best lemonade in the city. It's a routine that we repeat every Friday afternoon at noon, unless one of us has a lunch meeting and needs to cancel. I may be perpetually late, but it still gets on my nerves when others are to me. Do better, Reese. Be better.

Ebony saunters in around 12:15, breathless, as if she has literally run over to meet me. I'm at best a casual five minutes late, so today she is already beginning to test my patience, even though I figure she will be upset with me. I sit silently and sip my lemonade, tapping my foot, quietly pondering if she will get here before it is time for a refill. On cue, and as if she has heard my thoughts, Ebony walks straight up to me, hand on her hip, attitude front and center. "Girl, I can't believe you did my friend like that!" exclaims Ebony, clearly upset that her matchmaking skills have failed once again. Honey, I can't believe you did *me* like that! I thought *we* were friends?

Now what she is not going to do is act like *my* feelings don't matter in this situation. Nah, not when I'm the one actually meeting these rusty, dusty, and musty dudes my friends want to introduce me to. Do I compare them all to Phillip? Admittedly, yes. He wasn't perfect, but these guys still fall short. Do I even know what I'm looking for? The jury's still out on that, too. But I know exactly what I'm *not* looking for. If it's love, and if it's for me, it ought to be obvious. Not what my mother and father toiled through. Not what Tameka and Darryl are grasping for. If it isn't real, I don't have time for it. And I won't make time for it, either.

Narrowing my eyes, I cock my head to the side and glare at her before a single word finds its way out.

"Well hello to you, too Ebony! And how is your day today, may I ask? I'm doing fine, thank you for caring." I respond, my gaze meeting her own. Her eyes widen at first, then soften with compassion, but it's fleeting. In the next moment she's playing the victim again, doing that pouty face that drives me and Tameka up the wall.

"Don't be that way, Reesie. Why were you so mean to Clifton? He is a really great guy, anyone would be lucky to snag him" she says innocently, although her tone belies her words. I can't believe she isn't struck by lightning just for saying that bull. She knows as well as I know that the girl who "catches" him would promptly throw him back in the water. I won't let her off the hook, though.

"Whatever are you talking about, Ebony?" I say as sweetly as I can muster, even though I know exactly what she is talking about. She means well, she always does (at least I give her the benefit of the doubt and say that she does). But come on, get real, after another bad date I have had my fill of gator wearing, multiple baby mama having, toothless, jobless, classless fools that she thinks would make good husband material. As if she, having only recently gotten engaged herself, has become an expert on the subject.

Ebony is recently engaged to her dream guy, her "BAE", her "King", all of those ridiculous descriptors of the man she happens to be in a relationship with. Braxton seems to adore her, but I hate to admit that my dear friend is in love with the idea of being in love. She certainly won't admit it to herself. How else do you explain a grown woman changing her wardrobe, her diet, her hair color and even her church just to please a man who saw fit to put a ring on her finger? Nah, I don't think so. I love Ebony, but Braxton wants to run her life, and she's on board because it means she'll be a wife. I have no desire to lose myself like that.

"He said you said his eyes were too big? What's that about? You could at least be honest with me Reese", Ebony declares indignantly, her eyes as wide as Clifton's were last night. So she wants honesty, does she? Oh, I've got her honesty. I am sick and tired of her and her bootleg "good catches". She might not want to hear what is coming next, but I have to get it off my chest. It's been stewing for far too long.

"What do you want me to say, Ebony? How about his breath smelled like hot butt in the summer time? No, that was Derek…remember Derek? Derek whose baby mama stalked me on my job after one date with her man! Oh, I have more, you see, he expected me to pay for dinner *and* leave a tip because you said I had a good job and got *PAID*, no I'm sorry, that was Reginald, your friend from church, remember him? Let's see, he did compliment me, telling me that my rear end looked like two puppies fighting under a blanket, wait, that's right…that was your homeboy Tyrik from high school…I apologize, it must have been because he invited me to his Mama's house after dinner, because he had to have her car back so she could go to church, oh no, that was Curtis, your masseuse. The one who desperately wanted to lay hands on me. Cliff and I did not click, ok? The man was clearly not what I am looking for. He was at least five inches too short, at least 10 inches too wide, and his eyes nearly popped out of his head from across the room. Not just when he saw me, but across the dinner table and throughout the night. Freaked me out! Thanks, but no thanks, he's just not what I am looking for, ok?"

My question is much more of a definitive statement on my part. No desire to let Ebony set me up again. I don't care if he's Braxton's long lost twin brother, she can keep that mess to herself. I don't have the time or the patience to be bothered.

AND TROUBLES RISE

Ebony's dark eyes narrow into little slits as she quickly scans the room to see if any other patrons in the restaurant may have heard my little speech. She sighs heavily before opening her mouth. "Look, Reesie, you know I love you, but you aren't exactly the easiest person to fix up, you know what I mean. You come into a date expecting a man to fit your criteria of the perfect godly man. Before he even orders his meal you're over there making a list and checking it twice. Are you kidding me? Girl, you are 32, you're pretty but you are no Issa Rae, you're smart but you're no Mensa member. I know you're a local celebrity and all, but you are about to let another fine ship of a man pass you by. Like, buh-bye, do not pass go, do not collect $200."

I can't stand it when Ebony looks at me like that, lips tooted out, full on reality housewife style. And I could take the lips if it wasn't for the head roll that accompanied her little diatribe. She's going on and on, and I'm busy making mental notes about what portions of this convo I'll include in Candy Girl. Revelatory details hidden, of course. I'm nothing if not discreet about my blog. And Lord knows my friends and foes give me plenty of material to work with.

"I think you are a great person, Reesie-pooh, but I already have a man, and I don't get down like that. Have you heard the phrase 'Beggars can't be choosers'? That's you baby girl. A beggar, who is almost 33, never had a boyfriend for longer than six months, because married ones don't count, cold and lonely, bout to die from electric shock if the closest thing she's ever had to a man happens to short out during use because it's been overworked for the last 10 years. Ok? Shoot, it's not exactly like men are falling out of the sky for you", Ebony deadpans with little inflection, as if her normal tone would make the words less hurtful. Her brutal honesty cuts deep, though. Begging who? I am not the one.

    Still, it's hard to swallow the lump in my throat as I glance away, somewhat surprised by her harshness. A part of her is right, perhaps. What most people consider to be "quality" options are dwindling daily. My mother wants me to settle down with someone from my church, maybe an unmarried deacon that is in need of a churchgoing wife. In her opinion deacons, associate ministers and pastors fit the bill of what she wants in a son-in-law. Support personnel are too far down the totem pole for her. And he better not have a church at all. Goodness me, Mama wouldn't miss an opportunity to witness, but he better not ask for her baby girl's number.

    Deacon Hawkins, who just so happens to be 50, balding, and has a perverse affinity for day-glow suits, is a member of my church that Mama actually approves of. He *has* been eyeing me for the last few months, but he tries to get with any sister at church, regardless of age, stated interest or disinterest, or otherwise. One afternoon I just happened to overhear him and a few other brothers as they discussed various women of the church.

    "You see, my philosophy is, why go to a steakhouse and be served one type of food when you can go to an all you can eat buffet and have your choice? I like all types myself, young uns', ones drawing they pensions, and all points in between. But my choice would be a special sister like that fine specimen over there", and he had the nerve to motion in my direction. I shuffled by as quickly as possible, lest one of the others add a nugget of wisdom to the discourse.

My issue is not having men fall from the sky; I have "men" coming up to me all of the time. At the gas station: "excuse me, Miss, you need someone to help fill your tank?"; at the post office: let's just say I thank God every day for self-adhesive stamps; and even at the grocery store: "Uh, Miss, can you help me pick a melon that's just the right size...both firm and juicy?" I could go on and on.

Seriously, I want the right kind of man to find me. I pray for divine intervention in my life every single day, trusting that God will order the steps of my life in His word. Keep me in your will, Lord. But I've come to learn that you can't find what you aren't looking for. It doesn't help that everybody and their Mama's cousin is praying that I will find a husband. They're the ones that are desperate. Me, not so much. I figure, if he's out there, he will be headed my way soon enough. I mean, my goodness, this is not the Victorian era, and I am only thirty flippin' two years old. Ok, so there aren't any actual prospects on the horizon. So what? Am I less of a person because I don't have someone to share my life with? If Jesus is all that I need, shouldn't my relationship with HIM be enough? Should I really have to settle for what's less than His best for me? I don't think so.

"Reesie? Reese? Snap out of it girl, what is wrong with you?" Ebony waves her hand in my face to get my attention. I hadn't even noticed that the server has brought our food over.

"Reese, don't look so sad. It's not so bleak, I mean, it's just that it really makes me look bad when I try to find someone for you and then you feel like they aren't good enough for you. I'm your friend, girl. You know that. I want you to have someone to love. But when you decide someone isn't right for you, they come back to me and ask what went wrong. If I have one more brother tell me that you are too high-siditty, I don't know what I am going to do".

There she goes with the pout again. Always the victim, that Ebony. But not this time. She is not getting off just like that.

"Ebony, I have never asked you to set me up with anyone, not once, not ever", I reply evenly, although I feel my emotions boiling inside. "You have taken this on as your personal mission for my life, but you were never invited to do so." Her expression is a strange combination of surprise and mock horror. She has to know exactly where I am going with this.

"Wait, Reesie, don't be mad," she offers, knowing that I hate it when she calls me Reesie. Well, not really, it is my nick name but I hate her using it when she is getting on my nerves. "I really do want the best for you. And if it's more than you are willing to take on, just say no. I'd rather you say no than just go through the motions to please me. Don't do it if your heart isn't in it." She pauses here, and I consider what she says for just a moment.

"But girl, do you know how much fun it would be to help you plan your wedding?" I nod despite myself, betraying my own emotions once again. "Reesie, you are my girl…my very best friend from college…you're like a sister to me. I just want you to be as happy as I am. You above anyone else I know deserve it!"

The killing part is that on some level she is right. She does seem happier with Braxton than with any other guy she's ever been with. Every time I see them together I am reminded that I don't have my special someone. And it's not that I am jealous of who she has…I mean her guy is cute but not my type at all. More than anything, I am jealous of *what* she has: a committed relationship with the person she believes God designed just for her. I hate even thinking it out loud, because then it makes it sound like I am inadequate in some way. I know that I am not. I am intelligent, caring, beautiful from the inside out. More than anything, I am a Christian through and through. If that doesn't justify you, nothing will.

"E, I am not mad at you. I promise I am not". I can never stay mad at her for too long anyway. "Let's just promise one another to leave well enough alone, ok? I promise not to complain about blind dates anymore if you promise not to try and set me up, alright?"

Knowing that she has prevailed once again, Ebony triumphantly smiles at me. "I promise, Reesie,

I do! But, if you remember, there was Braxton's old friend that I wanted to introduce you to. Nothing fancy, but we wanted to ring in the new year together with a game night. It's been forever since we've hosted one. Anyway, I thought it would be a good time for the two of you to meet. Last time, I promise. Scout's honor". She says, hand raised in front of her like she was actually a Girl Scout. Ebony, who won't even climb the stairs at work when the elevator is down. And just like that, this girl has worked her magic on me yet again.

Ebony is not just a workplace confidant, she also happens to be my very best friend from college. Besides Tameka, she's one of my best friends in this world. I want to believe that she has my best interests at heart. So in spite of everything, I can't believe the words that are coming out of my mouth.

"That sounds like fun. What time should I be there and what should I bring?" Ebony is grinning like a Cheshire cat now. This diva knows that she has gotten over on me again.

"Girl, I thought you would never ask! Why don't you bring those lemon pepper wings you make, they are always slammin'!" They still don't know the wings I'm famous for are takeout from the local sports pub. And I'll never tell.

When it comes to others playing matchmaker with me, resistance is futile. Sometimes you have to just go with it.

CHAPTER THREE
Your Privilege is Showing

There are moments in time when it doesn't matter if you're the smartest person in the room. It doesn't matter if you're a subject matter expert, a proven authority, or have undergone months or years of education and training. None of it matters. Because in the skin I'm in, there will always be moments where no matter what you've done, and what you're capable of doing, you still happen to be black. In those moments, that's the only thing that matters. So here's to living and being unapologetically black. May the world never forget.

Always,

Candy Girl

It's the first Thursday of the month, so I find myself in my usual spot at lunch time today: the young professionals' board meeting for Build Them Up, a local non-profit that mentors area middle and high school students. Dylan Jacobs is our president; she's the public relations manager for Oak City's Chamber of Commerce and loves playing hostess in the Chamber's conference room each month. We're a fairly small board, just six of us in total, brought on for the express purpose of garnering support among other young professionals in the community. The agency's larger board is comprised of seasoned board members with varying wealth, expertise and connections. Most of them are in their sixties or so.

I breeze in the meeting, about five minutes later than usual, and Dylan's expression is tsk-tsking my audacity to show up a good fifteen minutes late for the meeting. Everyone else wears a smile, though, so I sit down at the table to try to join the discussion. Glancing down at the agenda, it seems they've already covered old business and are discussing the main item on the agenda today: The 10th anniversary celebration for BTU.

"Glad you could join us today, Reese." She says pointedly. "We were just discussing ideas for our upcoming fundraiser. I know it's a good nine months away, but I don't think we need to sit on this any longer. From a PR standpoint alone there is so much to do. This is the opportunity now to jump in if you have an idea." Dylan says, tilting her head to the side to indicate that she is open to listening to the group.

"I have an idea!" Megan Stewart, a junior associate at a law firm downtown, pipes up, holding her pen in the air as she does so. "What about a golf tournament? There are several great courses in the city to choose from, and it would be so simple to plan." Megan is downright mousy, sporting limp, dishwater tan hair and a perpetually wrinkled brow. She's only twenty-eight, but her manner of dress and could care less-demeanor make her seem far older.

"Thanks for that contribution, Megan. There are too many unknown variables at stake with a golf tournament. I for one don't think we should pin our hopes on an outdoor event, given our unexpected weather in the fall." Dylan says condescendingly. Megan nods and lowers her eyes. She's a sweetie, and hardly ever speaks up in our group, but Dylan's response probably killed her confidence just like that.

I usually try to give people the benefit of the doubt, you know, let them show me who they are instead of just telling me. Maya Angelou said that "When people show you who they are, believe them." And I'm a firm believer that Dylan is that mean girl who never outgrew her antics from high school. Working for the Chamber, she's extremely well connected and literally knows everyone in the city. She makes it her business to know everyone's business, too. I may have to love her with the love of Jesus, but I really. Don't. Like. This. Heifer.

"What about a progressive dinner at Bistro 334 and a few other hot spots downtown?" Suggests Will Bryant, an accountant in midtown. Will is a good guy, despite the fact that there were some not so great rumors out there about him and Dylan last year. Handsome, but in a goofy yet charming way, I can see how Dylan would be attracted to him. But despite Dylan's perfectly coiffed waves, her fashion forward style, her piercing green eyes and her lingerie model figure, I can't for the life of me understand how he would look past her personality flaws and date this woman.

Dylan smiles at Will just a little too sweetly to be convincing, then glides over to his chair and places a hand on his shoulder, still eyeing the rest of the group. She gives his shoulder a quick squeeze, but not quickly enough for me to miss it.

"Will, Will, Will. That's actually a great idea…so great that the foundation for the north side hospital hosted a fabulous one last year. It's a signature event for them now. I don't think copying them will set us apart, do you?" She asks rhetorically, and there are more robotic nods as the table again agrees with Dylan. I don't have to read the sweet tea leaves to see where this is headed.

"Dylan, pray tell, do *you* have a suggestion for a special event?" I ask on cue, having already prepared for her response.

Dylan lets out a little squeal and clasps her hands together in delight, having waited for precisely this moment to share her thoughts with the group. And by "her thoughts", I mean the idea that she wanted us to implement all along. Not exactly subtle, but definitely Dylan's style. Flashing neon lights are more subtle than this one.

"Oh my gosh, Reese Joseph, I am so glad you asked!" And she used my government name. Well now, let's see what she has cooked up.

"I've been really thinking on this one. What would be so fun, crowd appealing, generation spanning and has the potential to raise a ginormous amount of money for BTU?" She pauses for full effect, and a couple of board members actually lean forward in great anticipation. I sit there, wearing my best poker face, just waiting for the first shoe to drop.

"A celebrity-date auction. Attendees could bid on a night out with some very eligible bachelors and bachelorettes in the community. I even have a few people in mind to ask to participate." Dylan looks around the room for affirmation, and there are several expressions of interest. I'm cautious, though, not keen on any event that would involve people being auctioned off, if only for one night and most definitely a great cause. And honestly, I would still feel that way even if I wasn't the only person of color at the table. I'll be patient, though, and see where this is going.

"So, obviously it would take all hands on deck to pull off. But I'm picturing a raised dais for the participants to stand on, we could hire a professional auctioneer to present each person, or of course yours truly would be up for the task." Of course she would say that. "Each person would come out one at a time to stand on the dais. Maybe do a fun little twirl so that the crowd could see the goods." She giggles here and it is beyond inappropriate. I'm dismayed to see that the other board members seem intrigued by the possibility. My instinct tells me to speak now or forever hold my peace.

"Ummm, Dylan. Not quite sure an auction is the direction we need to go in…" I attempt to interject, but Dylan is more annoyed that I've interrupted her than the possibility of this being the wrong idea. She holds up a finger to stop me from speaking further. "Let me finish, Reese."

Oop, not a good move, Dylan. Not good at all. I exaggerate my hand motion, conceding the floor to her. But let her stop talking, I've got plenty to say.

"Ok then, as I was saying. We would need everyone to think about everyone you know that could be a great candidate for auction. Will, I know you were roommates with Orlando Peters in college. He's a pretty big get. I mean, if we could headline with a NBA player that would be amaze-balls!"

After pointing at Will, Dylan sets her sights on Carrie Thompson. Carrie's parents own several fine dining restaurants across central and north Alabama. "Carrie, I know you said your mom was great friends with Jamal Perkins. For those of you who don't know, Jamal is a two-star Michelin chef with this fantastic soul-food restaurant in Birmingham. His food is simply sublime. He is single…tall, dark, handsome. Perfect for an event like this." She smirks, and I'm remembering the recent feature on the Food Network about Jamal. He is one of a very small number of African American restauranteurs making a big splash in our state. He's going places, for sure. I'm disturbed by the trend that is emerging, but Dylan forges ahead, setting her sights on me next.

"So Reese, back to you. Would really love for you to take the lead on this next one. Cameron Pierce immediately came to mind, because he's amazing! And so debonair on camera! I think he would be a great addition to the lineup. And since you guys work for the same station and all, I think, I mean, it wouldn't be too much to ask for you to make the request of him. He's still single, right?" Dylan asks innocently, and I feel the knot forming from within. Cameron is our weekend anchor and my closest ally, other than Ebony, at work. She and Tameka have been trying to push us together for months, if not longer.

"Well, what do you guys think?" Dylan asks, self-satisfied with her skills. A smattering of applause breaks out across the table, but I sit there, shaking my head and stunned. The irony seems lost on the group, but I'm keenly aware that she has just offered up three African-American men to be auctioned off for a fundraising event. This is wrong on so many levels; I'm sickened by her ignorance.

"Don't you think it's inappropriate to auction off black men for an event?" I ask, and the eyes across the room widen as I hear an imaginary record scratch.

"Uh, what are you trying to say, Reese?" Dylan asks with total indignation. How dare I insult her privilege by asking such a question?

"Not sure if you noticed, Dylan, but every person you suggested is a prominent man of African-

American descent. Now imagine each of them standing on a dais, 'twirling their goods around' as they are being auctioned off to the public? What do you think about the optics of that?" I say, and Will's expression shows that the light bulb has finally gone on for him. Logan watches us intently, and both Megan and Carrie look everywhere except at me. Dylan, however, is still oblivious.

"I don't know why you are bringing race into this, Reese. They happen to be young, attractive, successful, well built, hard working, the list goes on. Race is not a factor here, and I'm offended that you are even trying to insinuate that it is." Dylan says, and her eyes reveal a mixture of shock and confusion.

"Who else made the cut, Dylan? Idris Elba? Michael B. Jordan?" I ask, giving her room to make a fool of herself.

"Don't be ridiculous, Reese. Idris Elba is off the market. Is Michael single now? Because if Michael is available, that's actually not a bad idea. Do you have a connection somehow?" She leans in, again oblivious to the irony of her response.

"Girl, if you don't stop while you're ahead… just, no. No. Not going to happen, not while I have any part of this committee. I doubt very seriously that the BTU board, or executive director, for that matter, would support such an event." I say, folding my arms across my chest. To my chagrin, Dylan is still unmoved.

"Reesie, Reesie, Reesie. Reesie Pooh, Reesie Cup. This is about making money for the kids of

BTU. I mean, the majority of the youth they serve are underserved minorities. Don't you think successful African-American men in this community would get behind this cause for the children?" Dylan asks innocently.

I consider my next words carefully. Though I want to unleash my best Angry Black Woman speech in her direction, I refrain from doing so. I can feel the eyes of the group on me. Megan and Carrie look tense, even fearful of what's to come. Will looks awkward, like he just wants us to move on without taking it further. Dylan is still wide-eyed and innocent, but at this point we all know it's just an act. The only person seemingly unaffected by the discussion is Logan Russell, an economic development manager in the Mayor's office. He's soaking it all in but remains silent. The last thing I need is to cause a scene for myself or the station. My peers have come to expect such stereotypical behavior from someone who looks like me. So this instead becomes a teachable moment.

"Dylan, I appreciate your enthusiasm for this cause, which is a great one. If we didn't share your passion for the young people in this community we wouldn't be sitting here." I say evenly. Glancing around, I notice several heads nodding. My gentle tone has caused shoulders to relax as well.

"But Dylan, a fundraising event with a great cause or not, that engages African-Americans in a way that is demeaning and exploitative is highly inappropriate. The mere thought of an auction evokes painful images of some of the ugliest moments in our nation's history. Imagine a male slave… someone's father, someone's husband, someone's brother, someone's son, on the auction block. His fate determined by his physical attributes, his broad shoulders, his bulging muscles, his inferred strength. He's sold for a fraction of his true worth. Because Dylan, a strong, intelligent, resilient black man is simply priceless. One can't place a price on his worth to his family or community. To his race. To humanity. So, no, we cannot move forward on planning an event like this. Even the idea of it is highly offensive." I say, grateful that the Lord held my tongue and gave me what I needed to say, not what I wanted to.

Dylan's eyes narrow momentarily, but her steely heart seems unmoved. Her fun has been spoiled, so she's more disappointed by that than anything else. She's pacing the room now…slowly, deliberately. She pauses behind Will again, this time giving his shoulder a little tap before she speaks.

"Reese, you articulated your argument very well, but please remember, this is a group effort. Guys, you all have a say here. If you disagree with Reese, this is the time and place to speak up now." She says, her mouth twisted into a terse grin. She's unprepared to go down without a fight.

An awkward quiet creeps over the room, and the only sounds you hear are people getting adjusted in their seats and shuffling the papers in front of them. I feel a sense of victory, thinking that surely no one will disagree with my impassioned plea, until Logan clears his throat. Not a peep the whole meeting, and now he has input? Here we go.

"Dylan, I'd like to give my opinion on the matter." Logan says, more gentlemanly than necessary, given our informal setting.

"By all means, Logan, please do. We are all ears!" Dylan says a little too enthusiastically. My balloon deflates a little, realizing that my words have meant nothing in this group.

"Reese is absolutely correct. There's simply not a way to frame this that keeps it from being offensive, which is the last thing we want for BTU or its standing in the community. While your intentions may be good, we need to be enlightened enough to realize that Reese offers a unique perspective on this subject. And she's right. We need to shelf this idea and consider a different special event for the anniversary celebration. We don't have a choice here." He says stoically.

And although I'm glad that Logan agrees with me, I can't even tell if it's because he also believes it is offensive or if he just thinks it will make BTU look bad.

"Logan, thanks for your input. Anyone else want to share an opinion on the matter?" Dylan asks, and there's total silence in response. She starts pacing the room again, gliding really, deliberately pausing to see who will dare speak up next. After several moments of silence it seems she has decided it's worth discussing another day.

"Well, then, in light of what Logan just shared, I think we should have a brainstorming session to come up with ideas." She whips out her phone to check her calendar. "Let's see, I have from 6:30-8:30 a.m. open on next Wednesday and Friday. We can meet at the Coffee Bean for an early morning meeting, get it knocked out right away. Please let me know what works best for you and I'll send a meeting invite out."

Everyone pulls their phones out, checking their calendars and personal availability. While everyone is looking, I take a moment to drink in the mood of the room. Because of what *Logan* shared, we can move the event in a different direction. The downside is we're back to square one and I have the pleasure of getting up at the butt crack of dawn to look at Dylan's pompous mug again.

Yeah, this is the kind of foolishness that I have the joy of putting up with on a daily basis.

CHAPTER FOUR
Déjà Vu

I have a problem saying no. I want to be the person that everyone can count on, I want to be the one that others turn to for encouragement and support. I can't solve the problems, but I know the One who can. And yes just sounds nicer on the ears, doesn't it? No is hard. No seems final. No brings disappointment. So I tend to say yes, and typically I'm the one who ends up disappointed. Maybe I'll start with a firm maybe instead.

Until next time,

Candy Girl

I have a bad feeling about tonight. It's the first Saturday night I haven't had to be the weekend anchor in quite a while, so I want to do my best to enjoy it. I've already taken much too long getting ready, but Ebony isn't expecting me to be on time, anyway. Well, I might have been more time conscious if Phillip hadn't started texting me this evening. It's irritating, but I feel like I need to at least be cordial and respond to his text messages. I try not to think about his wife when I do, though. But back to getting ready for the evening.

I want to make the effort to look my best, on the off chance that this guy is actually worth getting made up for. A lovely night awaits, with unseasonably mild temperatures expected for the evening, so I'm keeping it casual in my weekend uniform: skinny jeans, a stretchy t-shirt and a chic pair of ankle boots. I'll grab a jacket on the way out, too. My penchant for accessories, along with a fresh silk press that leaves my shoulder length hair bouncy and shiny, and artfully applied makeup that looks dewy and dazzling, while remaining natural, has me ready for my close up. It's the look for me.

After a short drive to her complex, I'm standing in front of Ebony's apartment, trying my best to figure out how to ring the doorbell without dropping the platter of lemon pepper wings I'm holding. God is merciful, and the door swings open before the welcome mat gets to sample the chicken I worked my tail off to find the time to pick up. I'm grateful and utterly shocked by the sight before me: a familiar face I can't quite place. He's a tall, broad shouldered man, sienna brown in tone, with deep brown eyes that have just a few flecks of gold. He smiles a welcoming smile and I notice two deep-set dimples framing full lips and a camera ready grin. I must be at the wrong door, I can't help but think to myself, until my thoughts are interrupted by the sound of Ebony's laughter traveling across the room.

Reverie broken, I'm suddenly sheepish as I realize that I just may have been staring. The handsome stranger is oblivious to my embarrassment, instead reaching to take the platter from my grateful arms.

"Here, let me get that for you. Come on in." He says, and dang it if his voice isn't pleasing to my ears, too. "So we do meet again. It's Davis." Ah, yes. Now I remember. So the friend of Braxton's that Ebony mentioned is the handsome fellow from the restaurant. Maybe it didn't work out with his date. Maybe. He's still as fine as I remember, but let's see what's behind the window dressing.

"Reese, there you are, girl! We were waiting on you to get started." Ebony says, rising from her seat to greet me. Tameka also stands up, leaving Braxton and Darryl on the couches.

"Now Ebony you know that Reese is going to be late to her own funeral, you already know."

"I know, Meka, that's why I told her six o'clock and six thirty to everyone else!" Ebony responds, and they both share a laugh at my expense.

I steal a glance at the clock on the wall and see that it's six thirty-five, so yeah, about right for me.

Still, I shoot them both a glance signaling they need to cut it out, knowing that Davis is nearby. He's oblivious to their banter, though, gingerly placing the tray of wings on the table. It's already spread with an array of tasty snacks: Tameka's famous spinach and artichoke dip, pita chips, bruschetta, a charcuterie board, fruit kabobs and a two-tiered tray of brownie and lemon bars, no doubt from our favorite midtown bakery.

"Enough, ladies. The fun has arrived so let's get this party started!" I say cheerfully, doing a little shimmy at the same time.

"Yes, yes! Chloe's babysitter can only stay until 9:00 tonight, so let's go. I hope you divas can stand a little competition." Tameka jokes, knowing that as the only mom in our group, a night out requires a little more planning than the rest of us.

"Gentlemen, the time has come." Ebony announces with a dramatic hand flourish. "Braxton, baby, will you bless the food so we can eat?" Ebony's voice is cloyingly sweet as she makes this request.

Braxton rises, his tall frame towering over the rest of the room. Braxton has been a councilman for District 3 for nearly two terms now. He's clean-cut, well educated, a sharp dresser and possesses the type of charm that appeals to constituents from all demographics. I find his personality to be a little too "shiny" to me, more gold-plated than twenty-four karat, but that's just me. Maybe it's because he's a politician, but I'm always a bit dubious of his sincerity. Ebony adores him, though, but I haven't quite figured out if it's him she's in love with, or just the idea of being his wife. That giant rock on her finger that she twirls around for anyone who'll notice certainly gives her a lot of reasons to think about.

"Most gracious and dear heavenly Father, we must begin our festivities by saying thank you. God we thank you for being a sovereign God. We are grateful for your most tender grace and mercy you have benevolently bestowed upon us on this occasion. And most high God, we must thank you for the fellowship of friends, loved ones, companions and new connections. God we gratefully acknowledge the blessing of the food that has been lovingly and painstakingly prepared and provided for us. May it richly nourish our bodies. May we cherish each morsel and savor each exquisite bite. And, God, dear God, Almighty God, Everlasting God, Holy God, I would be remiss if I didn't acknowledge my gratitude for the apple of my eye, my lovely and precious jewel, Ebony. Thank you for thinking enough of me to bless me with her.For these things and many more, we offer our humble thanks. It is in your most precious and divine son's Jesus name we do pray, amen." He prays, and I'm about to grab my purse, since church has been dismissed. I can barely suppress a grin as I notice that Darryl, whose hands were raised as if responding to the benediction, slowly lowers them as he looks around sheepishly at the rest of us.

"Are we done or is it time for announcements?" Darryl jokes, and we all laugh, saying amen in spite of the contrived prayer that Braxton offered before us, I mean, the Lord. Yeah, he's as slick as that Ultra Sheen our Mamas used to oil our scalps with when we were little. And if Davis, fine brother that he is, is friends with Braxton, that pretty much tells me everything I need to know about him, too.

The ladies start the line to get our food, while the guys linger behind as gentlemen. I offer a small smile to Davis as I walk past him, but he doesn't meet my gaze. Subconsciously, I wonder if my clothes are twisted or my hair is out of place. Surely he would have noticed me otherwise, I can't help but think. But I shrug it off as I see the mouth-watering snacks in front of me. I can worry about being cute some other time. I didn't have time for lunch today and I am starving.

Moments later, we're all seated around Ebony's living room, casually drifting from one subject to another, but not really discussing anything of importance. I jump in with quick responses here or there, but I'm trying my best not to dominate the conversation. Plus, the less I talk, the more I can eat. And as a reporter, I talk and ask questions for a living. Sometimes it's nice to just decompress and let others do the heavy lifting. To be honest, I'm already thinking about a nice glass of wine and my favorite fuzzy slippers that wait for me at home. But first, I have to get through this game night. I'm struggling to pay attention as fatigue from this week starts to set it. A warm baritone interrupts my thoughts, though, and I realize that Davis is speaking directly to me.

"And you, Reese? You're awfully quiet. I bet you've probably seen it all in your line of work. How do you feel about all of the protests going on?" He says, his eyes wide with interest. Looking up from fiddling with my goblet of water, I'm painfully aware that five sets of eyes are now staring at me. Dear God, why wasn't I doing more than feigning attention? I have no earthly idea about what protests he's even referencing. I take a quick sip of water before I formulate my response.

"Well, as you know, peacefully protesting is guaranteed in the constitution. So it's very important that citizens recognize their right to do so." I say, and I feel my cheeks turn hot as the words tumble from my mouth. Captain Obvious over here just added nothing of relevance to the discourse. The expression on his face is an odd mixture of disbelief and surprise. I think he was expecting more. I was expecting more, too.

"Reesie, girl, no need to be shy. You're among friends here. Of course we wouldn't dare share your feelings with the public. You have to overlook my girl, Davis. As station employees, we have to remain as neutral as possible when discussing current events. It just comes with the territory." Ebony offers, and Davis seems to buy this weak excuse, giving a small smile and nodding in response. Nonetheless, I'm grateful that Ebony has spoken up on my behalf. Appearing uninformed is never a good look, especially for someone like me.

"Hey, no worries at all. I get it. But in my opinion, not enough is being done by our state representatives. Braxton, man, I have to commend you for your part in the movement. I just wish Senator Stephens and Representative Johnson could get on board as well. They both talk a good game, but will they stand up on behalf of the children when push comes to shove?" I have to say I'm impressed by the level of passion and concern in his voice.

It finally dawns on me what he's been speaking about: the recent protests concerning the local school board's disproportionate punishment of African-American students. A local middle-school teacher is currently under investigation for slamming a male student on the floor of the classroom. Of course, several students recorded the incident and posted the video of it online. It even made national news. Unfortunately, it was just the latest incident in a long string of similar occurrences over the last few years. It's really struck a chord with so many people in our community, and given the tenuous relationship between law enforcement and others in our city, it has sparked a tremendous movement as a result.

"I can't speak for other teachers, but I'm in the classroom every single day. Now, obviously I'm with the lower elementary students, but some of those little rugrats really try my nerves, too. And don't get me started on the parents. One boy in my class has had disciplinary problems since school started. I contacted his mom to set up a parent-teacher conference, and she didn't even want to meet with me. She said it has to be my teaching ability, otherwise her child would pay attention and wouldn't cause distractions in the classroom. I mean, is she for real?" Tameka asks rhetorically, and I can't help but sympathize with her, at least to a degree. Tameka is a good teacher, but like so many, she is most definitely overworked and underpaid.

"I notice you didn't mention the boy's father. I'm guessing you reached out to him as well?" Davis asks, his deep brown eyes fixated on Tameka now. She is put off by his question, though, I see it in the curl of her lip in response.

"Listen, Davis, I know this is your first time hanging in our circle, but I've been teaching for over ten years. Of course I reached out to his father. It's not my fault that his daddy isn't involved in his life, either. He didn't give me the time of day. Not that I expected him to." She says, and I swear I hear a small gasp come from Ebony. Davis shakes his head, visibly disappointed by Tameka's offense.

"I meant no disrespect, Tameka. My mother is a retired educator who taught in the classroom for over twenty-five years. Believe me when I say I have the utmost respect for teachers. I simply asked about the child's father because I've found that, through personal experience and in conversation with friends and family members, people often overlook fathers and their roles in the academic success of their children. Again, no disrespect to you or your profession. I have great admiration for what educators like you must do each and every day." Davis says plainly, and I'm immediately in awe of his poise. Tameka's no pushover, and at times my dear friend takes a little too much pleasure in making the guys we know squirm just a bit. Davis is unruffled, though.

"Well, I can appreciate what you said, I just didn't want anyone thinking that I don't do my job. I do my job. I do right by these kids to the best of my ability." Tameka responds, crossing her arms and frowning.

"Aww, baby, it's alright. Give the man a break for asking a simple question. Shoot, woman, my food is getting cold. Now I'm gonna have to get a few more wings." Darryl says jokingly, rising from his seat and patting his stomach. He's good about breaking the tension when Tameka gets riled up. It's one of the things I actually like about their relationship.

Ebony, clearly annoyed by what has transpired, uses this moment to divert our attention. "Did you guys even get dessert? You know I got the dessert bars from Sugar & Spice." She says, motioning towards Braxton. He stands up and walks back over to the table, followed by Ebony. Darryl is still refilling his plate, and Tameka decides to join him. For a moment just Davis and I are left together. Our eyes meet, then we both look away quickly. When I glance back over I notice that he's watching me intently, but I don't mind a bit.

"Can I get you anything, Reese?" He asks, and I can't help the smile I feel creeping up at him.

"No, thank you. I appreciate it." I realize that I've asked nothing about him, satisfied with the view he's providing. Maybe it's better that way. I know that Ebony calls herself playing matchmaker tonight, but perhaps I'd rather just enjoy the evening without thoughts of becoming an old widow dancing through my head. Yeah, I'd rather just soak up the fine specimen of man that is Davis and not consider anything else. Much easier that way. But first things first, just so I can clear the air for my peace of mind.

"Are you still seeing the woman from Little Angelo's?" I ask, crossing my arms so he knows I mean business. He laughs in response and I'm left wondering what's so funny.

"I see her every time she's in town, since she lives in Nashville. You didn't really give me a chance to explain that I was there with *my little sister*, Daphne." He says, and I'm instantly regretful. Why do I always assume the worst?

"Oh, well, I didn't realize..."

"So, Ebony tells me that the two of you were college roommates? And the three of you ladies attend the same church?" He asks, unbothered by my assumption and rudeness that night.

"Um, yes. Ebony and I went to UGA together. Tameka and I are friends from high school. We're all members of New Beginnings...Pastor and Sister Bradford Houston's church. Well, we were. Ebony worships with Braxton now." And then, as an afterthought, I realize it would be rude not to ask something in return.

"Do you know the Houstons?" I ask, and his face instantly brightens.

"Yes, I know Pastor Houston. I'm a member of Third Day Missionary Baptist Church. Reverend Paul Dexter is my pastor." He beams. Oh yes, I know of both Pastor Dexter as well as Third Day. Our churches have fellowshipped many times over the years. His previous pastor, Reverend Allen Parker, was murdered along with his mistress nearly two years ago. At the time it was a major scandal for the church and community. But I doubt Davis wants to rehash that moment in history.

"And you and Braxton…have you been friends a long time?"

"Oh, yeah. That's my boy. We're more than friends. We're frat brothers, too. He's like my brother from another mother." He says, chuckling to himself. I don't find it funny, though. Braxton is not my favorite kind of black man. He's not my favorite kind of man, period. And this dude thinks he's like a brother to him? Mercy, Lord, I knew it would've been better if he had just kept quiet. About this time, the rest of our friends have made it back from getting refills.

"All right now, that's what I'm talking about. Are you two getting to know each other better?" Ebony nearly sings, a fake smile plastered on her face. She's basically bouncing with glee, or she would be, if she didn't have a plate in one hand and a wine glass in another. I hate to burst her bubble, but this ain't exactly Love Connection. Well, it could be, if it was an episode where the dream guy isn't what you thought he would be. Yeah, I guess it has more in common with Love Connection than I thought.

Davis rises from his seat before he says a word, but at least he's smiling.

"Heh, heh. Now that the line is clear, I think I will help myself to one or two of those delectable looking lemon squares. Reese, you care to join me?" He asks, extending his hand towards me. I don't really want to, but it has to beat Ebony's awkward inquisition. Reluctantly, I take his hand and stand up, but I release it as soon as I'm steady on my feet. I definitely don't want to give the wrong impression to him or the rest of the prying eyes that surround us.

"Don't mind if I do, thanks." I say nonchalantly, already walking towards the table. Davis follows close behind me. As soon as we reach the table, I find the tongs and grab both a lemon bar and a chocolate brownie. Finished, I hand them to Davis, but he doesn't take them from me. Not right away, at least. Instead, he smiles a sneaky smile and leans towards me and conspiratorially whispering, "I really just wanted the opportunity to speak with you alone again. I do want to get to know you better, Reese, but not necessarily under these circumstances." At least he's not excited about the prospect of Ebony serving as eager matchmaker, either. I take a bit of comfort in this, but yet say nothing.

"I don't know if you're a coffee person, or a morning person, or a lunch person, whatever. The time and location don't matter to me too much. I do want to share some one on one time with you soon, if it's convenient for you. How does that sound to you?" He asks, and at least he's not begging. That, in and of itself, is an improvement of some of my most recent encounters with men. So, in spite of my misgivings, I find myself thinking that he might be a good guy, underneath it all. Braxton isn't my favorite person, but

I can't hold that against Davis. He seems intelligent, passionate, spiritual, even. Not to mention good looking, too. All are great qualities to have in a man. So why do I find myself wanting to shut it down before we even have liftoff?

I consider Ebony and Braxton, engaged and seemingly in love. The wedding planning is rocking along, and as far as we can see they are enjoying the process. Will it last, I can't tell. But Ebony's parents are paying a small fortune for their wedding, and they will certainly take beautiful photos, at least.

Mama and Daddy are on the opposite end of the spectrum. Mama barely wants to share the same room as Daddy most of the time. Doesn't really want to feel his presence near her, after sharing a life, a home, and two children together. It's been that way since their divorce a few years ago, although things have thawed considerably since her illness.

And then there's Tameka and Darryl. Who knows where they stand? They'll get along one moment, and then be ready to tear each other to pieces the next. Little Chloe is caught somewhere in the middle of her married too young parents. Staying together for the sake of the children is best for whom, exactly? But back to the conversation at hand...

"That sounds nice." I say, and I'm surprised by the words that have come from my mouth.

"Really? That's great. How about sometime next week?" Even Davis sounds a tad surprised that I've agreed to meet with him.

"Sure. Why don't you give me your number so that I can reach out to you this weekend?" I ask, but the twinkle in his eyes is gone now. I can see it written all over his face: he doesn't expect me to call him. Well, there goes both of us. If I can help it, I don't plan on ever calling him, either. Still, he reaches in his wallet and produces a business card, which he promptly hands to me. I mutter my thanks, then walk away quickly to find my purse to place it inside. Tameka and Ebony eye me suspiciously while I rejoin them in the living room.

"Back so soon, Reesie? We were getting along fine without you." Ebony jokes, but I simply ignore her, smiling as I bite into the lemon square. My goodness, they are even better than I remember them being the last time I had one. Who needs to cherish a man when you can feast on dessert perfection? Not Reese Joseph, that's who. Davis walks back over to his seat, smiling and nodding at everyone. He glances at me, but I look back down at my plate. I'm not adding fuel to the fire for my meddling friends.

"So, y'all, I might as well tell you that Darryl and I are going to see the new Marvel movie next week. We already have Chloe's babysitter nailed down for the weekend. Does anybody want to join us?" Tameka asks, looking from side to side. Darryl is filling up his face with brownies in rapid succession, but he smiles and looks up at the mention of his name. He gives a thumbs up signal before continuing to eat more food.

"Girl, yes! A triple date would be awesome! Braxton and I are down…Davis and Reese, what about you guys?"

Our glances meet at the same time this time, but the resulting awkwardness is less than encouraging.

"Um, let us get back with you, how about that?" I say, more of a statement than a question.

"Yes, I agree. That sounds good, Reese." Davis concurs, and I can't help but notice the smiles of my friends turn into the slightest of frowns. Ebony lets out an exasperated sigh as if we've ruined her fun. Tameka rolls her eyes with great exaggeration, both of them taking great pains to let me know how they feel. Braxton, thankfully, has the good sense to change the subject before the last nerve I have left is stepped on.

"So, Ebony, baby, this is supposed to be game night. Can we get to the games already?" He asks jokingly, easing some of the tension that has started to creep up again.

"Reese is already playing games…I'm just saying." Ebony retorts, and that's when I make the executive decision that I'm just ready for the evening to be over. I rise from my seat, grabbing my clutch in one hand and my plate in the other.

"You know what, I hate to cut out on everyone, but it's been an incredibly long week for me. Ebony, thank you for the invitation. Davis, it was so pleasant to meet you. Everyone, please enjoy the rest of the night. I'm going to have to make my way home now." Not a hint of regret in my voice, I find the nearest trash can and place my plate in it. Satisfied, I make my way towards the door. The guys sit in stunned silence while Ebony and Tameka try to voice their protests.

"I was just kidding Reese. Please don't go." Ebony pleads.

"Girl, you know Ebony is crazy. Don't leave, Reese." Tameka joins in.

Their weak protests fall on deaf ears, and Ebony realizes how serious I am when I start to unlock the door. She runs up quickly, giving her best effort to keep me from opening it. I glare at her when she places an arm in front of me. My expression must be threatening enough, though, because she starts to lower it.

"Reese, I'm really sorry. You know I just wanted you and Davis to hit it off. Don't leave because of me, please." Ebony begs, and part of me wants to relent and join them on the couch. The other part is still livid with my friends. I refuse to sit here and let my love life, or lack thereof, continue to be a source of their gossip and fodder.

"I accept your apology, but I'm not staying. I just want to go home, unwind and clear my head. I won't be able to do that here. Good night, Ebony." I say with determination. Defeated, Ebony steps aside so I can leave her home. Head held high, I don't relax my shoulders until I'm safely inside my car. Sinking into the driver's seat, I breathe a sigh of relief.

AND TROUBLES RISE

A glass of wine and my favorite flannel pajamas are calling my name. Now what kind of woman would I be if I didn't answer?

CHAPTER FIVE
What had Happened Was...

Everyone loves a good story. The juicier, the better, but even little kids know that each one needs a beginning, a middle, and an end. Some stories would never be told unless someone was there to speak up for those who cannot speak for themselves. So I can pray, and I will pray, but like the late, great, Fannie Lou Hamer said, "You can pray until you faint, but unless you get up and try to do something, God is not going to put it in your lap." So today, this day, and each day after, I will do my best to tell the story.

Always,

Candy Girl

I never got around to calling Davis. At first I thought I'd be coy, play hard to get a little, but truthfully I didn't feel the pull to pursue a connection with Davis. Besides, he probably thinks I was being a bit of a brat during Ebony's get together. Not exactly the best start to a relationship. I'm embarrassed to admit that it's now been nearly two weeks since our first meeting. If I was going to get around to calling him, I should have done so by now. Moving on.

WLNN (We're Local News Now) is abuzz this morning, but I thrive off of the activity. Something about the frenetic pace of news keeps my adrenaline going…there's absolutely nothing like it, and I love being in the center of it all. And although I'm no shrinking violet, I've never been the one to have a wide circle of friends. People often think that I must be the life of the party, since I'm so at ease on camera. Not me. My squad is much smaller than most viewers expect, but I'm ok with that.

"Good morning Reese." Carol says, gliding by my cube as she makes her way through the office.

"Good morning Carol." I reply, but she's already steps ahead, too hurried to stop and chat. Her expertly coiffed, icy platinum, blonde bob, doesn't move an inch. Her designer suit game is forever on point and camera ready #careergoals. We're friendly, but definitely not friends.

Carol Parsons is the face of our station, and it's been that way for as long as I remember. She's pretty cool overall, a throwback to veteran journalists in her dress and demeanor, just a no-nonsense, consummate professional. Throughout my academic career, my college mentor, Sherry Healey, always stressed the importance of finding career mentors. I had hoped that Carol could be one for me, given her illustrious experience and career accomplishments, but for whatever reason, we've never meshed beyond the typical workplace courtesies. Still, in a career field as cutthroat as this one, it's best to play nice in the sandbox. For the time being, at the very least, Carol is several rungs higher than me on the ladder. I'm not trying to push anyone off, but I most certainly am holding on as tightly as I can.

  Rena, our station's receptionist, gave me the number of her brother-in-law, a local realtor that she highly recommended. Real estate is one of those tricky areas where word-of mouth recommendations always beats a glowing online review, at least in my opinion. I like to be able to put a face with a name, and a referral with the person who made it. Accountability makes all the difference. Sitting at my desk, I pick up the card she gave me and inspect it more carefully. Leonard & Richards Realty, LLC. I've never heard of them, but that's not necessarily a bad thing. I probably couldn't afford the commission rate, much less secure an appointment with a much larger firm.

  I call and am pleased when a cheery receptionist answers on the other end.

  "Good afternoon, Leonard & Richards Realty. How may I assist you?"

"Yes, my name is Reese Joseph. I'm in the market for a town home or starter home and I was referred to Mr. Leonard by Rena Thomas."

"Certainly Ms. Joseph. I see that Mr. Leonard has availability next Monday and Wednesday. Is there a day that works better for you?" Wow, that was sooner than expected. Monday would actually work out pretty great, I think.

"Monday looks good. Does he have any morning availability?"

"Yes, I see both the 9:00 and the 10:00 appointments available. Which do you prefer?"

"Monday at 9:00 would be excellent. Thank you."

"Oh, you're so welcome, Ms. Joseph. We look forward to seeing you Monday."

Now that was a successfully pleasant exchange. I'm already feeling nervous bubbles of excitement wash over me. I've checked the MLS listings online and have zeroed in on at least two or three properties I wouldn't mind having a look at. I hope this guy will be easy to work with. Fingers crossed and extra prayers regarding this. Hanging up the phone, my mood is instantly lifted. Maybe I'll figure out this adulting thing after all. Put down some roots, or something like that. I can't help but wonder how Mama will feel about it, but her last two scans have been clear. If they hadn't been, contacting a realtor would've been the last thing on my mind.

"Hey Reese, how's it going?" Cameron says jovially, sliding in to lean against the wall of my cubicle. Cameron Pierce is an evening reporter and substitute weekend anchor. He's only 28, but he carries himself with a certain level of maturity I've witnessed only in veteran journalists. Tameka and Ebony have been pushing me to ask him out for months, but that's just not my style. There's no explicit station rule that colleagues can't date, but we know management frowns upon it, especially since an intern was caught sleeping with the chief meteorologist two years ago. Besides, Cameron and I consider our relationship to be strictly platonic. We're the only two on-air personalities that happen to be people of color, so we've formed an alliance and rely on each other. He's not even my work husband, just a trusted and respected colleague and friend. I'd definitely like to keep it this way.

"I'm good, Cameron, how are you?"

"I'm good, thanks. Hey, you've got a minute?" He leans forward and asks, nearly whispering.

"Sure, Cam. What's up?" I smile back, knowing there is no telling what he is up to.

"Remember that girl I told you about, the one I went on a blind date with last week?"

"Yes. The teacher, right?" I try to recall. Cameron is boyishly handsome and a local celebrity. He usually has a bevy of attractive women of all shades after him. He's so dang goofy, though. Part of his charm is that he is oblivious to their interest most of the time. Most of the time.

"Right, yeah, that's the one. So, we kind of hit it off. She's really cute, seems nice, the whole nine yards. We had dinner Friday *and* Sunday night." He nods with emphasis. Ok now, Cam.

I'm genuinely happy for him. Cameron is one of those perpetual bachelor types, somewhat by his own design. I mean, he's only 28, but I think he feels the unspoken pressure that every unmarried southerner does. There's a certain expectation that you should be married by 30 or you are destined to a life of being alone. Left on the shelf, or some antiquated mess like that.

"That's great! I'm glad you've found someone you like." And I am. Cameron is a good guy. Any woman would be blessed to find her match in him.

"Me, too. And I do like her, I do. But the thing is, she invited me to go to church with her this Sunday, then have dinner with her mom afterward. Apparently her dad passed away a few years ago. Does that seem too soon to you? You know me, I'm all about church on Sunday morning, but does that give the impression that we're getting serious? I don't know that I'm ready for that yet." His eyes show concern and a genuine need for sage advice. Dear Lord, please give me the words to say. Let me be a good influence on him, not someone that leads him astray.

"Well, Cameron, I can see why you might be hesitating a bit. Church and dinner with her mom *does* seem a little soon to me. I mean, you've been on what…two dates and several phone conversations, right?"

"Right."

"I can see how that would give the impression that you are a serious couple. Where does she see your relationship right now?"

"I don't know. I honestly didn't expect to like her this much. I mean, come on, it was a blind date. Those almost never end up with a happily ever after. But she's a cool girl. She's smart, seems to have a good head on her shoulders. She's cute. Good sense of humor. I like her."

"Only you can determine what feels comfortable to you. If you don't have a problem with it, and she clearly doesn't have a problem with it, then what else matters?"

"But will her mom be expecting to witness a proposal at dinner?" He asks, and I can't help but laugh at this. It's too funny, but Cam looks dead serious.

"What, it's not funny. She might be a stalker or something. I don't know what she's telling her mom about us. I don't want to be referred to as a future son-in-law until I actually am one. And I certainly don't want her pastor singling me out during the worship service." I can't help but laugh at this admission. I've been the subject of a sermon more than once in my life. At least it felt like that. And the feeling was more than a little awkward.

"Well Cam, I hate to break it to you, but it sounds like you've already answered your question. I think if you explained, in a very respectful manner, that you're enjoying her company and would like to continue to get to know her better, but would prefer postponing attending church together or meeting her mother until you are further along in the relationship, she would be ok with it."

"You think so? You don't think she'll get upset?" He says, continuing to lean forward.

"Honestly, Cameron, I don't know her so I don't know how she'll react. But I can say that it sounds like a perfectly reasonable explanation to me." I say plainly, crossing my arms as I look up at him. His face lights up with relief. His shoulders are looser and more relaxed now.

"Thanks, Reese. You give the best relationship advice." Ouch. I felt that in my spirit.

"No problem." I smile back at him. He walks away satisfied, and I'm left wondering why I can help others get their love lives together but can't even snag a second date with a normal dude. Always a bridesmaid, never a bride. Story of my life.

I glance down at the clock on my desk and realize it's nearly time for our next news team meeting. Grabbing my trusty notebook and one of my favorite pens, I head towards the conference room, greeting a few colleagues along the way. I love coffee, but I try to limit myself to an occasional cup or two every now and then. I have to protect these pearly whites so they can stay ready for my close-up.

Walking in, I notice that I am one of the first ones here. That would normally be considered unusual for me, but here at work I don't come to play. You best believe I have to stay two steps ahead of everyone.

Finding my usual seat at the table, I'm quickly joined by Cameron, our chief meteorologist, two of the field reporters and our 6:00 p.m. broadcast anchors. Queen Carol glides in as well, her aura changing the energy of the room. Three producers straggle in, followed by two interns who bring coffee and bottled water in for everyone, then find seats in the corner of the room. Cameron and I always sit across from one another. This assures the opportunity to give knowing glances throughout the meeting if necessary, and you already know we're going to compare notes afterward. It's the non-competitive friendship for me.

Wes, our station's news director, waltzes in about five minutes after the meeting was scheduled to begin. This is pretty typical for him. He has a tall, wiry frame, boundless energy and a creepy habit of clasping his hands and tapping his fingers together when he thinks he's on to something. He's been here just over three years, a lifetime compared to some of the past news directors. Motioning in the air with his fingers, a female intern springs to action and brings him a cup of coffee. He nods at her but otherwise doesn't acknowledge her effort. He's not my favorite around here.

"Well folks, here we are again. This school board debacle is quickly becoming the song that never ends. I know what you all are thinking, how do we cover the protests in a fair way that accurately represents the thoughts and feelings of the community. Channel 13 took the wrong direction and I don't want us to follow their example. We are the leading news network in this market and we are going to act like it, damn it!" He exclaims, his voice rising and his manic energy filling the room.

I feel Cam's eyes boring a hole into my head, but I refuse to meet his gaze. Same old, same old with Wes. Not today, Satan. Not today. But these silent prayers of the heart come too late, and he's out of his seat, pacing the room now. Great. Wes having a bright idea is never a good start to a meeting.

"We need an angle here that can't be matched. I want a team in Wallace Heights today, yesterday, really. Human interest, talk to a few of the parents, get their feelings on all of this. Find the single mom who's working three jobs and barely sees her kids. Locate the ex-con who's trying to find a job, maybe one that never graduated, got his GED, whatever. You know the type, one who was in and out of trouble and got expelled, or something like that."

My eyes close so I don't have to offer a perfunctory eye-roll. Could Wes be more cliché right now? Next he'll be telling someone to take Cam with them so they'll feel safer.

"Look, I know Wallace Heights isn't everyone's cup of tea, but you have to go where the action is. We won't find the kind of parents we're looking for over in Rolling Hills, ok?"

There are a few silent nods around the room, but for the most part there isn't too much of a reaction. I glance over at Cameron, but he's not looking in my direction now. His eyes are downcast, I can't quite read his expression.

"And if it makes you feel safer, you can always take Cameron here with you. Ha, ha, not many guys or gals would give him a hard time, right?" The room erupts with laughter, an obligatory response to having a total idiot for a boss. But I don't find it funny. And Cam sure as…

"Why so somber, Cameron? Just joshing, just joshing. But seriously, I think we have something here. And I have a feeling we can create something special if you're part of it. And you, too, Reese."

"I'm sorry, what?" I stammer, a lump forming in my throat.

"The two of you are the perfect ones to tell this story. I just hate I didn't think of it sooner. So let's get to it, like, yesterday."

I feel Cam continuing to watch me, but I dare not meet his eyes. I know what he's thinking because face it: I'm thinking it, too.

"You want Cameron to work on this story, with me? Out of everyone in this room, we're best suited for this assignment because…"

"Because the two of you make a great team, especially for pieces like this. Because I'm not about to ask Carol to go out in the field. Because Tara's plate is already full, and Stuart will be on assignment at the capitol for the rest of the week. Because last I checked, I was the news director around here. Does that answer your question, Reese?" He asks, but he's already moved on from my line of questioning. Cam shakes his head in disbelief, but is otherwise doesn't offer a peep. And just like that, the last story I want to tell is the one I won't be able to get away from.

~

Thirty minutes or so later, and Cameron and I are sharing a car ride to Wallace Heights. Normally we would grab a station vehicle, but Cam has an errand to run afterward, so he suggests we take his car instead. The buttery smooth and supple leather of his Infiniti makes for a comfortable ride through the city.

"You know, he could've sent someone else for this. Not that I'm upset about working with you. You know I love working with you."

"And you know I love working with you, Reese. You're my true sister in this crazy work family of ours. But you know and I know that he wasn't going to send anyone else on this assignment. To Wallace Heights? You imagine Carol up in there, trying to sashay around to get a comment, tipping and toddling and afraid of her own shadow."

We laugh, but it's halfhearted at best.

"And that doesn't bother you?"

"Sure it does. But I'd much rather tell this story than have our colleagues do it for us."

I'm silent here, digesting what Cameron has just said. I know he's right, as much as I hate to admit it. Maybe I should be looking at this a little differently. Wes lacks the depth and nuance of realizing that the two black members of the news team have a deeper understanding of the issues plaguing Oak City's black community, certainly more than our counterparts, at least. Or maybe he's a genius after all, and knows that Cam and I are capable of bringing a unique perspective and humanity to our reporting that comes from our knowledge and experiences as members of said community. As black people, we get it. Maybe he feels that way. I don't want to get carried away and give him more credit than he's due, though.

As the car approaches the narrow road that leads to Wallace Heights, an apprehensive mood settles in the air. I feel it in the shiver creeping up my spine. I'm trying to relax, but my shoulders tighten involuntarily. Cam glances at me briefly, but then he looks back at the road. We continue in silence, uncertain about what lies ahead.

"Reese."

Looking out my window, I'm deeply saddened by the rampant poverty that is evident throughout this side of town. It's swift, jarring to the senses, the transition from the cookie cutter middle class neighborhoods sprinkled throughout Oak City into this. This unending row of deteriorating homes, shards of glass visible, boarded doors, barred windows. This blight on the community. This suffering people.

"Reese."

"Yes? I'm sorry, just lost in thought."

"It's ok. Just letting you know that an unmarked vehicle has been following us for the last several blocks. Don't be alarmed, just letting you know."

Oak City has built a reputation for having less than stellar law enforcement. A picturesque community that just can't seem to rise above the deep-seated resentment of race relations of the past... just can't quite move beyond the level of crime that inundates our small community (but that larger cities would give their eyeteeth for), just won't attempt to transcend the corruption that exists at its very core. Oak City's residents don't trust local law enforcement to protect the people, much less serve them. But local crime leaders would probably give the force its highest recommendation. It stinks, but it is what it is.

I inhale deeply, immediately on alert. Cam doesn't know this, but I'm suspicious every single time I see a police vehicle. Not just in Oak City, either. My experience hasn't exactly been one of feeling served and protected. Not that Cam knows about my experience, but at least I've felt a fraction of what he's gone through as a black man in America. Cam wouldn't know about the time in college, when Phillip and I once found ourselves detained by police officers. It was something silly; he accidentally left his bright lights on one night, something simple like that. He turned them off as soon as he realized it, but by then it was too late. The cops wasted no time in pulling us over, and took even less time for the incident to escalate from simply checking Phillip's license to asking us to exit the vehicle for a body search.

I was so scared that night. The car was cold and hard, my body pressed against it by his partner. The jerk was at my back, his hot, stale breath threatening as he whispered in my ear. His knee kept me pinned against the vehicle, and I had no choice but to remain in that position. Looking over to Phillip, I was heartbroken by what I saw. He looked up at me, meeting my gaze, silently apologizing to me. Begging forgiveness with his eyes. Apologizing for being black and fitting the description.

The other cop's knee was pressed again Phillip's back, holding him to the ground and daring him to fight back. Phillip watched as I was being frisked, the rough and calloused hands of the cop lingering over every curve on my body. He tried, in vain, to be there for me, but there was no use. We were both helpless in that moment, at the mercy of our legal captors, both miserable and unable to help one another when we needed it most. I still feel his hands on me. I feel the hot tears burning my cheeks. I hear Phillip calling my name. Just like it was yesterday.

I ease my notebook up across my chest, the creeping thoughts forever seared in my memory continuing to rise.

AND TROUBLES RISE

"You ok, Reese?" Cam says, and I exhale. Relax, Reese, I tell myself. Deep breaths. Don't get upset. Let Cam focus on the road.

"Yeah, I'm good." I say, smiling at Cam to signal it's true. But it's still a lie.

And that's when the blare of the sirens rings out.

Cam eyes widen, but he says nothing. I can only imagine what he's thinking right now.

Cam presses the turning signal, then slows down to a walking pace, easing over to the shoulder of the road. The silence that follows is deafening, both of us praying for the best but expecting the worst as Cam places the car in park. He rolls down the window, then immediately places his hands up where they can be easily viewed. Instinctively, I place my hands on the dash board as well.

Please, God, let this pass quickly. Protect us, Lord. I pray silently, as Cam and I continue to sit, motionless. We're at the mercy of whatever mood the officer brings to meet us with.

"License and registration."

"Good afternoon, officer. It's right here on my dash. I'm reaching for it now to hand it to you."

"Did I ask you for a play by play? License and registration." His eyes are hidden behind dark sunglasses, but his tanned arms are tight, his stance firm as he stands near the driver's door.

"Is something wrong, officer?" Cam asks, his tone lifeless.

"You're that news boy, aren't you? The ten o'clock one?" He intones, and he's leaning in to look a little closer. I glance at him briefly, but then look away. I still feel him watching me, his demeanor unsettling, and unnecessary, given the circumstances.

"I'm a television news journalist, yes. If that's what you mean."

"Yeah, I thought you looked familiar. And your friend, too?"

"Reese Joseph, WLNN," I say, automatically chipper in my signature sign off.

"Uh, huh. Thought I recognized you, too. Hope you two aren't looking for trouble today."

"Just doing our jobs, sir." Cam says, and this time there's an edge to his voice.

"That's what you call it? Ha, fake news, if you ask me." But neither of us did.

"Was there a problem officer? What was the violation?"

"There's been some suspicious activity in the area. Your vehicle looked suspicious. You look suspicious."

"I can assure you we are harmless, officer", I offer, leaning forward. Cam cuts his eyes at me and I realize I've spoken out of turn.

"Yeah, well we don't take chances around here. Not when people have a bad habit of nosing around in areas where they aren't needed."

"We know how to mind our business."

"That's all we ask you to do. That's all." He says, handing the license and registration back to Cameron. He doesn't wait for him to get it, practically dropping it in front of him. But Cam has quick reflexes.

"Take care of yourselves out here, kids." He says, walking away to head back to his car.

After placing his license in his wallet, he moves the registration to the console. Cam's jaw is clenched, his grip is tight on the steering wheel. Still, he's silent.

"That's a relief, Cam. That could've been a heckuva lot worse." I say, hopeful my tone will lighten the mood.

"And that's your takeaway? Naw, Reese. That was unacceptable." He's right, but I don't have an appropriate response to this.

We continue to travel in silence until we reach our destination mere moments later.

My spirit is in complete agreement with him, but I don't have the words, much less the energy, to take up this fight. It's too heavy at times, the weight of being black in this community…black in this world. And unlike most things, the burden doesn't get any lighter just because it's shared.

AND TROUBLES RISE

CHAPTER SIX

You Say Goodbye

Dear Lord, please send me a sign that the one, the one you've made for me, that he actually exists. That he's real, Lord, not action-figure sized, but molded and created in your image, custom made just for me. I'm not sick of being single, but I can be convinced about the wonders of monogamy. But send me a sign, Lord. Let it be clear that he's real. Let it be without question that he's been sent by you. I wouldn't, and I know you wouldn't, have it any other way.

Forever, Candy Girl

> *I want to see you. I miss you.*
>
> *I don't think I'm ready for that, Phillip.*

I'm not going to stop asking, Reese. Not until you say yes.

Phillip is relentless with his text messages, each a little more endearing than the last, and I can't help but wonder if maybe, just maybe, he's the sign I've been asking God to show me. Maybe. It's going to be a lovely day, I know that much. Bill Withers says so, as I sing along with him on the way to Leonard & Richards. A lovely day indeed.

Making my way through Oak City, I can't help but reflect on the afternoon Cam and I shared at work. Our journey through Wallace Heights was fruitful, but spiritually and emotionally exhausting. Cam and I pushed through, and struck gold with four different residents willing to speak with us on the record. We're confident that we got good material to work with, but Cam had a great idea to press a little further. If we can get Wes on board all of the toiling will be worth it. We promised to tell their story, and to tell it fairly and truthfully. We owe them that match. Still, this home search will be a welcome distraction from work woes.

Mama and Tameka lobbied to come with me to meet with the realtor, but I staunchly refused. I may consider letting them go on future trips, but this initial meeting is something I need to do for myself. His office is surprisingly easy to find, tucked just behind a midtown shopping center that I've been known to frequent. I had no idea it was right here this whole time.

Parking in a space near the entrance, I'm encouraged by how welcoming the office is. The property itself is neatly landscaped and the French doors are stately but not overbearing. Walking in, I immediately notice the lovely plants strategically placed at the entrance and throughout the lobby. The rhythmic, soulful sounds of the Black Pumas pulsate warmly throughout the space, and I find myself humming along as I ease over to the receptionist's desk. A young, auburn-haired woman is smiling as she talks into her headset. She notices my presence, smiles more broadly at me and places the caller on mute for just a moment.

"Good morning. I'll be right with you. Please feel free to have a seat and help yourself to some refreshments." She says, and I nod in response.

Turning towards the lobby I notice several plush, striped accent chairs and a small table with bottled water, assorted juices and a basket of baked treats. A short coffee bar stands to the left of the space. I walk over and find a bottle of water and a napkin, eyeing the tempting treats in the basket.

It's a blessing and a curse, loving dessert the way that I do, but when faced with temptation I just can't help myself. I settle on a couple of white chocolate and macadamia cookies that are wrapped in cellophane and tied with a bow. I place the cookies in my purse as a treat for later, then sit in one of the comfortable looking chairs. There are a few magazines scattered across the table, but I don't feel like aimlessly thumbing through one. Instead, I reach for my handy notebook and review the notes I made about properties I would be interested in seeing. I check again to make sure that I have my pre-approval letter folded neatly inside as well.

Mere moments later, the friendly receptionist walks toward me. She's petite, her milky, lightly freckled complexion a striking contrast to her auburn tresses and piercing, yet warm, emerald green eyes.

"Excuse me, ma'am. I apologize for the delay and hope you didn't have to wait long. I'm Casey, welcome to our office. Are you Ms. Joseph?"

I stand up and extend my hand to meet Casey's for a handshake.

"I'm Ms. Joseph, Casey. But please, call me Reese." A flicker of recognition crosses her face, and she lights up with glee.

"Oh my goodness, are you Reese Joseph from Channel 5 News?" I nod and smile in response, and Casey nods enthusiastically back at me.

"I knew it, I just knew it! It's a pleasure to meet you Ms. Joseph."

"Thank you Casey, nice to meet you also. I'm here for my nine o'clock appointment with Mr. Leonard." She's got the friendly customer service vibe down pat. Ok, Casey, between the cookies, background music and ready smile, we're going to get along just fine if you can keep this up.

"Yes, of course. I am so sorry, but Steve, I mean Mr. Leonard, was in a minor fender bender this morning. He was shaken up but is doing fine. He is, however, expected to be delayed by a few hours today. Hospital, then the insurance company and so forth. He is so very sorry that he couldn't make your meeting, but he has asked if his partner, Mr. Richards, can meet with you instead. Would you be comfortable working with him today? Mr. Richards usually handles our commercial clients, but he is very knowledgeable on the residential side and works closely with Mr. Leonard." I'm somewhat disappointed, especially because Rena raved about her brother-in-law, but I might as well make the most of the situation. I don't want impatience to get the best of me, but I really don't want to put off the home search any longer.

"Sure, that's fine." I say with nonchalance.

"Great, I'll ring him for you now. He should be just a moment." Casey walks back to her desk and pages him from her phone.

"Mr. Richards, Ms. Joseph has agreed to meet with you. She is waiting in the lobby."

As soon as she hangs up the phone she smiles back at me. "He'll be here momentarily."

I nod my thanks, then turn around to get a better view of the artwork in the office, which I hardly noticed before. Someone is a fan of ethnic art or hired an interior designer who is, I think to myself. I'm completely engrossed in a painting of a brown couple dancing closely together despite the rain storm around them. It's a stunning piece, so much so that I barely notice that Mr. Richards has come in until I hear a familiar voice.

"Ms. Joseph, good morning. How nice to see you again." His deep, rich baritone immediately grabs my attention. I turn around and can scarcely hide my amazement at looking into the face of Davis once again. His megawatt smile immediately lights up the room, charging it with electricity.

"Davis? I'm so confused, you work here?"

"Yes. I don't know that we ever received proper introductions before. I'm Davis Richards, partner here at Leonard & Richards. Steve tells me you are in the market for a home. Shall we continue our discussion in my office?" He smiles with a twinkle in his eye, no doubt relishing the surprise at my expense.

"Of course. Please lead the way." I say, pulling my purse a little closer to me. Maybe it can shield me from his charm. Davis thanks Casey, then starts walking down a small hallway, where I follow behind until we reach his office. The door is wide open, and I'm intrigued by the warm, masculine space. He has a rich, mahogany desk with two rust colored armchairs facing it. There's a large set of windows to the right of the room, drapes open, letting in a great deal of natural light and illuminating the office.

"Please, won't you sit, Reese. Can I get you anything?" He asks gently, but I decline the offer. Instead I sit down in one of the comfortable chairs and continue to look around his office. There's a massive whiteboard on one wall that lists various clients and their needs. A monitor is mounted near the ceiling in one corner of the room. His desk is disturbingly neat, either a tell-tale sign of someone who doesn't get much done or is completely anal-retentive, in my opinion. I haven't figured out which one Davis is just yet. He's still easy on the eyes though, I'll give him that.

"I know that Casey has apologized on behalf of Steve, but I also extend my sincere apologies for the inconvenience today. We're glad that Steve is doing well, though. Simply by the grace of God, because the situation could have been much worse."

"No need to apologize, but I thank you. I'm glad to hear he is well also."

"And he tells me you're in the market for a starter home…perhaps a town home, is that correct?"

"Yes, that's correct. But can I ask you something?"

"Of course, anything." He pauses, all ears as he looks directly at me.

"I didn't even know you were in real estate. I thought that you and Braxton were friends from work."

"Oh that? Well, technically we are. I think I mentioned that Braxton and I have known each other for years. But professionally, since I primarily handle the commercial end of our business, I've been able to work closely with the mayor and city council to acquire properties that represent redevelopment opportunities for the city. I specialize in fixer uppers, if you will."

"Ah, that makes perfect sense now. And Casey said you're also familiar with the residential side of the business?"

"Absolutely, I actually got my start selling and representing residential properties. I transitioned to the commercial side because the commissions tend to be higher, but I'm certainly comfortable in both arenas."

"That's good to know."

"Anything else?" He asks, and I'm beginning to wonder if he feels like I am grilling him about his experience. I promise you I'm not that chick. I'm not mentally calculating your net worth, not trying to pull a bait and switch. Just trying to feel you out. That's reasonable.

"I may have other questions later but I think I'm good for now." He smiles and nods when I say this. Looking at him again, studying his eyes more closely, I can't help but notice how kind they look. They crinkle nicely when he smiles. His jaw line is strong, self assured. And he looks pretty sharp in his khaki blazer, striped oxford shirt and neatly pressed, navy slacks.

"Great. Please feel free to ask questions at any time." He pauses here and reaches for a folder that's near the corner of his desk. Flipping to a blank page in the notebook in front of him, he quickly grabs a pen and looks ready to take notes.

"So, I took the liberty of grabbing the folder Steve had prepared from his desk. In it he has several one bedroom and one bathroom properties, mainly townhouses and a couple of duplexes, too. How does that sound to you?"

"Yeah, so, I had kind of envisioned a single family home, maybe, but I am certainly open to town houses or duplexes, as long as they are at least a two-bedroom, two bathroom home. Ideally I'd like an extra bedroom that can be used as a potential office slash guest space." I say, and I notice him jotting down a few things.

"Does yard size matter? If it's a single family home it would be more likely to have a yard. And parking…what are your feelings about a garage versus a two-vehicle parking pad or street parking?"

He's asking questions that I haven't fully given thought to, actually. Not that those things don't matter, because of course they do. I feel a warm flush creep up my neck now, and I know that I'm already starting to feel a little overwhelmed by all of this. Davis looks at me closely and I can tell that he senses my discomfort.

"No need to answer those questions right now, but those may be things you want to consider. It can broaden or narrow our search considerably. We can ease into this process, Reese, at a pace that feels comfortable to you." He interjects, and my heart skips a beat. Yes, Davis, please. Let's take it slow.

"While we're thinking about things, is there a particular neighborhood or neighborhoods that you wanted to focus on?" Hmm, now that's an interesting one. As a journalist familiar with all parts of Oak City, I most certainly don't want to live in certain areas. But as far as where *I do* want to live, I'm not so sure.

"Let me think about that. I'm pretty sure that I don't want to live too close to Winding Oaks. My mother lives there, I do too, I mean, I didn't, but then I moved back home when Mama got sick, and she's better now, and, well…" I stammer, feeling utterly flustered.

"It's ok Reese, you don't have to explain." But I do. I don't want you thinking I'm some hot mess afraid of adulting, still living in her Mama's basement. Even though the living situation is accurate, and if I'm being honest, the hot mess part is too, some days.

"It's just that, now that she's doing better, and I'm ready to make this transition, once I find a place I don't want her to feel the need to visit every single day." I say, nodding my head emphatically. Davis shakes his head slightly and stifles a laugh.

"What?" I ask, frowning at him. "Did I say something wrong?"

"No, of course not. I'm my mom's biggest fan, but we all know how they can be sometimes, amirite?"

"Okay? Amen, preacher!" I respond, and we share a laugh. The corners of his eyes crinkle when he smiles again, showing off his handsome grin. I feel a warm blush creep up my neck, but this time I look away before it gets the chance to reach my cheeks.

"I'd like to avoid downtown if possible. I love the look of some of the historic homes there, but I'm scared they might be more work than I'm willing to take on." Fixer upper and hot mess…what's the difference?

"How about some of the newer downtown properties…a loft, perhaps, or one of the mixed use spaces in the retail district?"

"No, I think I'd rather just avoid the traffic of the downtown area altogether."

"Understood. I'll focus the search outside of that area, then."

He writes down a few notes again, then pauses to type something on the keyboard. I sit there quietly, trying my best to avoid staring at him. I'm nervous about the prospect of spending one on one time with him, but with his partner out indefinitely, I don't know what may happen. He looks up at me, but I glance away again quickly. He smiles but says nothing, looking back at the computer screen. We play this silly game a few moments more, until I suddenly feel like a flirty schoolgirl instead of a grown woman. At some point enough is enough, and the flirty mood is replaced with a strange awkwardness that descends over the room. I'm feeling sheepish about the way that I behaved on game night, realizing that Davis might not be so bad after all. At the very least, I could have given him the opportunity to prove that he wasn't as bad as I thought he was. I feel compelled to address the elephant in the room, if but for a moment, to get these feelings out of the way.

"Davis?"

"Yes, Reese?" He says, looking directly at me now. There's such warmth to his gaze that I have a melting feeling from deep within. I take a deep breath and sigh before speaking again.

"I just wanted to apologize to you for the way that I acted on game night. Honestly, I'm usually not like that. I just felt out of my element and needed to get away. It was very rude, though, especially since you were being so gracious." He offers a reassuring smile to me, and I feel my shoulders relax a bit.

"You know what, Reese? I think we both were a little uncomfortable that night, and considering the circumstances, I think it was completely reasonable to feel that way. There is no need to apologize for it, but I appreciate you doing so." He smiles again and nods this time, a small gesture of respect. He's quickly earning mine.

"Nonetheless, I appreciate your attitude about it."

"Of course. All is forgiven, but there was just one sticking point for me that night. I can't seem to get it off of my mind." He says, scooting forward and placing his hand under his chin.

"What's that?" I ask, matching his body language, and leaning forward slightly in my seat.

"I gave you my number but you never called me. Did I make a bad impression?"

I sigh again, easing back now. That night I found him to be very attractive and he seemed to be intelligent and acted like a gentleman. He was quite nice that evening, and never gave me a reason not to call him. How do you explain that away, though?

"It wasn't that…I just didn't feel ready to pursue something with you, with anyone. My friends have a bad habit of trying to set me up with guys a lot. They think they're being helpful, but I'm just trying to live my life. I don't feel that I have to have a relationship to be happy."

"Whoa, whoa, whoa… I wasn't asking for your hand in marriage, Reese. But you do seem like an intelligent, lovely woman. You have a quiet confidence about you that I really like. I'm finally in a position where I am open to meeting someone, so when Braxton suggested one of Ebony's best friends, who also happened to be single, I was intrigued. I still find you to be intelligent, lovely and confident. If and when you find yourself ready to get to know one another better, I am definitely available for coffee, lunch or dinner. Name the place and time. That's just an open invitation."

"Duly noted, Davis. Thank you for your patience and understanding."

"Absolutely. And I thank you for your patience while I reviewed a few options. There are a couple of places in Midtown that are currently available and just might be a good fit for what you're looking for. Do you have time to look at them today?" He asks, his eyes wide with expectation.

"Oh, do you mean now? So soon?" I stammer, caught off guard by the suddenness of it all.

"Yes, we can go now if you have time. But if that's not convenient for you, I can have Casey schedule a date and time that works better for you.

"Yes, let's do that. Another morning would probably be better for me." Yes, yes. Let me have time to prepare and get my mind right to see you again. And outfit and beat too, of course.

"No problem, I'll have Casey set something up for you. My calendar is wide open next Monday, Wednesday and Friday morning."

"Sounds great, thank you." I say, standing up and reaching forward to shake his hand. He rises from his seat and meets my handshake with his, which is strong and firm.

"Allow me to walk you out, please." He says, coming around from behind his desk to lead me out of his office. Walking behind him, I can't help but glance down to notice how well he fills out his dress slacks. His gait is totally composed and assured, his head held high as we walk down the hall. For a brief moment I imagine what it would be like to walk arm in arm beside him. Feeling silly, I quickly push the thought out of my head. We reach Casey's desk in no time. She looks up and smiles as we approach.

"Casey, Ms. Joseph and I had a productive meeting this morning. Please schedule time for me to complete some showings with her. Let's say, about a two hour block of time for the morning that is most convenient for her. Thank you."

"Of course, I'd be glad to." Casey responds, continuing to smile with sincerity.

Davis turns to me now, a wide grin on his handsome face once more.

"Casey will take great care of you, Ms. Joseph. And it was a pleasure to meet with you this morning. I look forward to the next time and I hope you have a blessed day." We shake hands again, our eyes meet once more, then Davis walks back down the hall toward his office. I watch him walk away for a moment, then look back at Casey, who is watching me intently. I instantly feel embarrassed. Casey smiles but otherwise gives no inclination that something is amiss. She's nothing if not discreet, I can already tell. I like this Casey already.

"Mr. Richards has availability next Monday, Wednesday and Friday mornings. Do you have a preference, Ms. Joseph?" Casey pauses, eagerly awaiting my response.

"Next Monday would be great, Casey. Thank you." I reply, and a sudden urge to be bold overcomes me.

"And Casey?"

"Yes Ms. Joseph?"

"I know that Mr. Richards requested a two hour block of time, but I was wondering if he had at least three hours available that morning." She nods, then looks at his schedule before responding.

"He does. Were you thinking from 8:00-11:00 that morning? Would that work for you?"

"Yes, from 8:00-11:00 next Monday would be wonderful. One other thing, though. Can you schedule us to meet at the Coffee Bean downtown instead?" My request surprises Casey, who can barely hide her smirk as she meets my gaze. Her emerald eyes are sparkling with mischief now. Yeah, Casey. I can already tell we're going to be fast friends.

"Of course I can. I'd be glad to." She says cheerily, making the note in his schedule.

"Is there anything else I can take care of for you, Ms. Joseph?"

"No, Casey. You've been very helpful, thank you. I hope you have a wonderful day."

"And you as well, Ms. Joseph. Thank you!" She smiles again, but looks away when her line rings. She's all business now, answering in her usual professional manner.

Satisfied, I walk out the door and unlock the doors to my Avalon. I slide in, retrieving my sunglasses from their case and putting them on. On this lovely day, the week is already off to a good start.

People can think what they want about me, but it's really quite simple: I don't mind taking chances when the odds are in my favor.

AND TROUBLES RISE

CHAPTER SEVEN
Ready to Pop

Someone likes baby showers. It's a friggin' multi-million, if not billion, dollar industry. Every baby deserves to be celebrated, true, but someone please explain how diaper games and champagne toasts benefit the little darlings in utero? And what baby needs a pair of J's at birth? Nursery "street cred"? How, Sway? But the cakes are always good at baby showers, even if they are shaped like booties or bottoms. So I'll go, this time. If not for the mom or the baby, at least for the cake. Someone likes baby showers. Just not me.

Still here, Candy Girl

Mama's never really pressured me to start giving her grandbabies. Not yet, at least. Thank God for Thad and Peaches. My sweet niece has given her auntie a most precious gift (other than her, of course): a few more years until her grandmother starts pining for more babies to spoil. For a single girl, not to mention an only daughter, that gift is priceless. Thanks, Peaches. Thad could have a hundred babies and you'll always be my sweet girl.

"Reese are you ready yet? We're going to be late!" I hear Mama shout down loud and clear, but I'm still getting ready and don't mind taking my sweet time to get done.

"Catherine Reese Joseph, don't make me come down there. Are you ready yet?" Mama's voice calls out just moments later. Feeling like a teenager, I place my hairbrush on the vanity, sighing as I reluctantly rise from my seat in front of the mirror. I walk past my bed and turn the corner near the stairs.

Lord have mercy, I love my mother, and of course I'm blessed to have a living one to help take care of, but sometimes Mama still treats me like the sullen teenager that I used to be, the one who begged to move in the basement when her big brother went off to college, just to be able to have some privacy away from her parents. She even kept most of the décor the same from when I lived here before. I was doing just fine in the little studio apartment I had found after graduating from UGA, but of course I dropped everything when Mama got sick. Goodbye, fancy reporting job in Charlotte, hello, Channel 5 News in Oak City. I haven't regretted making that move to care for Mama, never, not once. But I still get a little annoyed with being treated like the teenager in the basement instead of the thirty-two year old, grown (and still growing) daughter.

"Give me five minutes, Mama. I'm almost ready." I yell from the base of the stairs, seeing Mama's curvy frame standing in the doorway.

"Five minutes, Reese. I'm not playing. I don't want us to be late." She responds, closing the door as she walks away.

And this is why I can't wait to meet with Davis next week. I definitely need to find a place of my own sooner rather than later. I know I haven't worn out my welcome, but Mama's health is in a good place now. This transition was only supposed to be temporary, anyway. It's time. And speaking of time, I could care less about getting in a hurry this afternoon. Honestly, for all I care we could just skip the whole event.

Today my mother and I have the displeasure of heading to Auburn for my cousin Shelby's baby shower. Shelby is my least favorite cousin in the whole world, but since her mother and my mother are not only sisters, but also the best of friends, I have no choice but to spend more time than I would like with her. I know a lot of people who live by the mantra "Family Over Everything", but sometimes I feel like I'm the only one clever enough to realize what the acronym means. And Shelby and I certainly aren't friends.

We're the same age (technically I'm three months older than she is), both educated, attractive and southern bred through and through. Our mothers thoroughly enjoy one another's company and have fostered a fantastically close relationship. But the latter didn't get passed down to the two of us. Shelby and I have always been unspoken rivals, but as we've aged the past animosity has become more akin to indifference. We genuinely are unbothered by one another, and wouldn't even make time for each other if not due to familial obligation.

Recent life events have necessitated the two of us spending more time together. Dale fell into Shelby's trap, I mean in love with Shelby, in two seconds flat. She tells the story of their meet cute as if they were star crossed lovers, but I heard from a friend of a friend that Shelby chased him down and wore him down. All I know is he came to visit one Christmas and asked her hand in marriage by Valentine's Day. First there was Shelby's engagement party, then the subsequent bridal shower, of course the wedding, and just over a year later we find ourselves here: attending the baby shower celebrating her newest life "blessing". She's ticking off boxes on her five-year plan like clockwork, and if anything, is well ahead of schedule.

I don't envy her life, but I'm not exactly comfortable with the fact that her life is a reminder that I'm still single, not even remotely attached and you can forget about being ready for motherhood. So instead I'll dress up and drink cutesy cocktails like "mom-osas" with Shelby and her dearest friends and sorors, pretending to be fine with her living her best life. I don't care that she's doing it, I just want to live mine, too!

"Reese! Let's go, now, I don't want to get caught up in the lake traffic." Mama shouts down the stairs, and I find myself picking at imaginary lint on my skirt just to delay the inevitable. Defeated, I reach for my purse and study my reflection once more. Do I really need the validation of a man and family to confirm my worth? Of course not! Snap out of it Reese Joseph, I tell myself. I smile a bright smile, but it doesn't reach my eyes. I blink away quickly, not liking what I see. It's best just to head up the stairs and get this day over with.

~

A short drive later and Mama and I are walking in to the dining room of the Auburn Manor, a lovely historic hotel in the heart of downtown. The space has been transformed into an ethereal blend of teal, silver and seafoam green. Gilded antique china adorns each place setting, and a beautiful mix of white lilies, teal green hydrangeas, blush colored roses and baby's breath serve as the centerpieces. A large dessert bar is set up on one end of the room, and carving stations are posted in three locations across the large space. A small army of servers are passing hors d'oeuvres from guest to guest. I see a few more already filling flutes with champagne, as well. Aunt Cora has spared no expense, I see. I swear I hear a small gasp from Mama as she mentally calculates the expense of the event. The room is breathtaking and tastefully done, I have to admit it.

Aunt Cora squeals as she notices that we have arrived, leaving a table of guests to come and embrace us. "Martha Louise and Reese!" she exclaims, extending her arms and enveloping both of us with a warm hug. "My favorite sister and my favorite niece!" she whispers in our ears, knowing good and well that Mama is her only sister and I am her only niece. Nonetheless, we giggle, happy to be in each other's company once again.

"Everything is so beautiful, Cora Leigh!" Mama says, and she is absolutely correct. "Where's Shelby?" We both scan the room to search for her. As if hearing our thoughts, Shelby takes this exact moment to turn around, the swaths of seafoam, gauzy material of her dress swirling about her like she's a goddess. And she looks every bit the part of one. Her frame is still slender, changed only by the gentle rounding of her growing belly. Pregnancy most certainly agrees with Shelby. She glides towards us in no time, her elegant presence as the honoree being rewarded by the adoring glances of her guests as she makes her way across the room.

"Aunt Martha! Thank you for coming!" Shelby beams, her smile straight and dazzlingly white. Years of wearing braces and regular brightening treatments will do that for you. She and Mama embrace as if reunited after several years, not merely weeks.

"Oh, Shelby honey, we wouldn't have missed this for the world!" Speak for yourself, Mama, I think to myself. I'm only here because you dragged me along. Shelby releases Mama from the hug and turns towards me.

"Reese, thanks for coming, too. So glad you could be here to witness this occasion!" The smile she gives me is forced and stiff, a sharp contrast from the one shared with Mama. I'm not surprised that she isn't too excited to see me. Truth be told, I'm not too keen on seeing her, either. Yet here we are.

"Glad to support you as we welcome our newest addition to the family!" I offer, wearing my game face once again. If my years as a journalist have prepared me for anything, it's simply how to be prepared. Thankfully we're interrupted by Aunt Cora.

"Girls, we'll let you catch up later. Shelby, darling, it's time for you to take your seat of honor. Martha Louise, Reese, just follow me. I have you both seated at my table." Aunt Cora motions us toward the round table seated near Shelby, who has her own throne to sit on and personal table. There are roughly eight guests per table, and I would estimate at least 40 people here, maybe more. Following Auntie, I'm not exactly pleased when I see that I'm the youngest person at the table by at least three decades. Buckle up, this should be an interesting afternoon.

Our table is filled with varying shades of beautiful black women, each a little older than the last. Shoot, even Mama and Aunt Cora are the spring chickens compared to this crew. Somehow I get seated between Aunt Cora and a woman wearing a bright, false-toothed grin and an ungodly amount of perfume. It wouldn't be so bad, except for the fact that Aunt Cora will likely spend most of the afternoon catching up with Mama. Besides, the woman to my left smells like a strange combination of White Diamonds and moth balls. Not the most appetizing aroma.

"Sit down, baby, don't be shy. Cora, you didn't tell me you had two daughters." She says, extending a chiffon blouse encased arm in my direction. "Ooh, Cora, she's a pretty thang, too. Where you been hiding this one?" The smile widens as she adjust her glasses to get a closer look at me.

"Pearline, this is my niece, honey. You know Shelby is my only child. But this one, she's my other baby." Aunt Cora replies, sweet auntie that she is. "Famous, too. Chile, all you have to do is watch the ten o'clock news to see her front and center. We're so proud of her." Aunt Cora beams, while the other ladies nod approvingly and say, "Well" and "You don't say".

"No wonder she looks so familiar. Baby you even prettier in person. Is you married?" Another woman pipes up, her eyes wide with hope and expectation. Well, now, can I at least get comfortable in my seat before we start with the third degree?

"No ma'am." I say both politely and confidently. Not today, Satan. You're not about to have me up in here feeling some type of way about being single. Not today.

"Baby you should try to find one of them mens on the computer internet."

"The what, Pearline?" Her nearest companion asks.

"The computer internet. They have this doo-hicky you can get on your phone and look at pictures of young, single mens. Old ones, too. Fine ones. Ugly ones. All kinds of men right there on your phone on the computer internet. Just like you shopping at the mall."

"Thank you for that suggestion." I say blithely, because what constitutes an appropriate response to that?

"Yes, honey. And if they don't tickle your fancy you just slide to the left. Or slide to right. Left right left. Honey, I gets mixed up. But it's on there. I heard about it." Ms. Pearline says, and I'm struggling not to laugh. Who knew that Ms. Pearline is a fan of Tinder?

I could entertain them with my one and only experience with online dating. It resulted in a restraining order at the time, but now I can laugh about it. A little bit, at least. Lesson learned, at least for me. One star-would not recommend.

"You ain't the type that don't like mens, is you baby?" Another woman asks, her curly wig struggling to hang on to her head. Her eyes narrow as she sizes me up, waiting for my answer.

"No ma'am, I am not. If God desires that I get married, I just don't believe He has sent my husband to me yet." I answer calmly, though I can feel my smile tighten. "Right now I am focused on my relationship with God, spending time with loved ones and continuing to grow as a professional journalist." A couple of the ladies nod politely at my response, while I look over to see Mama and Aunt Cora deeply engrossed in conversation. They are both oblivious to my discomfort in front of the Silver Inquisition.

"Honey, that's all well and good, but you can't wait too long. What is you, twenty-five? Twenty-six? Don't you wait too long, now, you hear me?" Ms. Pearline asks, and I am simply mortified. I blinked and I missed thirty-two, but I dare not let them know.

"I'll try my best." I say as cheerfully as I can muster, while Ms. Pearline just pats my hand.

"Sounds like what you need is some help, baby. Now my grandson, Trevor, is a nice young man. He's got a good job at the auto plant and he has his own car, too. He bout' near thirty now, but he could pass for someone younger. I just wish he would keep them pants up, he always wearing them down past his be-hind. He's a good boy, too. Don't do none of that drug slanging mess, in church every Sunday. And the boy knows how to keep a dollar in his pocket. Got all his teeth. He's a fine young man, and I ain't just saying that cause he my grandson. Sound good, don't he baby?" Her smile is scary now, her eyes holding a certain gleam that I don't quite know how to take. Is she trying to force her grandson on me? She seems to be trying her best to unload him on some unsuspecting, desperate woman. Thankfully I am neither.

"Now doesn't Shelby look beautiful?" I ask, deliberately trying to change the subject. "I wonder what she's going to have." Shelby and Dale have chosen to keep the gender a surprise for now. It seems to have worked, too.

"See how she sashays when she walks? That means she's having a girl." One woman whispers matter-of-factly to the table.

"No, Nadine, you wrong. That bump sitting way down low like that mean she gone' have a baby boy. Umm, hmm." Another guest disagrees with the first. Before I know it, all of the women are arguing animatedly, trading old wives tales that are surefire ways to guess the baby's gender. While I could sit and remain entertained by their antics, I instead take the opportunity to be excused from my seat and go in search of the nearest restroom. The other ladies are still talking as I walk away.

I walk past the remaining tables and find solace once I reach the hallway adjacent to the ladies room. I feel more relaxed as soon as I see the door, sighing with relief once I'm safely inside. Only one other person seems to be in the room, a vaguely familiar looking woman washing her hands and studying her reflection. She looks up when I walk in, looking away quickly, then looking back as recognition registers on her face.

"Reese?" She says, reaching for the paper towels to dry her hands. "Reese Joseph is that you?"

She asks, smiling warmly at me. For the life of me I can't recall who she is, and I simply hate that feeling. It happens, though, in my line of work. I've always been better with faces than names, anyway.

"It's me, girl. Tishayla Murray. From Valley Road Baptist, remember?" She asks, and I swallow the lump that has formed in my throat. Yes, indeed, I remember Tishayla. Her ex-boyfriend tried to holla at me last year, one of Ebony's many failed matchmaking attempts. This girl was a mess, too, calling me at work, coming to visit my church, just being an all around pain in the you know where. And Jamal and I only went on, like, two or three dates. Nothing serious, but you would've thought that we had gotten engaged or something. For the life of me I can't fathom why she is being so friendly towards me now, not the way she last treated me.

"Hi Tishayla. How have you been?" I inquire, not that I'm genuinely interested. It's just, at the moment at least, I'm temporarily blocking her path to the exit. I move away from the door for good measure.

"Girl, I am so glad you asked. I'm doing great! Jamal and I just got engaged over my birthday!" She exclaims, frantically waving her hand in front of me. I catch a glimpse of the sparkling diamond on her left ring finger, and I smile a tight smile as I offer my congratulations.

"Yeah, well you know, things just have a way of working out, don't they? The enemy tried to block my blessing, but I mean, who God has for you is for you, you know what I mean?" She looks down at my hands suddenly, apparently checking for evidence of my own relationship status. Satisfied at my empty fingers, she smiles a smug smile as she gently brushes past me.

"Good to see you, Reese. And don't worry, one day, maybe, your prince will come." Having said what she intended, she's confident as she walks on through the exit, flipping her waist length weave behind her. Undeterred, I use the restroom and wash my hands. Suddenly apprehensive about having to go back out and meet the lionesses once again, I deliberately take my time in washing my hands and checking my appearance a final time. Glancing at my watch, I realize I've been gone at least fifteen minutes. If I take any longer they'll be sending security to find me. I quickly exit the ladies room and make my way back to the shower.

Walking back into the ballroom, I see that the guests are deeply engrossed in a game of, "Who Knows Shelby the Best?" So doing my best to remain inconspicuous, I walk back to my table by passing through the back of the room rather than down the main aisle, successfully avoiding lingering stares and questions. That temporal sense of peace comes to an end as soon as I reach my table.

"There she is! What took you so long, baby?" Ms. Pearline asks, her face lighting up as I take my place beside her.

"I just had to use the restroom, but I'm fine." The gaiety of my tone doesn't match my discouraged spirit.

"Lawd, you don't have the runs, do you, chile? I get em' every time I eat this fancy mess. My innards wasn't made for no cucumber sandwiches and such. Pass the greens and cornbread, that's more my speed."

"No, ma'am, I don't have any bowel trouble. Thank you."

"You just let me know, now, baby. I keeps my Immodium AD with me at all times." She says, opening her large purse towards me so I can consider the contents. My goodness, Ms. Pearline is as well stocked as a corner pharmacy. I say nothing, but smile and nod politely.

"You just say the word, chile. Ole' Pearline will take good care of you."

"Pearline, you trying to pass off your medicine on somebody else again? I told you to stop doing that. Folks don't like that. They be thinking all sorts of things."

"Now I didn't ask your opinion, did I Nadine. Me and this pretty gal is having us a private conversation."

"Well, don't nobody want your old expired medications you done got off the clearance rack."

"Hush your mouth, ain't nobody's business how I spends my check. Surely not no Nadine

Walters." Welp, that escalated from 0 to 60 rather quickly.

"Ladies, I feel like I missed so much. What game is everyone playing?" I ask, cutting in before the wigs and teeth go to flying. My distraction works, because now they're all clamoring to pick up their answer sheets to see where they left off.

Most of the shower is a blur, and I find myself making polite conversation with the other ladies at the table to simply pass the time. When I do look to Mama for support, I find that she and Aunt Cora are spending their time fawning over Shelby instead. Shelby is glowing, clearly feeding off of the attention. When it's finally time to open the gifts, I gladly volunteer to record who gifted what, just to have the opportunity to escape the table. Walking towards Shelby's throne, I find an errant chair to rest in. Aunt Cora hands me a small notebook and pen. I smile at her as she turns to face the audience.

"Ladies, this is my dear niece Reese Joseph. She and Shelby have grown up together and have remained more than cousins, but also dear friends, through the years. Shelby loves all of her friends, but there is nothing like family. And Reese means so much to Shelby, I know that she is ecstatic to have her most favorite cousin here."

My goodness, why is Aunt Cora boring the guests with this drivel? I love my auntie, but she and Mama have never fully understood the dynamic between us through the years. As a matter of fact, Shelby is the last person I would refer to as a "dear friend" or a "favorite cousin". I look down at the notebook, but not before noticing that Shelby's grin has transitioned to a simpering pout instead. I don't know what's worse for her: The fact that Aunt Cora embellished our relationship or that she had the audacity to recognize me at all, thereby stealing, if only momentarily, some of Shelby's thunder. I have a strong feeling it was the latter.

    Shelby starts opening her gifts, with the crowd oohing and ahing after each one. I'm simply amazed at the over-the-top and expensive gifts she's received so far: a British style pram, a miniature rocking horse, a sterling silver infant grooming set, several cashmere blankets and countless smocked and heirloom outfits and dressing gowns. Is Shelby carrying an heir to the throne of some untold royal family? She glances my way from time to time, I guess to make sure that I am taking good enough notes about her gifts. Each time she does, I ignore her and continue to write. Sometimes you can't feed the beast, it just makes matters worse.

    I barely notice Mama come up behind me, placing her hands on my shoulders for just a moment.

    "Isn't it beautiful, Reese? I'm so glad we could be here to help support Shelby. I'm having the best time, aren't you?" Ugh, I hate to disappoint my mother. But the truth of the matter is that I am having a bad day. I'm not jealous of Shelby, I'm sincerely happy for anyone God chooses to bless, but it's making me all the more aware of what my own life currently lacks.

"You're right, Mama. It's beautiful." I say, simply ignoring her last question. No need for both of us to have a bad time here.

I swear I feel my hand begin to cramp as I continue to list all of the gifts for Shelby. There has to be close to a hundred gifts here overall. And Shelby has the nerve to sit there on her throne and look as though she deserves the utter and absolute adoration of her subjects. She doesn't even have the class to hide her disdain for gifts she isn't particularly fond of, especially the simple cotton onesies and polyester blankets she's been gifted. I guess certain gifts aren't special enough for her precious bundle of joy to come. I hope the baby has Dale's personality. It will at least give him or her half a chance in life. Shelby finally finishes tearing through her pile of presents, and this occasion is nearing its end. Thankfully.

A moment or two later, Aunt Cora hands Shelby a microphone so that she has the opportunity to give final remarks. I stop paying attention as she runs down her list of family members, dearest friends, sorority sisters, church members, and colleagues who have all made the trip to the event. Once she finishes offering words of thanks, she realizes that she may have made a mistake.

"Oh, and before I forget, I have to thank Reese for writing the names down of everyone who provided a gift for our little angel. I know it was a lot to keep up with, Reese, so thanks. Oh, and thanks for the gift you gave, too." She says, glancing at me and then turning her attention back to her more important guests.

From my table I can hear Ms. Pearline holler out, "Don't worry, Reese, baby. Your time may be next", and the room erupts in laughter, led by Shelby on the microphone.

Yep, I can't help but think. This day just keeps getting better.

AND TROUBLES RISE

CHAPTER EIGHT
Breaking Bread Together

A pulse is not potential. I mean, technically, it's the bare minimum of what one should expect in a mate. But why not swing for the fences? Shoot, if you're going all in, might as well wait for a #BlackUnicorn. Built to impress from the inside out. The real deal. All of that and a little extra. Unicorns are elusive, mythical creatures. You're not going to find one in any old neck of the woods. But when you find one, you'll know it. I've never actually met one, but they are among the most revered, beautiful, and precious creatures ever believed to exist. And I believe. But more than one? Child, now THAT is truly a blessing.

Until next time, Candy Girl

AND TROUBLES RISE

The sting of Shelby's baby shower has passed (somewhat) as I get ready for my coffee date, excuse me, home showings with Davis the following Monday. But I can't help but smile when I think of what could be. I take great care getting ready this morning, making the extra effort to be time-conscious as well. My fresh silk press from Saturday morning hasn't frizzed out yet, which is a good thing. I won't have time to change before I head to the station today, so I'm dressed more professionally than I would be otherwise. My go to navy suit will do the trick, with my favorite pair of slate gray pumps. I'll save the heavier makeup for when I get to the station, opting for a more natural, sun kissed look for now. It's unseasonably warm, so I'll save my jacket for on air as well. I have a silvery gray, sleeveless blouse that I'll rock for the time being.

I arrive at the Coffee Bean at 7:50 sharp, quite a feat for me. Usually they are slammed in the morning, but the parking lot is only half full. That's actually a good thing, because I want a relaxed, comfortable and quiet environment to speak to Davis in. I check my makeup one last time in the mirror before stepping out of my car to go inside.

The Coffee Bean was a welcome addition to Oak City a year or so ago, which was badly in need of such an establishment prior to its arrival. The quality of a big city coffee house with the charm of a small town corner coffee shop, this little gem has quickly found fans in the young and old alike. I'm especially pleased with their delectable array of pastries that are offered on a daily basis, plus their attention to detail with every new blend and recipe that's introduced. I stride in and am pleasantly greeted by the amount of empty tables and cozy booths that are available. I settle at a booth near the windows, one that lets in a good amount of natural light and feels slightly tucked away from the open floor tables. It also gives me a good view of guests arriving and departing.

Moments later Davis waltzes in, and I feel an unexpected warmth descend throughout my body. Definitely not the reaction I was expecting, but if I'm being totally transparent I feel so excited to see him again. He looks very distinguished and handsome, wearing the daylights out of his slate gray trousers, finely pinstriped, lavender shirt and charcoal blazer. Play it cool, Reese, dang, I tell myself. Chill.

"Reese! Good morning! How are you?" Davis asks, his voice barely containing his own enthusiasm. Somehow, this relaxes me a little. Clearly I wasn't the only one looking forward to this meeting today.

"I'm great, Davis. Thank you. How are you this morning?"

"I'm well, thanks. Looks like my work week is getting off to a great start." He says, grinning from ear to ear as he says this. He sits down across from me and even his eyes are smiling as he looks at me.

"You look lovely Reese. Quite a sight for these tired eyes." I murmur my thanks, somewhat embarrassed by his obvious flattery. A friendly server steps up to our table a moment later, ready and willing to take our order.

"Morning, folks. What can I get for you this morning?" She asks. Her stout frame doesn't temper her friendliness and charm. Davis yields the floor to me, and I order a slice of their daily special, the quiche Florentine, along with a white chocolate mochaccino and a glass of ice water. He orders the same, along with one of their massive cinnamon rolls that rival Cinnabon's. Our server nods politely, then is off to get our order filled.

"I hope you don't mind me requesting to meet here instead of the office today…"

"Are you kidding? It was a great surprise, actually. I'm so glad you made this call."

I look up at him and see the utter sincerity in his response. It's refreshing to meet someone who exudes honesty and integrity as if it is completely natural and ingrained into the fiber of their very being.

"I'm glad I did, too." I say, offering a sheepish smile in response.

"So Ebony tells me the two of you were college roommates. I bet you both have a lot of great memories together."

"Yes, she's one of my dearest friends. And you met Tameka as well. Tameka and I have actually known each other since middle school or so, growing much closer in high school. They're both my very best friends."

"And you mentioned attending UGA, right? I have family members who live near Athens."

"Right, Ebony and I graduated from UGA. Go Dawgs! What about you?"

"I'm a proud graduate of the University of Alabama. So one could say I roll with the tide." I look away quickly, pretending to cover my mouth as if nauseous. I'll try not to hold this disclosure against him, but it won't be easy.

"But you're originally from Georgia?"

"No, I'm originally from Montgomery, actually. I do have aunts and uncles, and several cousins, in Georgia, but many of my family members still live in Montgomery."

"And how did you end up in Oak City?"

"Once I graduated, I started working in Birmingham for a couple of years. Then I met my former wife, who was from Mobile. We moved there after the wedding and stayed there for a couple of years afterward…"

"You're divorced? I didn't realize you were previously married." I cut in, genuinely shocked by this revelation. I feel my eyes narrow slightly as I digest this. I wasn't expecting him to be a #BlackUnicorn, I guess…but I was really hoping he had no kids or exes of the matrimonial (permanent) variety. Maybe they aren't real, after all.

"Widowed, actually. Iris, she was my wife, passed away from ovarian cancer when she was twenty-six." I gasp inwardly, instantly filled with regret and sorrow for having pursued this direction of the conversation. Good gracious, Ebony, fill a sister in, will you. Now I have to take this foot out of my mouth without looking like a fool.

"I'm so sorry, Davis. I had no idea."

"It's fine, Reese. Really, it's fine. I was twenty-eight at the time, and I have to say, Iris represented all that is good in the world. She was grace personified. We married young, I mean, I was twenty-six, she was twenty-four at the time. We had no idea what we were in for. Certainly not cancer." His voice breaks slightly, and I can tell that this still affects him emotionally. How could it not? I thought Mama's breast cancer was bad…and it was. But I couldn't imagine losing my "life partner" at such a young age. I pray a silent prayer of thanks that Mama survived her battle.

"You seem so well adjusted after this. I couldn't even fathom dealing with a tragedy like that." His eyes are downcast now, and I'm trying to tread carefully. I've experienced love, sure, but never a loss like that. I can only imagine the devastation.

"Some days are harder than others. Years have passed, but if you ever really loved someone, and hey, I thought I loved Iris more than was even possible, but if you love someone they are always part of you. The love never dies. And that relationship was a catalyst for so much change in my life, so much growth. If it hadn't happened, I wouldn't be living in Oak City today. I probably wouldn't be sitting across from you at this very moment."

I'm captivated by the content and quality of what he's sharing with me. It hasn't been my experience to know men who are comfortable enough in their own skin to be vulnerable, yet strong. I consider my father, whose tug-of-war relationship with my mother has been exhausting to witness over the years. In the past she's been bitter about his rampant infidelity, and he's still clinging to the glory days, believing in his heart that he will win Mama back. I think about my brother, Thad, and how his failure to commit to his college boo has produced a beautiful niece, a resentful baby mama and years of missed opportunities. Then there's Phillip, my college love and the closest thing to a long term relationship I've ever had. But he never loved me enough. He never had what he needed in me, so he sought love elsewhere in the midst of our relationship. More than anything, he left me with a broken heart and more than a little skepticism regarding true love. My heart has healed, mostly, yet the cynicism has remained. But Davis is altogether unexpected. I'm not sure of what to make of him.

"Thank you for sharing that with me, Davis."

"Thank you for being willing to listen."

I nod, sipping my coffee, but saying nothing. Simply acknowledging that I am truly listening.

"Reese?"

"Yes, Davis?"

"What are you hoping to find?"

AND TROUBLES RISE

Lord, mercy. Have mercy, Lord. The sheer and utter weight of this question. I want to find the melody to my lyrics. I want to find my heart's twin, the one whose soul I was meant to be a rib for. I want to trust again. I want to love and learn and grow and be challenged by the one hand crafted for me. The one who sees my bed-head, and burnt toast, and short temper, and love for reality shows, and isn't the least bit intimidated by any of it. The one who laughs with me, and cries with me, and most of all, prays with me. That one. The one who knows he has found his "good thing" in me. But somehow, sitting across from this fine specimen of a man in the middle of the coffee shop, I can't take the mental gymnastics of trying to determine the best way to respond to this question without scaring him off.

"Well, Davis. That's a great question. I guess I'll know it when I see it."

"You don't want to make my job easy, do you?" He laughs gently.

"What? What do you mean?"

"It may be a better use of your time if you have a solid idea of what you want, a list, if you will, so you know what you're willing to live with and what you refuse to compromise on." Oh, I have a list. Baby, do I have a list. And you better believe I'm not willing to compromise on it. And, thank God, I am silently relieved that he's talking about homes. At least I think he is. He is talking about homes, right?

"Is that how you figured out what you wanted…in a home?"

"Absolutely. Of course, I had to be flexible, open to the market's conditions. But I wasn't willing to settle until I found the right fit."

The right fit. Like finding a perfect home is no different than finding the right cut of jeans for your body type. Or a killer, and comfortable, pair of heels. A dress with pockets. Just right. The kind of home I want to find is one made just for me. Come to think of it, that's the only kind of man I'm willing to settle for, too.

~

I'll give Davis an "A" for effort, but so far he's missed the mark when it comes to finding the right home. The first place we toured, a little bungalow in midtown, was ok, but a little plain for my taste. "Cosmetic changes", he kept saying, as I disliked the wall colors, the floors, even the bathroom fixtures. I'm not the handiest, but on a scale of Ebony, who doesn't know the difference between a Phillips and a flathead, and Tameka, who renovated their master bathroom one weekend, just for fun, I'm somewhere in the middle. But that doesn't mean I want a home renovation right off the bat. I want to unpack and get settled, with the only concern being how I plan to decorate.

The second home, a duplex close to a major shopping district, was not my speed, either. It was a new construction, which was actually pretty good, but bless it, the entire home was lacking in color and ambience. Slate gray and white everything, it looked more institutional than homey. I passed.

We're in the foyer of the third one on his list now. Davis is rambling on about the crown molding throughout the home, but I'm not impressed. All of the appliances are old, like 1970's sitcom old, and just gross. There was this strange, bolted door to nowhere, and I don't even want to know the story on that one. I want character, not Casper. Drama, not Dahmer. Maybe I should've been more specific.

"Was there anything you liked about the homes you saw today, Reese?" Davis asks, and I'm tempted to lie. I appreciate his effort, but this just isn't it. Not yet.

"Well…" I pause, struggling to form my words.

"It's ok Reese, no need to sugarcoat it. Please be blunt with me, brutally honest if need be. I want to be able to help you find your dream home, that's my job. Finding out what you like and dislike can help me better serve your needs."

What I like and dislike, what I like and dislike. I pace around the great room for a moment, taking in the view of the kitchen and breakfast nook. Thoughts of the other homes we've seen today replay in my mind. I sigh, crossing my arms and feeling disappointed by the way today has gone. I wasn't expecting a one and done situation, but that sure would've been a nice development.

"This house is creepy, Davis. Cable horror movie reject creepy. I'm almost afraid to say too much, for fear that the owner is recording our conversation." Davis is laughing heartily, but doesn't interrupt, so I continue. "And the second one, well, it was creepy, too, but in a different way. It was so sterile, and I know it was new construction, which I usually prefer, but something about it was so jarring to my senses, Davis. I just didn't like it." The laugh is replaced by a comforting smile, he's nodding along as I keep sharing the feedback that he earnestly requested, but will likely come to regret. "And the first one, Davis, the first one needed too many tweaks here and there. Paint here, new floors there. I'm not really interested in a fixer upper."

"But you don't want new construction?"

"I said I prefer new construction. And I do. But I don't know, the one we looked at today didn't feel right. No happy vibes at all."

"Are you open to a fixer upper at all? I don't know that you'll find everything you want unless it's custom built for you." Davis, you said a word right there. Because if it's custom built for me, you best believe it's going to be everything I want and more. In a home, of course.

"Yeah, so today was not great. I didn't especially like any of the homes you've shown me so far."

"I'm so sorry you didn't like any of these homes, Reese. But I still have a couple of properties in mind, and who knows what will be on the market soon…don't give up hope yet." I still believe, Davis. I still believe.

"And even though today wasn't a good day, I am happy about one development, and I hope you are, too."

"Oh, yeah. What's that, Davis?" I smile coyly, already feeling where this is headed.

"We get to see each other again. Sooner rather than later." He winks at me, and I feel the flush of my cheeks once more.

Take your time, Davis. You'll get to know me, and in the process, have no doubt what I am looking for.

AND TROUBLES RISE

CHAPTER NINE

Catch Me, I'm Falling

Labels. My man, my BAE, my boo. Should a grown woman be anyone's "girlfriend", except for her best girlfriends? I'm not a big fan of labels. I'll call you mine when I'm ready to be yours, and not a moment before. I wear enough labels as it is, not all of them by choice. I don't need you telling the world that I belong to you, as if I'm your latest obsession, your latest possession. If we're going to keep it real (and I don't live to fake the funk with anyone), the only one I belong to doesn't have to tell the world that I belong to Him. Everyone else should see it, as plain as day, written all over the life that I live. I'm reminded of the song we used to sing in the children's choir: If anybody asks you who I am, tell them I'm a child of God. That's the only label you'll ever need.

Keep shining, Candy Girl

So, Davis is not the best realtor. I mean, he seems pretty knowledgeable about all things architectural, and he seems to keep finding homes to show me, but I'd rather he just find the one I want already, if it's even out there. I'll never grow tired of his voice describing the quartz countertops in this kitchen, the stone fireplace in that one, the stainless steel appliances even sound attractive coming from him. But I'm getting tired of the looking. Home after home, three different days of home viewings at this point, it's becoming a bit much for my time and my patience. But spending time with Davis makes it a little better. Can an open house count as a date? Why not? How about one coffee-filled morning, two lunches, and several long phone calls? Because in the last few weeks we've shared those, too.

    I'm already focused on the next showing scheduled for tomorrow morning, when I should be paying attention to what my pastor's wife is saying right now. We had another blessed worship service this morning, with a message that was both timely and right on time. I'm so grateful to be a member of New Beginnings Missionary Baptist Church, not the largest church in the district (looking at you, Third Day), but definitely the one with the biggest heart. And that all starts with Pastor Bradford Houston and his lovely wife, Sister Donetta Houston. Otherwise known as Lady D. More than our "First Lady", I consider her to be a mentor and trusted friend. So when she asked to speak with me after service, of course I said yes. And now I can't even remember what she last said. Snap out of it Reese, dang. Quit with the Davis dreaming.

The daydreaming. The dreaming about Davis right here in the clear daylight. Pull yourself together, girl.

"Reese, I know you would be perfect for this opportunity. Many of the young ladies in the congregation already admire you. They see you on TV and think you've got it going on, sister." Lady D says, beaming with appreciation. I've got them fooled, though. I feel like I'm the last person who has her life together. Maybe not last, but next to last. Third from the end of the line, but who's counting?

"Do you think one of the moms in the church may be better suited for this?" I love the little ones, but I also prefer the more self-sufficient ones, like my BTU mentees. At least they've started puberty.

"You don't have to be a mom to be a part of the village, Reese. I'm sure Tameka and Darryl are grateful for your presence in Chloe's life. Bradford and I don't have any kids, but you best believe we love on our bonus niece and nephew, AJ and Alicia Parker, like they are our own. What these young ladies need is someone to be a positive example for them. Someone to cheer them on. Someone to represent what a Christian woman can and should be. You're all of that and more, Reese."

I consider what she's saying but I'm still in disbelief. She wants to start a new ministry for the tween girls of our church, and baby, some of these little divas are something else. Mouth for days, but I'm not the one to entertain foolishness from kids. Be respectful, we have nothing to worry about. Be disrespectful and we have a problem. With you and your mama. But I have prayed that God would use me to bless someone else, and what better place to start than right here in my home church. If you're not serving in your own church in some way, are you even truly a member? I know I'll want to weigh it more carefully, but Lady D knows that if she asks, the answer from me will always be yes. Reese Joseph and a rowdy group of 8-12 year olds… Jesus, be a fence! Talk about your new beginnings!

"Lady D, I'm so honored and humbled that you've even thought of me like this. You know to count me in for anything that can bless our church and community. Anything that can make a difference."

"Excellent! That's exactly what I was hoping and praying you would say. I can't wait for you to get started."

I'm glad she's so confident, because I don't even know where to begin. But Sister Houston's face is firm. She's one of those "I shall not be moved" saints when she has her mind made up, so I don't think she would've taken no for an answer. Use me, Lord, to be a blessing to others. To be effective in ministry. Let me see myself the way you see me, I silently pray.

~

Later that night, after I've had time to eat out with Mama, come home and grab a shower, change of clothes, and after a refreshing post-church nap, I find myself chillaxing in Tameka's living room. Darryl has taken Chloe to a friend's birthday party at an indoor trampoline park across town, and Tameka wanted to grab a couple of hours to hang with one another. Of course I'm happy to oblige my oldest friend.

Tameka's home is cute and cozy, the starter home they moved into when they got married, and have not quite felt the need to move out of yet. She likes the neighborhood, Chloe has several friends on her street, and Darryl has no desire to grow beyond his current station in life. A blunt assessment, perhaps, but also a truth bomb. Tameka, the usually ready to snap at anyone in her path Tameka, seems completely stress free with her husband and only child gone, completely relaxed in her stretchy lounge pants and tank top, a frozen drink in her hand. Her baby blender is basically a tiny magic bullet, and since Chloe has long since outgrown pureed veggies, we've found a second life for the margarita miracle, the cocktail creator, the wondrous wonder. Come through, baby blender. This virgin pineapple-coconut concoction is giving me life!

Phillip has texted me three times in a row, back-to-back, all within the span of an hour since I've been sitting here at Tameka's. She's said nothing, but keeps eyeing me curiously with each new message alert.

"So I guess you and Davis hit it off after all?" She says dryly, taking another sip of the cool drink.

"He's nice. Really nice. And you know, we've been spending a little time together here and there. He's trying his best to help me find a home."

"Ok then Reese, no need to get defensive."

"Defensive? Defensive about what?" I say, my voice involuntarily rising.

"Girl, you know you like that dude. Stop playing. 'He's trying his best to help me find a home'." She says with air quotes, laughing at my response.

"Hush, Meka. He's ok, He's nice and cute and all. That's all."

"Sure Reese, whatever. I know you'll claim him when you are ready to. When will you see him again?" Ugh, Tameka, with your nosy self. You know I'm not going to lie if I can help it.

"Tomorrow."

"When, girl? Speak up, honey, I can barely hear you." She says, cupping her hand near her ear with exaggeration.

"Tomorrow. We're looking at more homes tomorrow."

"You know y'all can just date, right? You don't have to have the man drive all over town back and forth to here and yonder when you can barely decide between sausage or pepperoni. I can't imagine how frustrating, and complicated, it must be, to try to date you AND be your realtor. Davis is a saint."

Tameka has tended to live vicariously through us for years, having been snatched off the market by Darryl at the tender age of 22. They dated for most of high school, and all throughout college, before then.

She's right on the mark with most of her comments, but sometimes she is out of touch and out of line. And where Ebony loves to talk about her love life, and frankly can discuss Braxton until your ears feel like they are bleeding, Meka is a little different. She'll throw out a nugget here and there about her relationship with Darryl, but other times she's not saying a peep. It's hard to tell if they are up or down this week, because they tend to avoid the in between. Taking in her spotless kitchen and dust free furnishings, not to mention how quiet and empty the house feels without the two of them, I would say this must be a down week. Tameka obsessively cleans when she's frustrated, and normally when she and Darryl are fighting you can smell the Clorox and pine sol through the phone. It's looking and smelling linen fresh around here today. Oh, Meka.

Trying to veer the conversation away from Davis, I instead want to bring up how Phillip has been reaching out to me again and again. And again. And I already know my dear friend won't be having it.

"So, Phillip keeps texting me. He's been, I don't know, pretty attentive lately." I slide into the discourse, hoping Tameka will be understanding. One look in her eyes means no such luck.

"He's not the dude, Reese." She deadpans, her lips pursed in response.

"What's that supposed to mean?"

"He's not the one, girl. He's not your prince, your soul mate, your one true love. None of that bull. He's not the one."

"You can't possibly know that, Tameka."

"I know that God didn't send you somebody else's husband, I know that much."

I sigh, exasperated by Tameka's attitude. Here we go. Now I'm regretting even bringing it up. She knows Phillip, she knows what he's meant to me through the years. What he means to me now. Still.

"He's separated from her. He said so."

"Of course he did. Saying, 'my wife is in the other room' would be a little inconvenient, don't you think?" Eyelashes aflutter, Tameka takes another sip while holding my gaze.

"Dang, Meka. I'm just trying to be a good friend to him, that's all."

That's not all, but if I tell her that I'm even considering starting fresh with him, that I'm even considering allowing him back into my life, I just, I don't even want to open up that can of worms. Don't get me wrong, I like Davis. I do. But if there's even a remote possibility that Phillip and I could ever be more than friends again then… then I guess I, …I just don't know. I'm not prepared to give up on that yet. Not for a guy I like. And I like Davis, but we're not exclusive or anything. Tameka doesn't say anything, just refills her glass. She places the pitcher back on the counter, picks up her glass, swirling the tropical goodness around a few times before taking another sip.

"Sure, Reese. Whatever. But don't let him play you again, that's all I'm saying."

I see no real harm in talking to Phillip. You don't stop caring about a person you've loved and known for twelve, thirteen, what, fourteen years? I don't expect Tameka to understand, misery loves company and she'd just as soon have me remain single forever as she would have me stuck in a lifeless marriage, like her. That isn't fair to her, I know. She and Darryl have been through a lot, but she just doesn't understand.

Me and Phillip, we have history together. He believed in me as a studying journalist, then a budding journalist, and even now he cheers me on as a blossoming journalist. He's been in my corner through it all. He's the one I cried my heart out to when I didn't get the CNN internship. He's the one that helped me study for finals, semester after semester. My goodness, he came home with me for Christmas, and took me to his family's home for Thanksgiving, for the duration of my college career. He was my first in every sense of the word. My first. I always hoped I would be his last. Maybe there's still time, maybe another chance for me to be his last. Unless Davis is a distraction, or is it a complication? Or more, perhaps.

"So what are you going to do? Keep texting him and living this virtual walk down memory lane? Or are you going to up the ante and see the fool?" Tameka says, casually tucking her feet under her legs on the couch. I swallow the lump forming in my throat, buying a few seconds before my next revelation.

"He wants to see me. Meet for drinks, or dinner, or something. But I don't know, I'm not sure I'm ready to."

"Girl, if you don't get out of here with that mess. You're not ready, after pining after him, ranting and raving over every single text message, whining about how great he is, for the last hour. As if my time to hang out with my best friend without Chloe clinging to my leg is limitless or something. Girl, please. How long have y'all been texting for this time? Days? Weeks?"

"Months." I say, lowering my head and refusing to meet her gaze.

"Reese. He's not the one, baby girl. You know I love you, right? I'd do anything in this world for you. But I'm not going to lie to you and tell you that Phillip's intentions are pure. I'm not going to lie to you and tell you that fate, or the universe, whatever, is bringing you back together. Naw, sis. This is some ungodly mess going on here. And if Phillip Martin is trying to breeze his way back into your life on a permanent basis, believe me when I say that he is most definitely not heaven sent. That's all I have to say. Do what you feel led to do, but don't expect me to support it."

I sip my drink in silence. Sometimes there just isn't anything left to say.

AND TROUBLES RISE

CHAPTER TEN
The Tipping Point

Have you ever stopped to think about the moments that made the difference in your life? Not the big moments. Nobody died. You didn't win the lottery. Nothing like that. The little moments. On a whim, you took a different path to work, and later find out that you avoided a car accident on your usual route. You kept having a nagging feeling that something wasn't quite right with your body, and instead of popping a couple of aspirin, again, you decided to discuss it with your doctor. Had you waited any longer, the cancer would've been untreatable. Is there a tipping point in relationships? What if the flowers, the phone calls, the shared conversations and meals, were all just a series of little moments that were leading to something spectacular? Nah. There is no tipping point, not in my book. Every moment matters. Make every one of them count.

Forever and always, Candy Girl

It's my weekend to spend with my Build Them Up group, and I'm distracted but trying my best to remain committed. I already had to get Dylan in her place this morning, she had the audacity to ask me to take her group today, too. She's really starting to work my nerves. Something's up with her, I'm not sure what, just yet, but lately she's been all over the place with planning the fundraiser. I reminded her that we all made a commitment to BTU and we all need to see it through. I'm not about to let these kids down. They're counting on us, at least my girls are. I refuse to be another broken promise in their lives.

    What started out as a workplace required community service project has quickly become one of the great joys in my life. My personal life was turned upside down when Mama got sick, and my work suffered, too. I needed a creative outlet, and Candy Girl was born. That platform has allowed me to be vulnerable in a safe space. To both tell and live my truth. I'm grateful for it, but for now, at least, I have to keep it to myself. I shudder to think about what my friends, colleagues, even church or family members might say if they knew about my online world. She'll continue to be my little secret, and I'm ok with that. And as grateful as I am for my blog, I'm even more grateful for my BTU mentees. We're supposed to be serving these kids, but I know in my heart that they are the ones who are blessing me.

    My pod includes three high school freshmen, Janae, Kiara, and Sheree. They're sweet girls, talkative and vivacious in personality. Kiara is the quietest of the bunch, but meeting as a small group has really allowed her to blossom. I'm so blessed to be able to spend time with them each month. Our discussions never disappoint.

BTU is sponsoring a college and career fair at the girls' high school next month, so for this session we have the assignment of setting three academic and career goals for each student. The girls aren't exactly enthused by this task, and have been dancing around the subject for more than an hour. Focus, ladies. We can do this.

"Hey Reese, wouldn't it just be easier to marry rich?" Sheree asks, and the other girls giggle in response.

"Put some respeck on her name, Ree. That's Miss Reese or Miss Joseph to you." Janae offers, and Kiara nods her agreement.

"Well I do declare, you have mighty fine manners, Miss Janae." I say, and the giggles are louder this time. "You guys know me, we keep it totally informal here. I don't mind if you just call me Reese. And you know it depends on the formality of the setting as well as whom you are addressing. I don't mind it, but others might. Just something to file away to remember." Dutiful Kiara takes notes, hanging on to every word I say as usual, but the others just nod.

"But to answer your question Sheree, yes it would be easier to just marry rich. But I know you want more than that out of life. I know you are capable of so much more than that."

"You say it like it's a bad thing. Always having money doesn't sound too bad to me." Sheree snaps her fingers for emphasis.

My mind races as I choose my next words. I have to remind myself that the background of each of these young queens is far different than my own. I need to see life through their lens, at least for a moment.

Janae has been in the foster system for two years now, ever since her mom began her struggle with addiction following recovery from a terrible car accident. Her battle with opioids continues, but at least she's in a residential rehab facility now.

Kiara's grandmother is raising her, and her mom is a few years younger than me. Kiara's mom was a teenager when she had her, and pops in and out of her life from time to time. She's incredibly close to her grandmother, but the sweet woman's own health struggles have overshadowed Kiara's needs.

And Sheree, bless her, has a relationship with her mother and father. But her father is in jail, and her mother works two jobs to care for Sheree and her three younger brothers. The time she spends at BTU is a respite from the heavy burdens placed upon her at a young age.

From their own mouths, each of these young women has experienced food insecurity, and none of them knows what financial security looks like, at least not in their own home. Social media ballin', yes, they are quite familiar with that.

My thoughts are interrupted by an unexpected visitor. Davis walks in, and the energy in the room is immediately electric. The girls straighten in their chairs, smoothing their hair and seemingly fighting the urge to smile too hard. Davis beams when his eyes meet mine, and I have a feeling my smile matches his own. What a pleasant surprise.

"Ladies, I'd like you to meet my dear friend, Davis." I say, and the girls ooh and ah in response. His grin dims a little, but he turns to greet the girls before placing two large bags on the counter.

"Good afternoon Ladies. As Reese said, I'm Davis. Davis Richards. It's my pleasure to meet you all Janae, Kiara, and Sheree." The girls are glowing because he knows their names, and I'm impressed that he even remembered. I think I mentioned it that first breakfast meeting at the Coffee Bean, but don't recall bringing it up since. That was ages ago.

"Are you hungry, Ladies? I brought lunch from Mimi's." Davis says, already unloading an array of culinary delights. Petite, artfully arranged trays of turkey club wraps, chicken salad sandwiches, grape salad, pasta salad, and powder sugar dotted brownies and blondies appear before our eyes. My jowls are watering, but he's not done yet. Miracle of miracles, this precious man produces half gallons of lemonade and sweet tea as well. Ok now, Davis Richards, I see you!

"Yaass, Mr. Richards. This looks amazing!" Sheree says, already out of her seat.

"Well, well, well. Just a friend, Ms. Reese, is that what you said?" Janae asks, trying her darnedest to bat those eyelashes innocently in my direction.

"Thank you for lunch, Mr. Richards." Kiara offers, cementing her role in front of company as the most well behaved of the bunch.

"Of course, Ladies. My pleasure to do so. Just trying to be a good friend." Davis says, winking at me. Thank God, I thought he was offended by my earlier remark.

"So tell me how I can get a friend like you, ok?" Janae responds, and the girls giggle again.

"Hold up, wait a minute. Are we going to keep chatting or are we going to feast on this spread that Mr. Richards was kind enough to share with us today. A girl's gotta eat, and I don't mean these tired snack bars that BTU provides." Sheree says, and we all laugh now. She's right, the snacks that are provided at each session are free, but that's about the best thing to be said about them. The Junior Board offered an alternative as a suggestion, but it was graciously declined. Just not in the budget. So

I've tried to spring for treats for my kids from time to time, and I know the rest of the Junior Board has done the same. Dylan was only too happy to tell us how she has her country club cater each session that she hosts. I hate to tell her that most of the kids find the burgers and chicken sandwiches dry and tasteless. But the snack bars are like perfectly portioned strips of cardboard in shiny wrappers. Lunch from Mimi's? Most definitely an improvement.

"Yes, of course. Why don't you all get washed up and we can get ready to eat?" The girls don't need me to tell them twice, already heading out the door to find the nearest restroom. The door has barely closed and Davis is beside me, arms outstretched for a hug, at least. Hopefully more.

"Reese, I hope you don't mind the surprise." He says, his strong arms enveloping me and his voice husky in my ear. I could stay here the rest of the afternoon, safe and warm in his embrace, but not at the expense of my time with the girls. Reluctantly, I pull away, seeing nothing but care and support in his eyes.

The girls return quickly, and I'm grateful that I broke away when I did. We gather together to bless the food, offering words of thanks for the wonderful meal that has been provided for us. Excellent co-host that he is, Davis encourages each of them to fill their plates to their liking, and truly there is more than enough food to share among the five of us, likely enough for them to take leftovers home, too. His generosity is heartfelt and appreciated. I make my plate next, with Davis close behind, then we sit down with the girls at the table. They're already digging in, clearly enjoying lunch, and I barely have a forkful of pasta salad in my mouth when they choose this moment to pick up where we left off.

"So Ms. Reese, we were talking about marriage earlier. Are you saying you don't want to get married? Like even if a handsome, eligible bachelor came along. Perhaps bearing lunch, for example?"

If Sheree was sitting closer I might've tapped her leg with my foot, or given her a good pinch, at least. Janae guffaws, but all Kiara can manage is an awkward smile. I finish chewing my bite of pasta, ruminating for a moment before speaking. Davis eyes me with curiosity, but is otherwise quiet as he awaits my response.

"I never said I didn't want to get married, Sheree. Perhaps one day I will. But marriage is a tremendous commitment. It's not to be taken lightly. And I would want to make sure that my motivation for marriage is for the right reasons, and most definitely, with the right person."

Davis' expression is blank, but I wish I knew what he was thinking. Sheree, Janae, and Kiara are all ears, their eyes wide with expectation.

"My advice to you all was not to see marriage as a ticket out of whatever circumstances you find yourself in. Marriage is a partnership, it requires work to make it work, it's placing your trust in God and trusting your mate with your heart. A marriage is what you make of it. Not what you can take from it. That's all I was trying to say." I can't meet his eyes when I say these words, not sure I want to see what they will tell me. The girls nod solemnly, continuing to eat their food. After a few quiet moments, Kiara looks over at Davis.

"And you, Mr. Richards. How do you feel about marriage?" Her large brown eyes are anxious, dear Kiara forever carrying the weight of the world on her shoulders.

Davis clears his throat, and if he's caught off guard by the question he certainly doesn't let on. He wipes his mouth with his napkin, takes a sip of his lemonade, then smiles directly at Kiara.

"I believe that marriage is a beautiful thing. What a unique and special testament to God's love for His children. Not the most important way, but truly such an important way for us to feel and know God's love for each of us. And I wholeheartedly agree with Reese, it's a tremendous commitment that should not be entered into on a whim. It's serious business. And with the right person, and with God at the center, it can be such a beautiful thing."

"Would you ever want to get married Mr. Richards?"

"He's already been married." I offer, but I instantly regret it.

"Oop, I need alllll the tea." Sheree exclaims, craning her neck around.

"No, I didn't mean it like that. You see, it's just that…" My cheeks are burning as I struggle to find the words to clean up my mess. They seem nowhere to be found, try as I may to grasp for them.

"Reese is correct. I was married to a lovely woman who left this earth far too soon. And we had a wonderful, albeit brief, marriage. But she is gone, and I am here. I will forever cherish her memory. And if God should see fit for me to do so, I would one day love to be married again."

I swallow the lump in my throat so deeply that I swear the rest of the room can hear it. Davis is so willing to share what's on his mind, so eloquent in how he expresses his thoughts and feelings, so profound in the simple way he honors what Iris meant, and still means to him, I can't help but be moved. I look over at my charges, each of them practically swooning from his words. Sheree's hand is even placed purposefully over her heart, her mouth open in surprise.

"That was so sweet Mr. Richards. We hope you find love again, don't we?" Sheree asks, daring the others to disagree.

"Yes, definitely. But only if it's with someone that can appreciate the kind of person you are." Janae agrees, her eyes pointedly narrowed at me. Kiara nods her agreement, and Davis offers a soft smile of gratitude.

"You know, Ladies, this was so sweet of Davis to stop by and visit with us today. And for treating us to this amazing lunch, too. But we really need to get back to our assignment if we want to finish today. And I'm sure that Davis has a million things to do." Groans follow this statement, and I hope I haven't lost their engagement, or this will be one long afternoon.

"Actually, Reese, I cleared my calendar today. If ya'll don't mind my help, I can hang with you all for the rest of the afternoon."

With this statement the mood instantly lifts, Sheree and Janae clapping their hands together in glee.

"Can he stay, Ms. Reese? We don't mind at all." Sheree says, her eyes begging me to agree to their request. I look from Davis, to each of the girls, and back to Davis again. How could I say no and disappoint them all? Clearly outnumbered, I feel like my only option is to say yes.

I'll give it to Davis, he's growing on me. But don't tell anyone.

CHAPTER ELEVEN

Made with Love

So I wasn't going to say it but it needs to be said. You can't eat everyone's cooking, and you shouldn't eat at everyone's table. I'm not talking about enemies, either. Some friends put raisins in the potato salad. I'll pass on that. Some folks don't know how to behave at the cookout. They want their share and yours, too. I'll just be over here, minding my business. Having my slice of cake, and eating it, too.

Living Life Abundantly,

Candy Girl

There's an air of familiarity that has settled between us, me and Davis. Davis and me. Us. We're feeling more and more like we could be an us. And I don't know what to make of us. Presently we're strolling through Oak City's Saturday morning Farmer's Market, just enjoying this beautiful spring day together. The weather is gorgeous, and the market is buzzing with young and old alike. We carefully weave our way through the crowds, not quite holding hands, but keeping the space between us close enough to do just that. Tiny, pulsating, tingles seem to tickle my senses every time our hands brush against one another. At least it seems that way to me, but Davis doesn't seem to mind.

"Let me cook for you tonight, Reese." Davis says, much more of a statement than a question, really. I smile back at him, but I'm beaming on the inside.

"So you cook?" I say, hoping my tone conveys my disbelief. I certainly hope he doesn't ask me if I do, though. Boiling water has to count for something.

"Sure I do. A man has to eat. Well, this one does. And take out grows old after a while."

"That's true." A nervous giggle escapes as I inwardly pray that he doesn't inquire about my own culinary skills, or lack thereof. Davis is oblivious as he continues to examine the vast array of delectable fruits and vegetables at the current stand we've stopped at to browse. The vendor, a silver-haired, portly gentleman, his face and forearms weathered by years of working the land, no doubt, merrily be-bops to the old school Motown blasting from his little portable radio. Diana says you can't hurry love, and Lord knows I can testify to that. He catches my eyes, and we share a broad smile.

"Howdy-do, ma'am. You folks let me know if I can help you with anything." He says, tipping his straw hat to me. We nod and smile, continuing to admire his rows and rows of fresh produce.

"These tomatoes are beautiful." Davis remarks, and I can't help but agree with his clear admiration for the plump, juicy looking tomatoes in the baskets. Think, Reese. Think. Name that tomato. Shoot! Red doesn't count, does it?

"Do you like heirloom tomatoes, Reese?" Heirloom, duh. Got it, heirloom tomatoes, I mentally file it away.

"Yes, I've always been partial to a good heirloom tomato." I respond, and it's true. Never knew what they were called, but I've always thought they were tasty.

"And do you like to cook, too, Reese?" Well, here we go. A fairly innocuous question, but of course every southern man wants a woman who can cook like his mama. How can I cook like *his* mama when I can't even cook like mine? Not that she didn't ever try to teach me; she did. I just wasn't a very good pupil. I won't dare bring up the time I tried to cook Thanksgiving dinner. That was the year mama started her chemo. And if I still don't talk about it, I don't want anyone else bringing it up, either.

"I still have a lot to learn." Maybe that will seem to be the perfect combination of honesty and humility.

"Don't we all, Reese. Don't we all." His smile widens, and once again I'm struck by his beautiful smile. Watching him now, I can't help but notice the painstaking consideration he gives to each item before placing it in our basket to purchase. His hands deftly move over the tomatoes, gently examining the heads of cabbage and lettuce, softly caressing the, Lord have mercy, I'm staring at this man. Heat rises in my cheeks as I try to turn my attention elsewhere. Be cool, Reese.

Davis is not the only cute guy I've ever been around. He's not the only attractive one I've ever dated. Why, oh, why do I get so flustered around him? He selects a small basket of tomatoes and makes his purchase from the vendor, who nods in my direction and makes a comment to Davis, I'm just far enough away to miss what it was, but Davis' smile grows in response. He walks back over to me and we continue through the market.

"What was that about?"

"Oh, Mr. James? He just said that I've got a lovely young lady with me and I better stay on my P's and Q's if I want to keep enjoying her company."

"Is that so?" I ask, turning back around to look at Mr. James. He's not watching us walk away, still dancing to the music as if no one is watching. We should all be smart enough to choose to live this way.

"And what did you say to him?"

"He was absolutely correct. So I told him so." Davis says, chuckling. I playfully punch his arm, laughing with him. Meeting his gaze, the rest of the market seems to melt away, and I look away, jolted by the intensity of the moment. Better to keep walking and just keep shopping. If I take a few deep breaths, maybe I can keep my heart from racing. Maybe.

Looking just ahead, I notice a lovely display of flowers and house plants, and of course I'm drawn to the hydrangeas. Their shimmering periwinkle blossoms make for a beautiful arrangement. They're my favorites, little clusters of happiness, something akin to the Pleiades lighting up the night sky. I make my way over to them, briefly separating from Davis. This display is lush and inviting, with a wide variety or perky blossoms and shimmering blooms. And in a booth full of beauty, the hydrangeas are clearly the standouts for me. Feeling warmth near me, I look up and see that Davis has reappeared at my side. I wonder how long he's been there.

"Beautiful, aren't they?" He asks, and I nod in agreement.

"They're gorgeous." I say, and his eyes brighten with interest.

"Would you like us to get some?"

"Oh, no. But thank you." I'd love for us to take some with us, but I don't want him to feel pressured. 'What is wrong with you, Reese? Girl, you better let that man get you some flowers', I hear Tameka's voice say in my head.

"Shall we go, then?" He says, looking directly at me as he extends his hand towards mine.

"Yes, let's." I respond, reaching for his hand and savoring the comfort of its warmth and strength around my own.

~

Davis drops me off at home to get ready, and I agree to meet him at his home for dinner in a few hours. I'm pretty easy to please, food wise, liking a little bit of everything, as long as dessert is good. And since I already know he purchased a red velvet cheesecake from Sugar & Spice, even if dinner is over-seasoned or difficult to chew, I can still look forward to an amazing dessert. Dessert first, words to live by. Can't go wrong with that.

Now if I could only figure out what to wear tonight. Something sassy but not too sexy. Fashionable, of course, but not too flirty. Elegant but not too eager. That's the vibe I'm sticking with for tonight.

"You betta keep that nickel between your knees, Reesie." I hear Ms. Bean's voice say. Not that I have any plans to let the night go there.

There was a time, soon after Phillip broke up with me, that it seemed like I tried to punish myself more than he ever did. I allowed his infidelity to make me feel unworthy of love. The real deal, at least. But a night with a handsome stranger, now *that* was a welcome diversion, and it provided me with a false sense of security. I believed the lie that the guy I shared a bed with was in it for the long haul, instead of racing to get out the door the next morning.

I'll admit it, I enjoyed it a bit at first. The newness of it, the departure of "good girl Reese", the feeling that I was in complete control and had total autonomy over my body. How I was wrong. After the third guy, Andrew, ended with a pregnancy scare, I knew I had to make a change. It was the wake-up call I needed before it was too late. I wasn't pregnant then, thank God, but a late period was all it took to show me there had to be a better way. Heart heavy, spirit broken and contrite, I found my way back to God. Thankful for His grace and mercy that sustained me through it all.

So even though I've "dropped the nickel" a few times before, tonight it is firmly in place, holding steady from my relationship with God instead of fear of Ms. Bean's, or my parents', wrath. My sexual appetite hasn't diminished, not in the least, but now I want to feast on the provision of a God-centered marriage instead of settling for fast food that still leaves you hungry afterward.

I settle for leggings and a ruffled tunic, casual yet cute, and twirl around to check my fit. Yes, this will work. Girl next door instead of red-light district. Yes, Lawd, let the church say amen.

But my hair, whew, is another story altogether. Alabama's weather is always hit or miss, and some days in between. Fine if you're a mole and don't plan on seeing the light of day anytime soon, not so fine if you spend your career in the public eye. Strolling through the farmer's market with your man is cute and all until you break a sweat and your fresh silk press frizzes out. So these tresses will be tightly wrapped in a printed silk scarf tonight. Davis says he likes a more natural look on a woman, but I've heard that one before. Let's see if his words are more than lip service.

~

"Reese, you look great. Please, come in." The door is open wide as Davis beckons me to come inside. The aroma wafting through the entrance is simply intoxicating. Everything smells wonderful, and I admit it, I'm more than a little impressed. And hungry. Not playing when it comes to food this evening. I never do.

"It smells glorious in here, Davis."

"Thanks, Reese. I hope you brought your appetite with you. I've tried my best to whip up a little sumthin, sumthin." Davis I've brought my appetite and the neighbor's, too. I hope it's not in vain.

"A little something? Davis, this is enough to feed the multitude." I say, looking around at the offerings spread on his table. I'm so focused on the food that I barely notice the rest of his town home.

Davis has taken great care to artfully arrange an elegant table, the place settings gleaming, the cream linen tablecloth draped just so, and a gorgeous centerpiece of periwinkle hydrangeas, framed by softly flickering candles. A small moan escapes as I take it all in. There's a familiar sound in the air, the melodies dancing around the room. I recognize Ellington and Coltrane's "In a Sentimental Mood", and my head swims a bit with the restrained beauty of it all.

Davis guides me over to the table, pulling my chair out so that I can sit down. I'm silent, speechless, really. The spinach salad that appears before me is delicate and lovely, and I look up to see Davis holding a carafe of lemonade. No detail is overlooked. I'm amazed at how well he already seems to know me. After pouring the lemonade, Davis is gone again, but only momentarily. Next he brings a small basket of fluffy, golden, yeast rolls. Each little pillow of happiness looks buttery smooth and delicious.

"Davis." I say, hating to interrupt his carefully choreographed display.

"Reese." He stops at the mention of his name, signaling his focus has shifted to me.

"Davis, thank you for making this effort. Thank you for inviting me over for dinner." I hope he knows how sincere I am when I say this.

"Reese, believe me when I say that it is an honor and privilege to share the evening with you." His warm eyes are deep and dark, inviting me to escape with him. His sincerity exceeds my own. I have no doubt that his desire to be here with me is great and true.

After checking on the other components of our meal, Davis returns to me. He's so handsome, his strong arms highlighted by his knit polo and slacks. He reaches for my hand, and a pulse of electricity shocks us both. We smile, our hands continuing to tingle as they are intertwined. He bows his head respectfully, and I do the same. And then he thanks God for the joy of our day together, and he prays for our meal and evening, which already feels blessed. Saying amen, I feel the slightest mist gathering in the corners of my eyes. Are my feelings betraying me, Lord?

We feast on the salad, then the balsamic glazed chicken he's paired with root vegetables and roasted new potatoes from the market. Each bite tastes better than the last. I'm blown away. Davis said he liked to cook, he didn't say he could rival a chef with his talent. What other mysteries and wonders are in store? There's something, there's got to be something I'm not seeing. He's a mama's boy? He has bad credit? His feet are ugly? There's got to, got to be something wrong with this guy. There's chemistry between us, and the conversations flow so easily from subject to subject. I feel safer just being in his presence. He's not perfect, no man is. There's got to be something, I just can't see it because of the smile, and grace, the intelligence, and warmth, I'm missing it somehow. That's the only reasonable explanation.

Davis excuses himself from the table, offering to start a pot of coffee as he plates dessert, but I pass. He's just a room away, but it feels like he's close enough to hear my thoughts in my head. I sip the lemonade and question everything I've been feeling over the last couple of months. What was life like before I met Davis? Why has every moment of my life seemed better since?

"So Reese, I know this is a relaxing evening together, not a business outing, and I don't want to make it awkward. But I was wondering had you given any thought to the last home we saw. You seemed to really like that one, but weren't sure if you wanted to make an offer?"

Ah, yes. That one. The single family home that felt like home the moment I stepped across the threshold. It's crossed my mind several times over the last few days, but I don't know, I don't know. I loved the kitchen, and the size of the master bedroom and closets, all of the storage was great for growing into. The whole house was, to tell the truth. There was a cute yard, but it was manageable, and I think I could handle it. Daddy taught his little girl pretty well. At the very least, I know how to pick up the phone and call someone who can. The place felt warm, inviting even, like I could picture my things on the shelves, my art and photographs on the walls. Like I could share movie nights with Davis on the couch. It was too good to be true, right? Surely there was a busted pipe lurking under a sink, or an uneven foundation, a tree leaning against the home, something? But alas, no, it seemed to have everything I said I wanted and needed.

"I liked it, Davis. I really did. I'm just not sure if I'm ready to take that next step."

"You want to keep looking?" He's dubious, knowing how much I seemed to like the home.

"I don't know what I want to do. I don't want to waste your time, you've been great, but I don't think I'm ready to put in an offer yet." His crestfallen expression shows me everything I need to know about that.

"Reese?"

"Yes, Davis?"

"I think I know what the issue is." He says, putting a finger to his chin.

"Oh yeah? Enlighten me."

"I think you know that's the one, you know that everything you needed, and said you wanted, is right there. After looking, and hoping, wishing, and praying for so long, now that God has placed it in your path, you just don't know how to handle it. Maybe the blessing is more than you expected." I feel the tears spring to my eyes now, and I'm powerless to stop them.

"Hey, hey now. Hey, Reese. I didn't mean to upset you. I just don't want you to miss out on what God has for you." He says, gently rubbing my shoulder. Davis, sweet Davis. You are much more than I expected. But we're talking about homes. We're talking about homes, right?

Davis leans over, gently tracing the contours of my face with the soft caress of his fingers.

Stopping at my chin, he cups it, lifting it ever so slightly so that our eyes meet. Locked together, I dare not look away.

"I care about you, Reese Joseph. These last few months have been amazing, every moment with you has been a wonderful time together. And I know you've been hurt before, and I know that you're a strong, intelligent, beautiful, and independent woman, but I also know that we are good together, Reese. I know you feel it, too. Whatever your reservations, I'm willing to work through them. Whatever barriers you see, I know that we can overcome them. Because I like you, Reese. I really, really like you. I like where this is going. And I want to spend a lot more time with you. I don't want either one of us to let this blessing pass us by."

My mouth parts, ever so slightly, as much out of surprise as it is inviting him to come closer, and Davis, answering the call, leans forward to meet his smooth and taut, pillowy lips, with my own.

Who needs dessert? Kisses from this man are sweeter than any confection I've had the pleasure to enjoy.

CHAPTER TWELVE
Guess Who's Coming to Dinner?

I have a simple relationship rule about meeting the parents: I don't. I did, once, and the subsequent relationship, and finally the separation from them was almost as painful as the breakup from their son. Not that I have anything against parents, because who am I kidding, I love my own. Wouldn't trade them for anything. But there's this thing with meeting the parents. Beyond the getting to know you phase, now I'm getting to know where you come from. Now I'm auditioning to make my position in your life more permanent. And don't start on the wrong foot with the parental units, either. Baby, hell hath no fury like a boyfriend's mother scorned. So while I don't mind receiving the approval of others, it's not required for my existence. Last I checked, we are full grown, so let's keep our parents out of it.

My two cents, Candy Girl

Why am I dreading church this morning? Any other time I would be praise dancing around the house, singing songs and preparing for worship, but today, today somehow feels like an event I am dreading instead. Davis invited me to worship with him at his church this morning, followed by dinner with his mother afterward. Afraid of disappointing him, I quickly said yes while my heart screamed, "NO"! But Sunday has arrived, and I find myself struggling with the knots that are twisting in my stomach. Fix it, Jesus!

    I keep pacing between my closet and the mirror, never quite satisfied with the outfits I have chosen. I definitely want to look my best, but there's so much more to it than that. For one, Mrs. Richards will be there. I'm feeling the pressure to impress his mother, much more than I would care to admit to. For another, this will be our first time attending church together. My church is a fraction of the size of his, with many less members, too. But Third Day Missionary Baptist Church? Chile, it is one of the largest churches in Oak City, and the largest predominantly African-American one by a mile. That's hundreds of eyes watching us today. Hundreds of people he knows, and I likely know as well, suddenly invited to pay attention to our relationship. Things are going great with Davis, so great, in fact, that I don't want to do anything to jinx it. I just want to enjoy it while it lasts. Heaven knows I'm keeping my expectations low, just in case.

    I settle on a scallop-sleeved, turquoise sheath dress. Davis likes me in bright colors, and frankly, I feel pretty darn good in them if I do say so myself.

My taupe heels and printed clutch will be appropriately neutral, and I walk around my room for a few minutes to make sure the shoes are still comfortable. The last thing I need is to make a fool of myself tripping in the aisle on the way to give my offering. My makeup is super simple, my hair falling in loose waves on my shoulders. Normally the humidity would be too much for me, but thank God that Alabama's discombobulated weather has afforded me at least one perfect hair day in a lovely spring weather package.

Davis arrives on time, as usual. I hear the bell and dash up the stairs, stopping in the foyer to smooth down my hair and dress. I try to open it casually, as if I'm accustomed to being on time for any occasion. But Davis knows better, and the glimmer in his eyes says as much as he breaks into a wide grin when I open the door.

"Reese, Baby, you look wonderful." He says, leaning forward to envelop me in one of his strong hugs. I lean against him, inhaling his cologne and relishing the comfort of his embrace. He pulls away first, but the heat emanating from his body lingers.

"You clean up nicely yourself, Mr. Richards." I wink at him, happy to flirt with my man.

"Shall we go and give God some praise this morning?"

"Is there ever a bad time to praise Him?" I ask, my arm finding its natural place in the crook of his. He shakes his head "no" in response, and I reach back to close the door behind us. A small step or two down the front walkway, and before we know it we've made it to his car. Davis releases my arm only to lean forward and open my car door.

"Thank you." I smile up at him, grateful that chivalry isn't dead after all. Tameka says that a man doesn't have to open doors for you, and she's right, he doesn't "have to". But in my opinion, if he's a real gentleman he should at the very least want to. So I sincerely appreciate that Davis wants to open doors for me every time we're together. As simple as the gesture is, it's still appreciated.

After gently closing my door, Davis makes his way around to the driver's side. Sliding in effortlessly, I'm finally noticing his own attire. His cologne instantly warms and fills the space, and this dashing man looks so handsome in his chestnut plaid suit, a hint of French blue threads weaving its way through the pattern and highlighted by his shirt and bow tie. Yes Lawd, he can wear a suit. Starting the car, I hear the sounds of Tasha Cobbs-Leonard and I know that everything is going to be alright after all.

~

We walk into Third Day and lo and behold, there's a sizeable crowd with more than a few inquiring minds. Based on their curious looks, they want to know what's going on between us, but Davis and I are quiet as we walk hand in hand to our pew. I started to release his hand as we entered the sanctuary, but Davis didn't give up too easily. If anything, it seemed like his hand squeezed mine a bit instead. I'm not at all ashamed of the man, but dang, let me get a little comfortable with this development, at least. The last thing I need is viewers calling into the station or sending nasty emails about their opinions about my love life. I'll never forget my social media cleanse from a couple of years ago. I had posted a photo from an event for the city, the Mayor's Annual Gala, I think, and I was escorted by a local minister. The hate and vitriol I received in the comments, many from his members, no less, was more than enough for me to think twice about advertising my personal life again. I'm proud to walk beside Davis, but more than a little skittish about the response it might generate.

We find a pew that's not quite in the front, not quite in the back, but somewhere right in the middle. It's a pretty good spot, actually, at least for saint watching. Church viewing. Whatever you want to call it. Davis points his mother out, she's several pews away from us, and not looking in our direction at the moment. She's serving frowning church mother realness, I can see that, even from this distance. I'll plan to glance over from time to time, casually really, just to see if she's noticed us. Or maybe not. One pinched glare would be all it takes to kill my vibe.

We've arrived during the brief interlude between their Sunday School and morning worship service, so the church is still buzzing with saints filing to their seats. Third Day's many pews are starting to fill up, and I'm glad we came when we did. I'm also glad our arrival wasn't a distraction to the worship service, and soon the attention of the congregation will be focused elsewhere. Maybe there's something to the whole being on time thing after all.

AND TROUBLES RISE

The former First Lady of Third Day, Rachel Parker, is glowing in her pew. She's always been an attractive woman to me, but the Kelly green dress she's wearing is especially pretty on her. She looks elegant, regal even, her arm entwined with a handsome, milk chocolate brother that look pretty dapper himself. Sister Parker, I see you girl, boo'd up at church, finding love after all you've been through. When her husband was murdered a couple of years ago it was a huge scandal for Oak City, tragic and so sad for her and her children. It took nearly a year for them to find the killer, too. Shock of all shocks when the whole world learned who the killer was… I just don't know how she got through that mess.

But I don't know, there's a completely different vibe here now. I don't know much about Third Day's new first couple, Pastor Paul and Sister Marianne Dexter, but Davis has had nothing but good things to say about them. And as service begins, I have to admit, it is definitely not like the Third Day I remember. I guess I'll give it a chance. Who knows what good things are in store for us today? I give Davis' arm a little squeeze, nodding slightly toward Sister Parker. He smiles a sheepish grin, but says nothing. Now I know this is not the time or the place for gossip, but I'm here for all of the news, at least what I can get. Tameka isn't here, which is a shame, because she always has the "church announcements", i.e., the tea on the members of the churches in our community.

"My cousin, Grayson Shepherd." Davis says, in a tone so low it's nearly a whisper.

"What did you say?" I ask, unsure if I heard him correctly.

"Sister Parker is dating my cousin, Grayson Shepherd. He's a chaplain on base." Hmm, interesting. Not a pastor, but still a preacher.

"And is it serious?" Stop it, Reese. Don't get too nosy up in here. You're supposed to be here for the message, not the mess.

"They've been a couple for a while now, at least a year or so. He seems really happy, and just look at her. She's glowing. She seems much happier now, lighter in spirit, than she ever was when Pastor Parker was still alive." That's what it is, what I couldn't put my finger on before. Her whole countenance has improved considerably, she's in a happier place. Bless you, Sister Parker. To come out from the storm to see the light of day. Yeah, she is living her best life now. And if that isn't encouragement to keep pushing and praying, I don't know what it is. Ok now, Reese Joseph. Back to the service. I don't know what you came to do, but I came to praise the Lord!

~

Worship service was on fire today! The Spirit of the Lord was felt throughout the sanctuary. I don't know what I was expecting from Third Day, but it most certainly wasn't that. I guess God was preparing me for the battle ahead, because despite the angels and crosses hanging on the shelves and walls, Mrs. Esther Richards' home feels like leaving a tropical oasis and walking straight into Siberia. Be with me, Lord Jesus.

After a lovely Soul Food Sunday meal of baked chicken, macaroni and cheese, collard greens, cornbread, field peas, and sliced tomatoes, we're sitting around the dinette in her eat-in kitchen, grateful for the food, if not for the conversation. At least there's peach cobbler. A rich, decadent, luscious, melt-in-your-mouth, slap-your-mama kind of cobbler. She may not be the friendliest, but this woman can cook. That's the truth.

"Remember how Iris used to love my peach cobbler, Davis?" Mrs. Esther asks, since no one brought up Iris, last I checked. She's been doing this for the last hour or so, subtly, and sometimes not-so-subtly, working her name, her heroics, her memories, into the conversation. Mrs. Richards has a short, wider frame, and a deep, ebony complexion, but she seems to stand a little taller each time she notices my discomfort. Surely I'm just imagining her disdain? One can only hope. I take another spoonful of this gooey deliciousness, the peaches a perfect balance of sweet, with just a hint of tartness. A bit like me.

"Yes, she did, Mama. She really did."

"Honey yes. She could eat half a pan by herself." Mrs. Esther folds her arms across her middle, releasing a big bellowing laugh. Davis joins in, and I'm the intruder of this cherished, and shared, remembrance from the past. I'm feeling more than a little outnumbered when it comes to capturing Davis' attention. How would one compete with a tragically lost daughter-in-law, anyway? I haven't minded the conversations where he's mentioned Iris, not between just the two of us, at least. I've discussed my past to him, too, sometimes more open than others. Iris isn't coming back, and Phillip, well Phillip…it's a little more complicated with Phillip, I think, swallowing another mouthful of cobbler. I figure now's a good a time as any to offer a compliment.

"Well, it's truly delicious Mrs. Esther." Probably the best peach cobbler I've ever tasted, but I know that saying this would seem disingenuous to her.

"And I know she would've perfected the recipe, too. I'm sure of it. That is, if she had been given the chance." She moves away from the counter and walks over to Davis' chair, gently placing her hands on his shoulders. She stops and stares at me, compelling me to meet her gaze. "She could do anything she set her mind to."

"She sounds like she truly was a wonderful woman." I say, keeping my tone even as I look directly at her. Davis is oblivious to this silent battle, he's seemingly unconcerned that his dear mother is sizing his girlfriend up, and so far it doesn't seem like I'll measure up.

"She was a wonderful daughter-in-law, yes she was. More like a daughter, she was." She's crossed her arms now, continuing to hold my gaze. "Of course, she wasn't on TV or anything. Not a celebrity by any means, but she was beautiful enough to be famous, yes. She could've been a movie star.

And she was a star, to us. She just so happened to be a real and regular, amazing young woman." I try to overlook the clear dig at my profession, but it stings a bit. I've heard it all before, people asking about my "little" TV career, or folks joking that I get paid to read, silly stuff like that. And of course, I get comments that I must think I'm "big time" because I happen to be on the news. I've worked incredibly hard to achieve what I've done, and I continue to work hard each day. I've been seen as a pretty face before, and have overcompensated to show that I belong in news. More than anything, it has been God's hand on my life that has brought me this far, and I'm grateful. But I doubt Mrs. Richards would understand these things about me. She thinks she already has me figured out.

Davis is being extra quiet, unusually absorbed by the dessert in front of him. So that's how it's going to be? The two most important people in your life are dancing around each other, and you can't so much as give your girl a little support? A middle-school dance would be less awkward.

"So Mama, Reese volunteers with some of the local teens through a community group, Build Them Up. She's a mentor and truly encourages them. I had the pleasure of witnessing her in action one day, and she's really, really great with the young ladies." He's beaming when he says this, the words for her but the smile in his eyes is fully for my benefit.

"Don't say? Well, that's nice. When's the last time you talked to Daphne, Davis?" She asks, already clearing some of the dishes off of the table. I rise to help, but she shushes me back to my seat.

"I would be glad to help, Mrs. Richards." I offer, still trying my best to earn at least a portion of her favor.

"That's not necessary, Reese. Davis, you were saying?"

"Oh, I uh, I talked to her last week, Mama."

I try to make eye contact with Davis again, but he's preoccupied with his sweet tea now. I guess this seems like a good enough time to leave the room. Being polite is exhausting at this point, and I could use a mental break.

"If you'll excuse me for just a moment, please, Mrs. Richards. May I use your restroom?"

"Of course. Davis, please show your guest the way." She responds, turning back to the pans on the stove.

Davis rises, extending his hand towards mine. I grab it gratefully, allowing him to guide me to the restroom.

"I'm so glad you're here, Reese." He says when we are safely out of earshot.

"I'm glad somebody is." I say, and I know he knows full well what I mean. You could cut the tension between us and the room would still feel stifling. His expression darkens, the smile in response is tight instead of the warm one that is so familiar.

"Don't mind Mama, Reese. She's still an old school educator at heart. If she's impressed with you she's not going to show it, but I suspect she is." There's no relief in this admission, though. Despite his claims to the contrary, I doubt very seriously that his mother thinks much of me at all. We're at the entrance to the hall bathroom now, so Davis gives my hand a little squeeze for support. I guess my official escort is over now. I smile, then go on in, gently closing the door behind me.

A modest guest bathroom greets me, stylized in the same faith-based motif of her great room and kitchen. Sweet haloed angels on the shelves. Framed scriptures hanging on the walls. And the owner fresh out of hospitality. Not exactly Christ-like, you think?

After using the restroom, I wash my hands, agonizing over my reflection in the mirror. Is something on my face? Stuck between my teeth? Are my clothes too tight? I had low expectations coming into today; I'll be the first to admit it. But I was still hopeful. Hopeful that we could hit it off. After all, the whole reason we're even sharing a meal today is because of our common interest, Davis. We care for him in different ways, but still, he means so much to both of us. Surely that's enough?

I exit the bathroom, slowly sauntering down the hall back towards the kitchen. A wall of family portraits seems to watch my every move. I see a large family portrait of Mrs. Richards and all of her children: Davis, Elliott, and Daphne. There are various pictures of the kids, all at different ages, too. Then a large family picture at the very end, this one is of the entire family together. I study this one more intently, allowing my eyes to rest on each member of the Richards Family. While Daphne and Elliott clearly favor their mother in skin tone and features, the resemblance between Davis and Mr. Richards is nothing short of astounding. He looks exactly like a younger version of his father. Same build, same coloring, everything. I'm floored by this. The final one is a wedding portrait of Mr. and Mrs. Richards. She was a lovely young woman in her high-necked, long-sleeved lace gown, her thick hair arranged in artful curls to frame her face. And if I didn't know any better I would think it was Davis standing next to her. How did I not ever know how much he resembles his deceased father? Standing here, mere steps from the kitchen, I'm suddenly aware of the conversation taking place nearby.

"I didn't think you would ever disrespect me like this, Davis. Elliott, maybe, he's always been something else. But not my Davis. And to disrespect Iris' memory, too? I expected better from you, son."

"Mama, disagreement is not disrespect. You know that I will always love you and respect you as my mother. That doesn't mean I have to agree with everything you say or do. And I know you don't agree with everything I say or do, either."

"You got that right. What makes you think I want you bringing some woman in here, sashaying through my house like she's part of this family? Iris was family, Davis. She was your wife."

"And she's gone, Mama. After years of fighting for her life she is finally at rest. You know how much I loved her…I still do. But I am glad she is no longer suffering. And I am glad God brought Reese into my life…"

"The enemy could've sent her your way, ever think about that?"

"Mama, you don't mean that. If you gave her even half a chance you would see just how special she is. If you looked a little closer you would see just how happy your oldest son is again. For the first time since I don't know when I am truly smiling again. Don't you want me to be happy, Mama?"

"Of course I want you to be happy. You were happy with Iris, Davis. You made each other happy. There's no one that can replace what the two of you shared together. No one."

"You're right, Mama. Iris is irreplaceable in our hearts. But I don't want Reese to replace her. I don't want her to destroy her memory. Iris is gone, Mama. She lived a good life in her short time on this earth. I am a better man because of her. And she loved you, Mama. She loved you so much. But we are still here. Right here in the present. And I don't want to destroy Iris' memory, but I do want to build new memories with Reese. In the here and now. If God ordains it, for the future."

I hear her gasp, and can only imagine the expression on her face. My heart swells by his words, though, with my respect for Davis intensifying with every word he says. He's willing to stand toe-to-toe with his mother to defend our relationship? I can respect that. I see you, Davis Richards. I see you.

My enthusiasm is tempered as the floor creaks because of my sudden movement. I'm mortified, knowing that they must have heard me eavesdropping on their conversation.

"Did you hear something, Davis?"

"No, ma'am. But thank you for listening to my heart, Mama." She sighs again, and instead of disappointment, I breathe a sigh of relief.

"I listened to your heart because you are my heart, Davis. You always have been, And if you care about Reese, the least I can do is give her a chance. I'm not saying she'll grow on me, but if nothing else I'll pray more. How about that?" He chuckles softly now.

"Mama, just give her a chance. That's all that I ask. And I promise I won't give you a hard time when she changes your mind."

Sensing a natural conclusion to their heart-to-heart, I breeze back in, hoping to very casually reenter the room.

"Thank you, Mrs. Richards. That was just what I needed." I say, smiling at her. She purses her lips in response, but says nothing.

Well, so much for second chances. But if nothing else, at least this afternoon of breaking bread together has revealed a key truth about Davis: He loves his mama, but he is *not* a mama's boy. And I am grateful for the difference.

AND TROUBLES RISE

CHAPTER THIRTEEN
Full Plates and Empty Cups

It's too much sometimes. From work to family to friends to dating and living and volunteering, it's too much. My plate is full and my cup is empty. How can I be a blessing to someone else when my own tank is merely existing on fumes and a prayer? Yet and still, I press on. I'm in this race for the long haul, and my greatest competition won't go down without a fight. The race isn't given to the swift, and your girl plans to endure until the very end. But can a sister get a timeout, a water break, or just a moment to catch my breath? A little bit can go a long way.

Not easily broken, Candy Girl

Spring has given way to summer, and the sweltering heat is merciless this time of year. Every nook and cranny of my body is begging for a cool shower, for the second time today, and it's only ten a.m. Alexa, find air conditioned bras. Is that not a thing yet? It should be. I can't even try on sundresses in peace because of this disrespectful heat.

Davis will be here around 11:00, which means I may actually be on time today. Who am I kidding? I'm nowhere near ready to accompany him to his aunt's get together this afternoon. He's framed it as a simple outdoor barbeque, but his mom will be there, so take that for what you will. If his family can cook like him, then I'll just have to enjoy the ribs prepared in the presence of my enemies. Well, enemy.

Thinking about you Reese.

I'll be your way in a few weeks. Can we link up?

I'd love to take you to dinner.

Why, Phillip? Why move our friendship beyond its current stage? I know that eventually he will wear me down, he always could, he always has. But there's something innocent about a text here or there. Meeting for dinner feels much more foreboding. And what would I tell Davis? I consider my words carefully as I text my response.

I don't know. I'll think about it. Swamped right now.

No lies detected. I don't know if I'll ever feel ready to meet up in person. I'll think about it, but that doesn't mean I'll say yes. And I am swamped right now. Dylan accepted a position with a firm in North Carolina; she's leaving in two weeks, and take a wild guess as to who she asked to take the reins? It's not so much that she wanted me to take over, but since no one else on the committee volunteered to do it, I felt compelled to say yes. But I could have said no. Not to mention work, with the upcoming special election for mayor. Three dynamic candidates are making this one a real nail-biter, and since our station's resident political reporter accepted a position with our sister station in St. Louis, we've all been stretched a bit until his position is filled. Then there's Mama's upcoming appointment with her oncologist. She's optimistic about her last scan, but I know it will weigh on me until she gets the all clear. This plate isn't just full, it's getting heavy, too.

~

We arrived without incident, and the last hour or so has been enjoyable, for the most part. Standing in line to get another lemonade, I take in my surroundings with a rumbling stomach and nervous energy. Swaths of members of the Richards Family are sitting and standing, mingling together in a beautiful mosaic of shades of lightest brown to rich mahogany and deep ebony, adorned in bright and colorful summer wear. And I'm not half bad in the teal maxi dress and gladiator sandals I settled on, either. Though a yard full of Davis' closest relatives and dearest friends isn't exactly what I call a relaxing afternoon, I appreciate his bravery in sharing our relationship with his family. I'm not feeling so courageous myself. Of course he already knows Ebony and Tameka. And he met Mama over a lovely lunch between the three of us one recent afternoon, but we're going to hold off on anything further for now. I'm just not there yet.

A lovely, elegant woman stands beside me, her floral sundress swirling about her in the balmy breeze. And her golden sandals are too cute, setting off a precious pink pedicure. Time continues so slowly, and I'm admiring her attire for a moment too long when she finally notices.

"Great turnout, isn't it?"

"Yes, yes it is. Beautiful weather, too." I stammer, suddenly embarrassed for staring too long. I look up into her beautiful brown eyes and feel so silly for not recognizing her earlier. She's none other than Rachel Parker, the former First Lady of Third Day. Davis said she was dating his cousin, Grayson. No wonder she's here, too.

"Sister Parker, I'm so sorry. I didn't recognize you at first." An easy laugh flows from her.

"Please, call me Rachel. Just Rachel." She says, and I'm intrigued. Most of the clergy members in our district wouldn't dare acknowledge a greeting if it didn't have a "Reverend", "Pastor", "Sister", or "Minister" attached to it. Some might, but not many. But I guess since she's no longer a pastor's wife…

"Reese, isn't it? From WLNN? You always do such a great job. Way to represent out there." She says, and I'm deeply flattered. I want my work to have meaning, to have purpose. And Lord knows it isn't easy being a black woman in news, especially in the heart of Dixie. So even a little encouragement goes a long way.

"Oh, well, thank you Sister Parker. Rachel, I mean. Thank you."

"You're most welcome. Are you part of the Richards Family, too?"

"No, no. I'm just a guest. I'm here with Davis Richards. He's over there at the end of the red table." I say, pointing him out to her. He's deeply engrossed in conversation, completely oblivious to me singling him out.

"Davis? Of course I know Davis. He's a member of Third Day, and an excellent one at that. Are you enjoying yourself today?"

"Yes, I certainly am. Everyone is so nice. This is my first time being around so many of his family members, though. To be honest, I wasn't expecting this many people." She laughs in response to this, then simmers down when she realizes I'm dead serious. How was I to know that a quick get-together for his family seems like a family reunion for most folks?

"The Richards Family is pretty big, true. I had to get used to it myself. I'm here with Grayson Shepherd. He and Davis are cousins. Grayson is the tall one over there in the navy polo." She gestures in his direction, and I see him standing there, tall and handsome. He's laughing and carrying on with a small group of men.

"What's the occasion? Davis said today was just a weekend barbeque." I ask, and looking around his aunt's setup, one would think we were either celebrating a grand occasion or memorializing the passing of a loved one. There are just that many people here. My own family is so small and closely-knit, the size of this one just blows my mind.

"He's right. That's one of the things I've learned about the Richards Family. They don't really need an excuse to get together. Good food, good company, that's really all you need anyway." I nod my agreement but say nothing.

"Well, you look great, Rachel." I say, hoping this simple statement can communicate what I don't feel at liberty to say. "Truly great."

"Why thank you, Reese. I feel great, too." She says, winking at me. Yeah, I see she's wearing "living her best life" like it's a new outfit. Whatever she has been doing since Pastor Parker passed away, it is most definitely working for her. She looks good.

"And I'm assuming Grayson Shepherd has something to do with that?" I ask, hoping my tone comes across as playful interest, not sheer nosiness.

"He hasn't hurt, that's for sure. Grayson is a wonderful man. But this joy that I have, it's that deep in my soul kind of joy. Not to take anything away from Grayson, but I dare not steal the glory from my Father."

I feel a twinge of something akin to both appreciation and admiration. To the average onlooker, Rachel Parker looks changed by love. And I guess, in a way, she is. But who would've thought that she was talking about God, and not her man?

I glance back in Davis' direction, noticing how he's surrounded by a group of young children. They're taking turns being swung in the air by him, peals of laughter coming from the little ones as they squeal with delight. Those waiting their turn gaze adoringly at him, their eyes bright and shining with anticipation. My goodness, he's so great with the children. I can only imagine the type of father he will be.

"I'd say you've done pretty well in the 'boo' department too, Reese. He sure looks like a keeper to me." Rachel says, interrupting my thoughts. My cheeks feel warm, and suddenly I'm feeling sheepish. He's my really good friend, I keep telling myself, but it seems like I'm the only one who believes that. He's sort of my man, I guess. He's God-fearing, intelligent, warm, caring, and funny. He gets my jokes, too. He's so great that it's maddeningly annoying. He's a tender kisser. He's easy on the eyes. The list goes on. Why do I continue to make this harder than it has to be? It shouldn't be this complicated to admit that you want a good thing in your life. And I do, I do, but this is more than a little overwhelming. Meeting his mom, meeting his family, and we're just a few months in. These rising waters feel like they are closing in around me. Will we sink or swim?

"He's a good one, Reese. When God blesses you with a good gift, you ought to show him how much you appreciate it." Amen to that, Rachel. Louder, for the folks in the back.

~

Monday is here, it's 7:30 a.m., and I'm still recovering from the weekend. Davis was attentive throughout the cookout, a little too much, actually. He hasn't done anything wrong, I just need a breather. Maybe take a few days to refocus. Friendly space. Davis seemed disappointed by my request, but he didn't press it, which I can respect. The BTU Junior Board is throwing a farewell coffee meeting for Dylan today. Good riddance, if you ask me. We're at the Coffee Bean, each of us pretending to care that Dylan is leaving Oak City for greener pastures. I'm drowning my personal, non-Dylan related sorrows in a caramel frappe and cheese Danish, while Dylan continues to complain about the weight she's gaining while watching us eat the tasty pastries. Honey, this is a celebration!

"Obviously I've always felt a special connection with my pod, but *all* of the BTU kids' lives matter. I feel like I'm abandoning them in their time of need." Dylan whines with as much sincerity as she can manage. She's never been a believable actress.

"Don't feel that way, Dylan. I'm sure they understand. And of course we'll be there to support them in any way possible, even after a new junior board member is added to the team." I offer, and it's true. We will gladly step up to support our kids.

"I'm sorry Reese, I know it must have been hard growing up without a father. You of all people know what these kids must be going through. And if anything, it helps you better relate to them, don't you think?" What foolishness is Dylan spewing now?

"Dylan, not sure where that came from, but I absolutely grew up with my father in our household."

"Oh, you did? Hmm, I just assumed…"

"You just assumed what? That the black girl on the committee grew up in a single parent household? You know what happens when a person assumes things." I snap, still feeling a bit on edge as I await Mama's results.

"Whoa, whoa, whoa, Reese. Lighten up on Dylan, it was an honest mistake." Will says emphatically. He's already out of his seat in her defense.

"Thanks, Will. But I've got sister girl." Dylan responds, and all of the heads in our corner of the store turn simultaneously in my direction. Here we go. I feel the heat of my temper flaring at her obtuse remark.

"Who are you calling sister girl, Dylan? Do not ever refer to me in those terms. Call me Reese or do not address me at all." Dylan's eyes narrow, Will looks increasingly uncomfortable, and Logan moves a little closer to us. He's holding his palms up towards me, his eyes pleading for us to be civil.

"Reese, Reese, Dylan was totally kidding. You know how she is, just playing around. No disrespect meant, I'm sure." Will says as Logan offers a gentle, yet nervous smile.

"Will, perhaps I would feel differently if the words had come from you, but they did not. They came from Dylan, a legal adult responsible for her own comments and actions. And, given our previous discussions, I would venture to say that disrespect was most definitely her intent."

"Reese, you can't know that." Will interjects, much too eager to cape for Dylan's antics.

"You're right, Will, I can't. But I also can't help wonder if you would defend me so vociferously if I was the microaggressor in this situation?" Dead silence follows this question, and I've already received the confirmation I needed. Logan continues to watch us, but his brooding eyes won't meet my own.

"I think all of us have a lot on our plates right now, I'm not the only one here with a professional and personal life outside of this committee. And frankly this is a critical time for us to be placed in this dilemma. We'll be lucky to find a replacement venue in time." I say, and now the other heads nod in agreement. Dylan says nothing, though, already preoccupied with her manicure.

"How can we help, Reese?" Logan asks, his eyes expectant.

"Let me start with my station contacts. I'll see what's available and we can go from there."

"Um, Reese, just one thing." Dylan interrupts, and Megan sighs with exasperation.

"What is it, Dylan?"

"I was just going to say to try to avoid any unsavory parts of town, you know. Just because I'm not leading it doesn't mean it has to go downhill. Ghetto fabulous, and all that jazz."

And this is where only the Holy Spirit can keep me from going off on this girl, this nuisance, this utter and unnecessary pest in my life. I want to give her just enough so she won't bother reaching out to Oak City from North Carolina, and all points in between, for the foreseeable future.

"Ok Dylan, I think we're good here. We appreciate your leadership up to this point, but the anniversary is in more than capable hands. Reese has got this." Logan says, finding the role of peacemaker to be a difficult one.

"I was just going to offer a bit of advice to Reese." Dylan interjects, clearly not reading the room.

"Didn't you hear Logan, Dylan? We're good now, Reese has it from here. Buh-bye and we wish you well." Shock of all shocks, even timid Megan has found her voice. They might not say as much, but the relief of finally being rid of Dylan is written all over their faces.

      So long, farewell, and please don't come back soon.

CHAPTER FOURTEEN
Keep Calm and Carry On

Today we celebrate the gift of time. Cancer sucks, it stings, it steals away moments, but it can't erase memories. Not your average Sunday dinner, no, this time it represents so much more. For one, my entire family will get to share dinner together for the first time since I don't know when. For another, I don't know if or when we will be able to do it again. But I trust God, and I pray, and I hope. Lord, let it be enough.

Always, Candy Girl

The songwriter said that "Every Day is a Day of Thanksgiving", and today I am most thankful that I am here with my family. Mama and Daddy are at least on speaking terms, and Thad is home from his latest assignment. My beautiful niece, Paisley (we call her Peaches), is with her mother for the weekend, but otherwise the Joseph Band is back together. And sweet Ms. Bean decided to spend Sunday evening with us, too. Her children are all grown, and live out of state, so a visit from them is rare indeed. She's our honorary Auntie anyway, and is always welcome when we get together. Aunt Cora and Uncle Luke are planning to stop by at some point, too, but Mama said that they probably won't make it until dessert. There's enough laughter to go around until they get here.

    I started to invite Davis, too, but wasn't quite ready to introduce him to Daddy just yet. And I already know that Thad would give him a hard time. So no invitation for dinner with my family. He'll have to make do with Mrs. Richards today. Friendly space. It's preserving my mental health, I keep telling myself. And besides, he's already met Mama, they hit it off just fine. He can wait to meet the rest of my crew until I feel good and ready for him to.

    Mama is simply glowing today; her dewy skin is positively luminescent. Could it be Daddy's presence with us around the dinner table? Maybe she's bursting at the seams to share good news with us. I know that's she's met with the oncologist by now. I thought she would've said something to me in private, but she insisted on telling us all together. Her animated energy is a blessing to behold. Mama's been in her element, doing what she loves best: cooking for her family and having us all around her table. She's glowing today, and I am so grateful.

Ms. Bean has been regaling us with a tale of the two men in Pappo's fighting for her telephone number. We all can't help but laugh along. Of course she's always known how to keep us in stitches, shooting straight from the hip. Now, Ms. Bean is every bit of seventy-five, but she will wear a jumpsuit or a pair of heels better than women half her age. She'll have a male companion every now and then, but she's the first to say that she'll watch a Hallmark Movie at home, on her terms, rather than spend the evening with someone boring. Uptight. Clingy. Annoying. And most certainly, unfaithful. She was Mama's sounding board for years while Daddy strayed. Back when she thought Thad and I were too young to notice. She's a shero to Mama, and me, too.

"Reese, you won't believe who I ran into the other day." Thad interjects during a brief lull in the conversation, and the rest of us look up, anxious to hear about Thad's mystery friend.

"Yeah, who was that?" I say, noncommittal but somewhat interested. Thad typically has a gift for storytelling that makes a visit to the DMV seem entertaining.

"Phillip Martin in the flesh. Can you believe that?" Thad's eyes are twinkling as he looks at me. Mama and the others are oblivious, but he knows that I've been in communication with Phillip for a little while. Well, a lot of while. Much longer than I would care to admit, especially at this table.

"Phillip? Reese's Phillip? Oh, how nice, Thad. We haven't seen Phillip in ages. How is he doing?" Mama asks sincerely, and Daddy seems to have perked up as well. Ms. Bean is all ears, as usual.

"Ha, ha. He's not my Phillip, Mama. He hasn't been my Phillip for a very long time."

"I know Reese, but he was such a sweet young man. We always did like having Phillip around." Mama says, and Daddy nods his agreement. Of course, neither of them is aware of the scars on my heart that Phillip left behind. Mama knows it didn't work out, and Daddy, too, but neither is aware of the full scope of our relationship, or its eventual demise. I shared more with Thad, but not enough to endanger future encounters with Phillip. He was never a fan of Phillip's while we dated, but I always chalked it up to him being an overprotective brother. Thad continues to watch me, completely amused by the mention of his name.

"Yeah, he asked about you, Reese." Thad says, searching my poker face for a response. I feel a nervous twitter of excitement, though I try my best to play it cool.

"That's nice." I say flatly, meeting my brother's gaze but refusing to lose in this game of chicken.

"Oh, I wonder what he's doing now. Is he single now, Thad?" Ms. Bean asks earnestly, and I'm bothered by the perverse grin that spreads across Thad's face.

"No, Ma'am. I don't think so. It was my weekend with Peaches. He and his wife, and their son, were at the playground, too." The air of the room deflates like a flat tire. Thad looks at me, but suddenly I don't feel so good. An uneasy knot forms in my stomach.

"Oh." Mama says, one syllable expressing years of disappointment that her only daughter still isn't married.

"But he's doing good, doing real good. His son was just a bundle of energy, he and Peaches are about the same age, I think."

"That's nice Thad. Good to hear he's doing fine." Daddy says between mouthfuls of food. "Martha Lou, you put your foot in this dressing, woman. This meal is outstanding!"

Mama rolls her eyes at Daddy, but is too polite to keep from saying thanks.

"Thank you, Thomas." She says dryly, not even bothering to look in his direction. Daddy's enthusiasm doesn't waver, though. He's savoring every bite, smiling at Mama every so often to show his appreciation for her culinary skills. Mama seems to care less, though. And Ms. Bean just laughs with incredulity. She's never been Daddy's biggest fan.

"Yeah, so I told him Reese was doing great. You know I had to brag on you, sis." Thad's megawatt smile is on full display as he says this. I smile back at him, appreciating his show of support. But I still feel uneasy about what he just disclosed about Phillip. It doesn't make sense, him being there with Julie. Of course, PJ is his son, no issues there. But Julie? When he's told me time and again that they are legally separated, with no hopes of a reconciliation? When he said they barely talk, and hardly even interact with one another. A family park day is a far cry from what he's said they've been up to. It just doesn't make sense to me. I chew in silence, each bite a little tougher going down than the last. Phillip has some explaining to do.

    I take a sip of my sweet tea, and I notice that Mama is a little jittery in her seat. She's so cute, nervous about giving us her good news. Out with it, woman, so we can toast you! I could use a good distraction from the Phillip nonsense.

    "Ahem, ahem. Everybody." Mama says, clearing her throat. Ms. Bean is still smacking loudly, but the rest of us freeze to give Mama our undivided attention. She smiles broadly, taking a moment to look at each of us. Her eyes rest upon mine, and a nervous tingle travels down my spine. She looks directly at me when she continues.

    "Thank you all for joining us for dinner today. Hopefully Cora Leigh and Luke will get to stop by for dessert. But my goodness, I cannot tell you what a blessing it is to have Thad and Reese around my table this evening! Thomas, our babies are all grown up."

Daddy and Thad are smiling from ear to ear, while Ms. Bean has the nerve to toot her lips out, pouting that she didn't get a personal shout-out.

"And you too, Verbena. Of course, you're part of the family, too." Mama continues, and Ms. Bean crosses her arms and nods her approval.

"You all know I met with Dr. Rogers last week. I thank you for your prayers and encouragement, your concerns and your messages of hope. Lord, how they lifted my spirit! They did. I thank God for each of you."

Mama continues to thank us for the outpouring of love and support, and I am in awe of how beautiful Mama looks, resplendent in her pale lavender blouse. Something shimmery in the material, iridescent threads, perhaps, frame her lovely face. Her smile is genuine and the light in her eyes is bright and upbeat.

"I would love to share the news that we all have been praying for, but I cannot. Dr. Rogers said that the cancer has returned. She's hopeful that we can treat it, and she wants us to remain optimistic. I'm a fighter, and she knows it. Breast cancer didn't take me out three years ago, and I don't intend on losing this battle now. I'm not alone in this, I know I have each of you in my corner. And my heavenly Father will never leave me nor forsake me. We will overcome even this trial." Mama says, never once taking her eyes off of me. The rest of the table sits in stunned silence. I hold her gaze, refusing to look away. She needs me. And Lord knows I need my Mama.

Mama, I think. Oh, Mama. This extraordinary woman is the picture of grace and resilience, not just throughout her battle, but even in this moment. Not my Mama. Not again, Lord. Please, not again. I want to cry out, but I restrain myself. I feel as though the wind has been knocked from me. I can't seem to catch my breath, on the inside I'm desperately gasping for air. Mama's countenance is not one of sadness, though. It's not one of despair. If anything, the gleam in her eyes signals that she is ready to fight again.

"So we are still going to toast today. C'mon now, why the long faces? We are going to get through this. Now, c'mon, raise your glasses with me. We are going to toast to faith and family. And we are going to toast to fighting on!" Mama raises her glass of ice water in the air, and we all join her, united in our support. We are powerless against her warrior spirit.

~

A few hours later, and Ms. Bean is taking a leisurely nap in Mama's recliner while Thad watches basketball with Uncle Luke. He and Aunt Cora will be heading to Shelby's house soon, and won't be able to stay long, but of course knew Mama would be disappointed if they didn't stop by to at least hear her news. While Mama and Aunt Cora are talking, Daddy asks me to join him on the front porch. Of course I'll forever say yes to my Dad, and moments like these aren't as frequent as either one of us would like them to be.

I'm rocking slowly in Mama's favorite chair, while Daddy occupies the one that he used to, the one that's saved for guests now. He's reserved, deep in thought, content to just be here with together, I guess.

"Did you know, Baby Girl?" He asks, a slight break when he finally finds his voice to say this.

"No, Daddy. It caught me by surprise, too." He grunts at this, sniffling just a bit.

"You know I'm just a phone call away, right? I can stop by in the evenings, some mornings, too…as much as she'll let me."

"I think Mama would really appreciate that, Daddy."

"Ain't nothing. That's the least I could do. Wish I could do more. Your Mama's so stubborn, though. She doesn't have much use for me anymore."

"Mama would be glad to have your support." I say plainly, not willing to admit that my own father brought most of this on himself. We continue to rock, back and forth, back and forth, gently rocking and enjoying the warm breeze. I know he hurt Mama. I know he did. But I still remember how much they loved each other. When they were on good terms, they were really, really good together.

"Your Mama was the prettiest gal at the spring dance the night I fell in love with her, I ever tell you that?" He says, smiling a small smile.

"You never told me that, Daddy." I say, wrinkling my nose up at him.

"Yes, yes. Prettiest one by a mile. And smart, too. I was a little older, see, we were in different grades. But I heard how smart she was. Still is. You got all the good stuff from your Mama, Reese. Good head just like her. You look so much like her, got her ways."

"And you, too, Daddy."

"No, I never wanted you to be like me, Reese. You or Thad. I wanted you both to be fine people, like your Mama."

"I think you're a fine man yourself." He's sniffling harder now, pinching his eyes together from time to time.

"Can't be too fine. Martha Lou won't hardly give me the time of day. What kind of man gives up his family just to have a little fun?" He says, sniffing harder now.

"Them women didn't mean nothing to me, not a single one. Your Mama has more class in her pinky than all of them put together." It's the first time he has ever acknowledged his infidelity to me. I already knew these things, but it still hurts to hear them. It still pains me to hear my father have to say them.

"Then why wasn't Mama enough? Why weren't we enough?" I ask, my voice even. I've forgiven Daddy, I had no choice but to. But since he's taken us down this road, I have to ask him. I need to know these things.

"I ask myself that every single day, Reese. Not a day goes by that I don't regret hurting your Mama. Hurting our family. Not a single day goes by."

"It's in the past, Daddy. It's all in the past now. You have to let it go and move forward."

"Feels like it has a chokehold on me. I want to be there for your Mama, Reese. I wasn't there for her the way I should've been. And she might not want it, but I can try my best to be here for her now." He says, reaching his hand out towards me. I lean over, reaching across to squeeze his hand.

"Just keep showing love to Mama, Daddy. Keep showing her that you support her. She'll come around eventually. And if she doesn't, you just keep trying. All you can do is your best, Daddy. You can't make someone forgive you. You can't force your way back, either." I say, looking him in the eye. Daddy's shoulders continue to slump, he's still sniffing, but it's quieter now. He nods his response and squeezes my hand back.

"I told you, Reese. Smart, just like your Mama." He says, his smile matching my own now. We go back to rocking, trying our best to forget what was lost, giving our best effort to remember what's most important in the here and now.

~

The pile of dishes on the counter won't wash themselves, so reluctantly, I start filling the sink with soapy water and prepare to get started. Normally I would tug Thad on the ear and make him help, but

Mama wants to talk, it's written all over her face… and if she wants to talk, then I most certainly want to listen.

"Do you want a cup of coffee, Reese?" Mama says, already getting her favorite mug out.

"No thanks, Mama. I'm good. I'll probably just have some water."

Mama finds her favorite creamer and a bottle of water for me in the refrigerator. Pouring her coffee, she adds her creamer, then places the container back inside. She places the water on the table, but says nothing. I hear her sighing, again and again, letting me know that I'm taking too long. We bought her a dishwasher several years ago, but Mama refuses to use it and won't let you use it in her kitchen, either. She said she doesn't trust a machine to get her dishes clean. I am about halfway done when her patience wears thin, and I hear her tapping her fingers on the table. She knows that is one of my pet peeves, but does it anyway.

"Reese, come sit with me for a spell. The dishes can wait, baby." She says, and I reach for a drying towel to wipe my hands. I sit down across from her, taking the water and opening it. The sip is cool, refreshing as I savor the liquid. I smile at Mama, signaling my desire to engage in conversation with her.

"Everything was so good, Mama. Dinner was wonderful." And it was. The macaroni and cheese was jumping, as usual. And I can already taste the velvety smooth richness of my soon to be second helping of sweet potato pie.

"Yes, yes. God is so good. It's been a lovely day. Both of my babies home, too! More than I could ever ask for."

"And Daddy, too." I can't help but slip in, smiling at her deliberate omission of him.

"Sure. Thomas, too." Mama says, giving me her best "Good Christian" smile. I have to laugh at this.

"Daddy said he's missing you, Mama. He said this has been the best day he's had in the longest time." Her expression changes quickly, shifting from a superficial smile to a focused frown in seconds.

"Reese, baby girl, I forgave your father a long time ago. But that doesn't mean I have to continue to entertain his foolishness."

"Daddy still loves you, Mama."

"And I love him. I truly was in love with that man. I gave him my all. But sometimes your very best still isn't enough." It wasn't enough with Phillip, either, if I'm being honest with myself. Close, but no cigar. It just wasn't enough. But maybe, just maybe, my parents' love story can be different. Especially now that Mama's cancer has returned. Maybe there is a future for them yet.

"Mama, I think Daddy would jump at the chance to be there for you." Mama guffaws at this, her eyes wide in disbelief.

"And he would certainly look silly, jumping up and down for no reason. Ha, he might wear himself out jumping!" Her laughter continues, and she shakes her head emphatically. I join in the bubbly mirth of her mood, sharing a good laugh with her. Perhaps laughter will truly be the best medicine, because Mama seems to have it in spades. And though she thinks Daddy's interest is funny, it's not so far-fetched, if Mama ever had the notion to "entertain his foolishness" once again.

Daddy had more than one affair in their nearly thirty year marriage, and Mama forgave him every time. Until she didn't. Spirit weary, she realized that Daddy wasn't going to change anytime soon. Until he did. For whatever reason, maybe because of her first round of cancer, maybe not, Daddy has tried to prove time and again that he is truly a changed man. Mama barely acknowledges his presence when we're all together, and in my heart of hearts I hope he isn't pining after her because he thinks she's playing hard to get.

Of course her cancer had to play a part in it, too. I think he came to the realization that life is but vapor; that Mama, forever a constant in his life, might not always be. It awakened a side of Daddy that Thad and I never witnessed while they were married. Suddenly, my too cool, always smooth Dad was reduced to a bowl of jello whenever he came around Mama. His compliments became heartfelt, no longer the insincere calling card of a proven womanizer. He checked on Mama frequently, not always stopping by, but calling and texting as much as he could. Sending flowers to brighten her spirits or small creature comforts to make her convalescence more tolerable. But the ice around Mama's heart still hasn't seemed to thaw out. I can't help but wonder if she'll warm up to him now.

If Daddy is as determined as he was last time, and our porch chat certainly has me convinced, then Mama won't have any trouble finding a personal nurse and assistant for her beck and call.

"Reese, you and Thaddeus are full grown. I have no reason to enter into relationship with him again. Not when he didn't respect boundaries and protect my heart the last time. No ma'am, I'm not interested." I nod my head in response, but say nothing.

"But this isn't about me and your father, is it Reese?" How does she always know what's on my heart before I even say it? Oh Mama, I don't want to burden you with my troubles. Not when you're still dealing with your own stuff. Not when you are in the fight of your life once again. Looking into her eyes, I see the hidden concern that has taken up residence there. It made itself at home the moment she first noticed a lump in her right breast, and that was more than three years ago. Just like then, her worried expression is not out of concern for her own health, it's about the needs of her children.

"Reese, I'm going to be alright, sweetheart. I am. God has me, baby. You don't have to worry about what's happening with me. Reesie, you placed your life on hold to take care of me when I needed it most. I'll never forget that. I will always cherish that time together. But now it's your time to live. I don't need your daddy to take care of me. He can barely take care of himself." She winks when she says this, and I see Daddy's puppy-dog eyes pining after Mama at dinner earlier.

"Of course, he's still welcome in my home. We'll still gather at holiday meals, and I love it when we all get together like this. But I'm not trying to relive the glory days of our relationship. Those days are long gone. I need his friendship more than anything else from him. Thomas is forever family because of you and Thad. But that is all. And that's enough for me." Mama says, succinctly and earnestly. Dark brown eyes widening, Mama's gaze holds steady as she clasps my hand with her own.

"Live your life, Reese. This Davis cares deeply about you, I saw it written all over his face when I met him." I didn't realize his feelings were that obvious, even though he's never shied away from showing me how he feels.

"Reesie, you don't have to be afraid to love him." Mama says plainly, and this is the part that pierces my heart the most. The tears are searching for release, and I feel the warm wetness of them before I can stop them.

"I know you've had disappointments, Reese. But what if this time it was different? What if Davis is the man, the love that God has meant for you all along? What if everything you've been through was so you would finally know what the real thing feels like?"

What if Mama is right? What if everything I've experienced, this long and winding, and don't forget bumpy road, was just part of my journey to happiness after all. Mama needs me, Lord. And I need her presence in my life. I need her wisdom, I need her guidance and love. I need her healed and whole and here with us for as long as you allow her to be, God.

But whether or not I care to admit it, I just might need Davis, too. Lord, let me bypass the detours and take the nearest exit to Davis Richards Boulevard. And please give me traveling grace, Dear Lord.

CHAPTER FIFTEEN

Revolving Doors

Is a closed door a reason to celebrate? Was the blessing blocked, or were you protected from harm's way? What about an open door? Do you stand there, unsure, or do you walk on in? The God I serve doesn't play Let's Make a Deal, so I have to believe that if a door is opened, it's for a reason. And if it's closed before me, well, there's got to be a reason for that, too. We'll understand it all better by and by.

By Faith, Candy Girl

Phillip is officially becoming a stalker. He's left me no less than three voice mail messages on my cell phone today, plus another two with Rena at the station. Not to mention the repeated text messages he's sent me as well. The old Reese would be flattered by the interest, but the current Reese is annoyed beyond description. First of all, I can't stand someone leaving multiple voice mail messages, unless it involves my parents or closest friends, literally the house could be on fire and I'll wait to hear the sirens. Secondly, to leave messages at my office, inviting my easily tempted to be nosy colleagues into my personal affairs, is pretty much where I draw the line. "Report the news, don't be the news" is what has been drilled into my head throughout my career. I have neither the time nor the patience to explain this away at work, especially since Phillip hasn't been a part of my life in years. Especially since the only flowers sent to the office have come from Davis. Especially since I'm still figuring my way out of this mess. It makes me look unprofessional, and I simply refuse to tolerate that. I'm not just competing with my colleagues, I'm competing against myself. I've worked too hard to cultivate my brand and image to let it go down the drain because of my old college boyfriend.

Still, he's persistent, and when he begged for the two of us to meet for dinner I couldn't find the willpower to say no. I'm not going to fool myself into thinking that we could ever be a "we" again, but I want him, no...I *need* him to be out of my system once and for all. I need to close this chapter of my life and move on.

I started to tell Davis, but how would I even begin with that? Phillip has this inexplicable hold on me; it seems, even after all of these years. How do you explain that? I don't want to upset Davis, but truth be told, I would probably want to meet with Phillip regardless. I need him to see that I'm happy now, I'm in a good place; I don't need him and the drama he brings any more. As a preemptive measure, I told Davis I would be having dinner and catching up with an old friend from college tonight. I conveniently left out specific details, but that's probably for the best. He didn't ask about Phillip, and I didn't tell him. No harm in that, I hope.

Getting dressed, and more importantly, mentally prepared for tonight has already left me exhausted. After trying on no less than a half dozen outfits, soon I'll have to take another shower, too. I finally settle on a cap sleeved, slim fitted black dress and simple stilettos. Not too sexy, not taking myself too seriously, but definitely giving the impression that I am older and wiser now. I slip on an elegant pair of chandelier earrings and my Pandora charm bracelet, a just because gift from Davis. Maybe it will serve as a reminder to stay on my best behavior.

We decide to meet in Auburn, just an hour's drive away, but far enough to where I don't feel like I may run into Davis or someone from our circle. My plan is to get this evening over with and forget that it ever happened. I hope it's that easy.

Phillip has chosen Salerno's, a fine dining Italian restaurant near the university. I find valet parking quickly, exiting my Avalon to make my grand entrance. I know Phillip is already inside, he texted me moments ago to let me know that he had our table. I walk slowly, deliberately taking my time, even though I'm nearly ten minutes late. Of all of the things he's forgotten about me, surely he's remembered this one.

Salerno's is lovely inside; its décor is tasteful and elegant. The muted lighting and gently draped tablecloths are the perfect accompaniment to the candles and fresh flowers on each table. A dozen or so couples are already seated; some leaning intimately across their tables as if celebrating a romantic occasion or much needed date night. I look around the room and see that they even have a jazz trio playing this evening. My thoughts immediately drift to Davis, but I'm trying to push them to the side, at least for the moment. But why did it have to be jazz?

Still quiet, I glance again at each of the couples, each seemingly more in love than the last. The hostess points over to our table, and time stands still. There's Phillip, looking as if he's stepped off the cover of GQ to join me for the evening. The nerve he has to still look good after all of these years. Darn him. His smooth cocoa brown skin is rich and luxurious in the light, his jet black waves are more closely cropped than I remembered. He looks sexier than I hoped he would. I notice him before he sees me, so my stride slows down even more, expecting to ease up to the table inconspicuously.

I reach the table as he looks up from his cell phone and our eyes meet, his own widening with approval. I hope my expression doesn't do the same.

He's smiling now, showing off the smile that looks like a paid political ad, it's so perfect. This man is so fine, no wonder he played me like a violin, and most definitely like a fool. He almost can't be held responsible for the abundance of physical riches he was gifted with.

"Reese, Reese, Reese. I've been looking forward to this for so long. I must say, Ms. Joseph, what a blessing it is to be in your presence once again." The sexy drawl of his voice envelops me before his arms have a chance to. I lean into the hug, but bristle when he whispers "You are absolutely stunning" huskily in my ear. Heart beating faster, I pull away before he gets too familiar with me once again. I allow him to pull my chair out as I prepare to take my seat, and when I'm comfortably settled he slides back around to his chair across from me.

"So, Phillip. I was surprised that you still wanted to meet for dinner. I figured I wouldn't hear from you after Thad saw your family in the park that day." I say, changing my BS frequency to its highest setting. I have to with this one, he knows how sprung I was on him.

"Jumping right to it, are we, Reesie?" He replies, the corners of his eyes crinkling as he smiles. "It was good seeing Thad that afternoon. It's been ages man, ages. You know I had to ask him about you." He pauses, relishing in my obvious discomfort. That dazzling grin of his is blinding.

"If I'm being totally honest, I have to admit that I've never stopped thinking about you. Never."

His eyes are gentle now, and I find myself looking away momentarily, remembering the good times between us. Long repressed memories easily flood back of being so young and so in love with him. Remembering our breakup snaps me back to reality.

"And Julie…how *is* your wife doing, Phillip?" I ask coolly, choosing to ignore his last comment. Don't come in here trying to play me again, dude, not after all we've been through. Not when you know my brother didn't just run into you at the park, but you *and* your little picture-perfect family.

"I told you we're not together anymore. We're trying to figure out how to co-parent PJ, but that's all. It's for the best, really. One of those things where the relationship just ran its course, you know."

There's a hint of sadness to his voice when he says this. His eyes are steady, unwavering, when he looks at me now. Don't forgive him, don't forgive him, I think, but it's already too late. My anger softens as I hold his gaze. The flickering candlelight illuminates his face before me.

Something, the tiniest of twitches, catches my eye. There's a gleam in his eye that wasn't there before. His smile is a little too self-assured for me to relax in his presence. Still the same old Phillip. An excuse and a smile and he thinks he has me fooled yet again. I wonder if this is what Mama used to feel like when Daddy tried to explain his actions. "Don't get burned by the same flame twice, Martha Louise," Ms. Bean used to always say. Perched around the corner while they gossiped in the next room, as a teenager, I never knew what she meant before. It's crystal clear to me now.

"You're divorced? Oh, I didn't realize that had taken place. When did this happen?" I ask, feigning genuine interest as I lean forward.

Phillip is so cool that calling him out on his mess wouldn't even faze him. He left me for Julie, fled my arms and ran into those of his wife; now the mother of his only child. Well, I guess it's his only child. Phillip's panty dropping antics were bound to catch up with him after a while.

"Not exactly, but we've been separated for more than six months now." Aha, I think. Now we're getting to it. You're probably not even separated by more than a pillow. He thinks this is going somewhere because things "supposedly" didn't work out with his wife. Not happening.

"And you wanted to have dinner with me because…?"

"Because I have never, ever stopped thinking about you, Reese. I know that I hurt you, but you are without question the one that got away for me. You've always been an extraordinary woman, and I hate that I was too young, too immature, and frankly too foolish to realize it." There's a steadfast sincerity in his voice that seems to chisel away the edge in mine. We *were* young, and stupid, too. But I was a faithful fool for this man. I risked my personal health by allowing him to be the first person I'd ever been intimate with. I gave him my heart and then some. But not this time.

"I should let you know that I have someone in my life now. I only agreed to meet with you because we have history together. I cared about you a great deal once; you know that you will always have a special place in my heart as the first man I loved. Even after all of that, and even with the person I'm seeing now, there's only room for one at the top, and His name is Jesus." I say, little inflection in my voice. Maybe he will see that I'm in a different place now than the young woman he once knew.

I was so inexperienced in college, so sheltered. Phillip walked into the student union that fateful day and rocked my entire world. Suddenly I had found "my person", and with it came a built in social calendar for the next three years. By the third date I was truly, madly, deeply in love with him; by the fifth I had given him my virginity. There was an immediate, and intense, backlash of guilt and shame that washed over me afterward. Entering into this kind of relationship with him went against everything I had ever been taught at home and at church. But it was too late: I had already committed to being all in with him.

The next years flew by, and even when we were on bad terms I was deliriously intoxicated by him. I was obsessed with him; I never seemed to get enough. When we had to be separated, I was counting the moments until we would be together again. I could spend an entire weekend with him and still wonder why it never seemed to be enough. My heart was a void that never seemed to be filled by his love. I didn't understand it in college, but my growth in Christ has shown the wiser me the many reasons why.

I was devastated when he broke up with me, seemingly without reason, the month before graduation. And I was simply inconsolable when I found out he was marrying the woman I later understood he cheated on me with throughout college.

"I hope he appreciates the jewel that he has."

"He does. He's an exceptional man and person of integrity."

"Then why are you here with me tonight?"

"Phillip, that's a great question. And I believe I have the answer. You see, I thought I needed to see you to realize what a special person I have in my life. But the truth of the matter is, I needed to see you to realize what a special woman I am now. I'm grateful for our time together. If anything, it's taught me the way I never, ever want to be treated in a relationship once again. And God has brought me from a mighty long way. So I thank you for your invitation to dinner this evening, but frankly I'm not very hungry. I've forgiven you, Phillip, and I wish you well, but I have someone very important that I would rather spend the evening with. I do hope you understand." Resolute, I rise from my seat to prepare to leave.

"Don't go, Reese. Spend the evening here with me. No sweet talk, no flattery, just a pleasant dinner between old friends." Phillip reaches for my hand to stop me, but I retreat from him.

"No, Phillip. I can't. Time is a precious commodity. You can't get it back once it's lost. And I don't want to lose another minute here when I would rather be somewhere else. I'm glad you're doing well, Phillip. I wish you all the best." Grabbing my clutch, I walk away quickly, refusing to be Lot's wife in this situation. No turning back.

Walking straight out of the restaurant, I fumble with my clutch for just a moment before I find my valet parking ticket. The valet seems surprised to see me so quickly, but smiles and says nothing as he retrieves my car. Feeling generous, I tip him twenty dollars for barely ten minutes of service. He smiles and nods, escorting me to the driver's side and closing the door behind me. Adjusting my seat, I crank up the volume on my latest Todd Dulaney CD and am engrossed in worship music until I reach Oak City.

I can't wait to see Davis, and I don't stop until I arrive at his home. He told me he was staying in for the evening, grabbing take out and maybe watching a movie. Maybe this can turn into a casual, impromptu movie night instead. I would text him to let him know I'm here, but I think that would ruin the surprise. Checking the backseat, I'm pleased to see my trusty overnight bag is back there. Not that I go around spending the night with people. I'm still a Girl Scout at heart, always prepared for the unexpected. I keep extra clothes at the office, in my car, even over Ebony's house. You just never know. I'm going to maintain boundaries in our relationship, but I also know these stilettos are killing my feet. At the very least I can change into something more comfortable. So although I'm saying no to the slumber party for two, I will say yes to the yoga pants and tank top in my bag. That's a decision I can easily commit to.

Walking toward his door, I see the flicker of lights from the television. Good, he must be downstairs still. I glance at my watch and note that it's nearly 9:00 now. I ring the doorbell, then wait on the porch until he answers. He lives in a great garden home neighborhood, otherwise I would be hesitant to be out here at this time of night. I hear the peephole slide open, then step back as Davis opens the door.

My man looks all kinds of handsome in his lounge pants and fitted t-shirt, his muscular frame bulging through. His eyes are surprised, but I'm so pleased when a charming grin breaks out across his face.

"Reese? Baby I thought you were going out for the evening."

"Surprise!" I exclaim with purposeful gaiety, leaping towards him to fall in his arms for a hug. The warmth of his body envelops mine and I find myself getting lost in his embrace. He smells so good: earthy, like pine and sandalwood. I arch my body into his, gently nuzzling his neck before my lips find their way to his. He pulls me closer towards him, closing the door behind us and returning my kiss. His soft, succulent lips are like a desert oasis, and I stand there, drinking him in. Finally, he pulls away, keeping his face inches from mine as he gazes into my eyes.

"What a wonderful surprise." His deep voice bellows, and he leans forward to kiss my forehead. I melt a little every time he does. Pulling back, he chuckles again as he guides me towards the living area.

"I could at least offer some refreshment...where are my Southern manners? Why don't you have a seat, Reese. What can I get you to drink?"

"Just water would be nice, thanks." I say as he walks to the kitchen. I find a seat on his comfortable couch, looking around to see what he was up to. A half eaten hoagie sits next to a large bowl of chips on the coffee table. A twenty oz. bottle of Sprite rests beside it. Looking up at the television, I notice that Davis has paused a showing of Coming to America, a classic among pretty much every black person I've ever known. It's the scene where Akeem and Simi are in the bar, searching for a suitable wife for the young prince. Davis is walking towards me now, a bottle of water and a napkin in his hand. I smile and offer my thanks as I reach for the water.

"You look absolutely beautiful, Reese. Did you enjoy catching up with your friend?" Davis asks, sliding on the couch beside me. I scoot over a bit to make room.

"Thank you. Um, it was ok. We really didn't have all that much to talk about." The last thing I want to do now is to go into too much detail.

"Yeah, sometimes it can be awkward when you haven't seen someone in a long time. I know she was glad to see you, though. At least you got a good meal out of it. Did you meet somewhere great?" I feel my heartbeat speeding up when he asks this question. I don't want to outright lie to him, but I don't want to risk making him upset, either. Dinner tonight provided the closure I needed. I've moved past Phillip, I'm ready to move forward with Davis now.

"Salerno's in Auburn. Have you heard of it?" I ask nonchalantly.

"Salerno's is great. I haven't been since, well, since Iris was alive. But it had a great vibe, a romantic ambience. More of a special occasion restaurant, in my opinion."

"Yes, beautiful restaurant. But it wasn't a romantic occasion, just a meeting of old friends. The setting made it more awkward, I think." I keep my tone measured, buoyed by the fact that this much is true.

"I bet, with a bunch of couples hanging around. Do you think you'll meet up again?"

"No. Some people are in your life only for a season. That time has passed." I say, the sentiment resonating deep within my soul.

"That is so true. It doesn't mean that your time together wasn't meaningful, or an important part of your life. It just means that your journey continues. What's that quote, 'Don't be sad it's over'..."

"Be thankful it happened."

"Yeah, that's it. Is that how you feel now?" I feel tears spring up in the corners of my eyes, even as he asks the question.

"That's exactly how I feel about it." I say, my voice breaking slightly. Davis is looking at me now;

he sees that I'm overcome with emotion. He moves closer and I feel his strong arm around my shoulders.

"Baby, are you ok? I wasn't trying to upset you." He asks gently, and guilt washes over me.

"I'm ok, Davis. I just, I need to tell you something. But I don't want you to take it the wrong way." I say, pulling back from him. I can't quite look him in the eyes, but I know he feels how serious I am about it.

"You know you can tell me anything, Reese." His voice is quiet, his shoulders starting to slump.

"I wasn't just meeting an old friend tonight. I met with Phillip, my old boyfriend from college. He begged me to have dinner with him and I finally relented." Davis moves his arm from around me now, his demeanor stiffening in response. Still, he says nothing. I guess he's waiting for me to continue.

"Phillip and his wife are separated now. He thought it would be a good time for the two of us to get reacquainted, but I told him about us. I told him how wonderful you are and how happy I am with you. I walked away from dinner before the first course began, and I'm not looking back." I move my hand towards his hand, but I'm surprised as he pulls it away. I look up at him now, and see the sadness and confusion across his face. I feel a deep pain within my chest now, as if even my heart is troubled for keeping this from him. I should have been honest with him from the beginning. I should have been honest with him, but I couldn't even justify it in my own mind. How could I have explained it to him?

"I don't quite understand. You're telling me that you didn't meet up with an old female friend from college, but the old college boyfriend you told me broke your heart? The man, if I can call him that, who dumped you before graduation and later married the woman he had been cheating on you with? You had dinner with that person tonight?"

"Yes." I say flatly, and now I'm really feeling like an idiot for even agreeing to meet with Phillip.

"And, because it didn't turn out as expected, after meeting him, dressed to the nines, no less, at one of the most romantic restaurants in Auburn, which is a good hour's drive away, you waltz over here to surprise me like nothing happened? After you initially lied about tonight?" His eyes narrow but never lose their laser focus.

"That's not exactly what happened. I wanted to see you. I want to be with you." I say, waving my hands with emphasis. Make him understand, Dear Lord.

"So badly that you drove an hour away for a secret date with some dude who doesn't even respect you. You're better than that, Reese." The tears are falling now, more rapidly than I expected. It made perfect sense at the time, and nothing seems to make sense now.

"Davis, I wasn't trying to lie to you." This is true. I wasn't trying to lie; I just wasn't forthright in offering the truth.

"Lying by omission is still lying. You left me with the impression that you were meeting a college friend for dinner to catch up and reminisce, not rekindle a failed romance."

"I wasn't trying to rekindle anything with Phillip. I was trying to show him that I'm different now, I'm better now. He hurt me but he didn't break me. I wanted to show him that I don't want or need him in my life. I've moved on and I am better for it. I wanted to get him out of my head, don't you understand that?" I ask, hoping he'll relate on some level. He's already shared how difficult it was to move on after Iris passed away. Surely he'll understand this, too.

"What I know is this, Reese. I know that for the first time in years I am in a relationship with someone that I can picture a future with. I know that, tonight, I learned something that makes me question what I thought I knew about you. I don't understand why you felt the need to meet with him tonight. I don't understand why you felt the need to lie about it. I don't understand why you think I shouldn't be upset about this." He stands up now, walks towards the door, and looks back at me.

"I think you should leave, Reese. I think we need some space for a while. I really need time to think about a few things." The tone of his voice is flat now, not a trace of emotion when he says this. I'm embarrassed by what I did, embarrassed that I'm being asked to leave his home, a place I always thought I would be welcomed. So I stand up, adjusting my dress and grabbing my clutch from the couch. My confidence is shattered as I walk toward the door.

"Davis, I…"

"Don't. Please don't say anything else about it. Now is just not the time. I'll call you when I'm in the headspace to discuss it appropriately." He's opened the door wide now, his arms are folded across his chest. I walk past briskly, holding my head high and refusing to cower in front of him.

"Please let me know you made it home safely." His parting words pierce my heart but I turn, nod at him, and offer a small smile. He's silent and stony faced, closing the door as I retreat inside my car.

A cascade of tears falls down my face on the way home. I made such a mess of everything today, when I could've done what my gut said to do when Phillip first reached out to me: I should have simply said no. Now I've hurt the person that I truly love in all of this, too. And Davis said he could picture a future with me…now everything about our relationship has been called into question. I reach my home, slipping inside without waking Mama, and finding comfort once I reach my bedroom. I send the shortest of texts to Davis, simply typing "I'm Home" before I press send. I plug my phone into its charger and place it on the nightstand. Getting undressed, I find a pair of comfortable pajamas and a satin bonnet for my hair. Brushing my teeth and wiping the makeup from my face, I use the restroom and wash my hands, completing my bedtime routine.

But when I slip under the covers, emotionally spent and utterly exhausted, I can't seem to fall asleep. Instead, I lay there and pray until I can no longer remember when the conversation with my Lord draws to an end.

AND TROUBLES RISE

CHAPTER SIXTEEN
One Step Forward

You know what heals all wounds? Forgiveness. You thought I was going to say 'time', didn't you? Time does its part, but it's forgiveness that does the heavy lifting when it comes to restoring and repairing relationships. We all have someone or something to forgive: the unfaithful love, the so-called friend, the abusive parent, the micromanager from work, the wayward child. Yeah, it helps to forgive others. But what if you're the one who messed up? You would do anything in your power to earn the forgiveness of the ones you've hurt. You would gladly start over again. But more than them forgiving you, more than you forgiving them, a deeper cleansing must take place. Forgiving yourself is the place where healing can begin.

Truly, Candy Girl

I blinked and it's almost fall. The dog days of August have been replaced with milder, and rain-filled, days of September. Davis still hasn't called. A text message here or there to check on each other has been the gist of our communication. It was jarring to the senses at first, but I guess I'm starting to get used to it. In my mind, at least, we're just taking some friendly space. We'll find our way back, sooner or later.

Cam and I are counting the moments until this news meeting is over. Wes has been on it today, he's on a tear because Channel 13's special election coverage scored higher ratings than our own. People in Oak City can be fickle, and I know we'll bounce back soon, but we'll have to incur his wrath until then. Good times. Several viewers have written petty little emails to the Station VP, as if that's just what we needed. After making several unnecessary comments about our on-air attire, I quickly determine that these remarks don't apply to me. Oh, I'm going to do a fit check long before I make my way in front of the camera. And you best believe the tailoring will be on point. But now the direction of his comments seems a little closer to home…

"And ladies, you know I applaud just about everything you all do. You're amazing, am I right team, aren't these ladies amazing?" A smattering of unenthusiastic applause follows. I glance over at Carol, who's wearing a pasted on smile.

"And you know I find you all to be modern, stylish representatives of our station. Our on-air personalities are literally the face of our station. So keeping that in mind, I want you all to look more deeply at how you're representing WLNN. We want to present a persona that is sleek, professional, trustworthy. I know it may be fashionable to experiment with hair and makeup, following these trends or those, but it's important that we get this right. Our viewers want to see our team as one worthy of trust. Think classic news. Cronkite. Walters. Sawyer, and the like. Now, I'm no fashionista, I'm not a cosmetologist, either. But let's return to the looks that brought us to this market. Let's explore hairstyles more in line with what the viewers expect, got it? Great, great, moving on." He says, not even waiting for a response.

Carol glances at me now, still wearing the same grin, but this time with knowing eyes. Who else could Wes be talking about except me? I've worn my hair in its natural state for the last two nights, a far cry from the sleek silk press or blowout I normally wear, but still professional, in my opinion. But clearly Wes, and our viewers, disagree. On top of everything else, now I have to think about my hair on camera? I am much, much more than that.

Cam and I couldn't get out of there fast enough, and although Ebony and I encouraged him to join us for lunch, he politely declined. His teacher friend dropped him when he wouldn't commit to meeting her Mama, and he's been dating here and there ever since. She's out there, Cam. You'll find her when it's your time.

So Ebony and I are sitting here at the little deli around the corner from the station. Not our usual jaunt, but still a good choice on this rainy day, when we account for travel time there and back. Ebony heard Wes' remarks and has plenty of her own. We have a lot to catch up on, actually, so we easily jump from work, to the wedding, and now to Davis. Davis, who never fails to cross my mind each day. That Davis.

Of course she gives me an update on him, I knew she would. I can't help that Braxton and Davis are close friends. But then she says that Braxton told her not to keep me informed about Davis. Wait a second, what was that?

"Wait, what? What did Braxton say, Ebony?"

Ebony's smile is strained now, it's clearly paining her to reveal what her precious fiancé had to say about my relationship. The nerve.

"Well, Reese", she hesitates, "He wasn't completely for the two of you, to tell the truth."

"And why not? What have I ever done to Braxton?"

"Reese, come on. You and Meka have never been big fans of Braxton. He knows that."

"He's just so fake all the time, Ebony. So phony about everything."

"Ahem, that's my man you're talking about. I'd appreciate it if you at least pretended to respect our relationship, okay? Dang, I'm trying to be supportive of you and Davis." She's right, and instantly I'm remorseful. I don't have to like Braxton, but the very least I can do for my friend and sister is to support her in their relationship. Unless he hurts her. Then everything goes out the window, figuratively and literally.

"Sorry E, you're right."

"Already forgotten. I know you just want the best for me. I get it, I do, too. Heh, heh, that's why I'm with Braxton, boo, because he is THE BEST." Ebony chuckles, and I can't help but smile. Like it or not, she is loyal to this dude. That's an admirable quality, I guess? Whatever she sees in him, I didn't get the memo.

"So what did Braxton say?"

"Just that, well, you're not exactly known for keeping a man, Reesie. He said your standards are 'too high' for him, that's all."

I can't even wrap my head around this comment. My standards are too high? How is this valued in anything else except finding a mate? Folks will let only the finest artesian water touch their lips, but any old person can do so. Make it make sense, Lord. Ebony watches me, trying her best to remain upbeat.

"Reese, don't act like that. Davis is a wonderful guy, he means a lot to Braxton. He went through so much when his wife died. He just doesn't want his friend to be hurt, that's all. So even though I thought you guys would be a perfect match, Braxton asked me to hit the brakes a little. Just to give it a little time. Not push it, you know?" I nod but say nothing. Suddenly I'm fascinated by my pasta salad, picking at it and swirling each noodle around in the sauce.

"I like Davis, I really do Ebony. So much that it scares me a little, if I'm being honest. But I had no intention of hurting him, you have to know that. I would never deliberately hurt anyone, especially not someone I'm in a relationship with." Ebony isn't sold on my speech; it's written all across her furrowed brow and smirking grin.

"Then what was that Phillip nonsense? He's never been worth your time, but still, you've kept in communication with him…for what, exactly? What's your end game, Reese?" Ebony says, her tone more dubious than I expected.

"It was a misunderstanding, that's all. Whatever Phillip and I had is dunzo, long gone. I should've never let him back into my life. Ebony, I really messed up. I know I did. And I don't know how to regain his trust. If he'll ever forgive me."

"He already has."

"You don't know that."

"Yes, I do. And it has nothing to do with you and everything to do with the caliber of man that he is. Not saying it doesn't hurt, I'm sure it does. But he's mature enough, he's gracious enough, he's gentleman enough to forgive you and not hold a grudge. What happens next, though, that's up to you, Reese." Ebony sips from her glass of sweet tea, fluttering her lashes and sugar sweet in her delivery.

"Maybe it's for the best. Maybe we weren't meant to be, anyway."

"Reese Joseph, you better wake up and smell the coffee, the roses, whatever the saying is. Wake up, girl! Men like Davis Richards aren't just falling from the sky. The sisters at Third Day are probably on standby waiting to snatch him up! Look what Jasmine did to Pastor Parker, and he wasn't even available." Ebony places her glass back on the table, holding it forcefully as she looks me squarely in the eyes.

"If you ever want a good man in your life, you better not let Davis go. You better leave it all on the field and go after your man. Believe me when I say this, Reese. I know what forever looks like. It looks like you and Davis."

"And you and Braxton?" I say, smiling so hard my cheeks are hurting.

"Well of course, ma'am. How do you think I know what I'm talking about?" Ebony says, laughing enthusiastically. I can't help but laugh with her. Ebony truly believes every word that comes out of her mouth. And as much as I hate to say it, I really don't know if she is right about her and Braxton. But Dear Lord, I truly hope she is right about me and Davis. I get adjusted in my seat, drawing in a deep breath before I continue.

"How do I win him back?"

"Girl, please. You never lost him. The man is still in love with you, he's just in his feelings right now. Pull out your best lingerie, girl. Or get something new. Pull out all the stops." I hear what she's saying, but my spirit screeches to a halt.

"Ebony! You know we haven't taken our relationship to that level yet."

"What? You haven't? Well then, girl, you better level up, you know what I mean?" She laughs again, but I'm still dubious. Not saying there won't be a time and place for that, one day, but not this day. I feel like that's where I've made too many mistakes in past relationships. Confusing love with lust. Trading permanence for passion. I want to experience the freedom of intimacy with Davis, I do, but not until I have the honor of being his wife. A wife. Someone's wife. Did I just think about being this man's wife? Lord have mercy, I know I'm in trouble now!

CHAPTER SEVENTEEN
Nobody Likes a Shady Beach

Investing in yourself is always a smart move. I'm all about professional development and continuing education, not to mention retail therapy, but there are moments where all it takes is a good glass of wine, uninterrupted thoughts, a literary escape, tasty treats, whatever it takes to recharge mentally and emotionally. Invest in yourself, honey. Take the time that you need to unplug from life and feed your soul. Prayer helps, of course. Time with the Father that requires nothing but your undivided attention. Offering your presence to experience a close encounter with His presence. I'm there, I'm in that place. So while the world passes me by, I'm going to take a rest stop and catch up later. I'll send you a postcard.

With Love, Candy Girl

AND TROUBLES RISE

One of the things I love most about Alabama is the ability to hop in car, leave the mess behind, and find yourself relaxing on the beach mere hours later. Gulf Shores is calling my name, and this is the weekend that I will get away and, temporarily at least, forget about work, forget about Davis, forget about that nonsense with Phillip, forget about everything. I owe it to myself. I've earned this weekend.

The drive down the interstate is uneventful, delayed only by a stop in Fort Deposit for some pecans to snack on down the road. The weather forecast this weekend could not be better: balmy, breezy, perfect beach weather. Thank you, Sweet Home Alabama, for fall temps that have extended the summer. Swimsuits packed. Beach reads selected. Fresh mani-pedi completed. I hope this weekend is one to remember.

Three hours later, I'm walking through the lobby of the oceanfront condo I've reserved for the next three days. It looks straight from a travel magazine spread, shiny marble floors, spiral staircases and all. It takes but a moment to realize that I'm clearly the only person of color in the nearest vicinity. I make my way towards the check-in desk, noticing as the clerk seems preoccupied by her cell phone. Her tan is clearly manufactured, her hair dyed an unnatural shade of blonde and her hot pink acrylic nails are frightening in length. She doesn't even look up when I'm standing mere inches away from her.

"Ahem." I clear my throat in an effort to get her attention. She looks up, but otherwise doesn't attempt to greet me.

"Can I help you?" She asks, clearly bothered by the interruption.

"Yes, I'm here to check-in for the weekend."

"Really? I'll need your picture id to confirm the reservation." She says.

I guess she's genuinely surprised that I am even a guest in this establishment. Swanky as it is, if the customer service doesn't improve I have no interest of making a return visit. I slide my driver's license across the granite counter, hesitant to even hand it to her. Her large blue eyes narrow as she reviews my license, turning it over to review the back as well. She looks from the license to me more times than I am comfortable with.

"Reese? Like Ree-cee, like the candy? Or like the actress? No it, must be like the candy." She says, carefully eyeing my brown skin, my comfy travel attire, and finally pausing to take in my weekend Bantu knots that are most definitely not WLNN approved.

No, this woman did not, she did not. I draw in a breath, not willing to give her more energy than it's worth, but I will get my point across to her. That I will do.

"It's Reese. Like the way I just said it: Reese. One syllable, double e sound like whee, it's Reese.

Reese, it rhymes with piece and also peace, like I will give you a piece of my mind until you pronounce it correctly, but if you can get it together we can be at peace. Reese. Got it?"

"Got it." She says, the expression of her round blue eyes showing that what I've just said registers loud and clear.

"Good", I say, practically snatching the key cards from the counter. Don't play me today chick, not about my name. Not when I'm supposed to be relaxed and enjoying my vacation. It's not what you're called, it's what you answer to. I answer to Reese.

"We hope you enjoy your stay with us, Ms. Joseph." She says, and for the first time I notice that her name tag reads "Heather". Yeah, I'll store that tidbit away for later.

"Be certain that I will let you know if I do not." I say, walking away triumphantly. Though off to a shaky start, I'm still giving this trip the benefit of the doubt. Now, if I could only find the elevator. I look from right, to left, to right again, sure that I can figure this out on my own. I'd hate to have to walk back to the counter and ask for assistance. Mercifully, I spot an elevator just down the hall. I walk towards it, my Louis Vuitton weekender bumping my hip every so often, matched by the rhythmic click-clack of my toiletry case as it swings from side to side. Pressing the up button, I wait patiently for my ride to arrive.

The door slides opens, and I'm somewhat taken aback by the two men inside, locked in a romantic embrace. They are kissing passionately, oblivious to the door opening. I pause a moment, but neither comes up for air to the realization that they've arrived. Sighing, I hesitate before taking the plunge to join them. Let them keep riding; it's no bother to me, I think as I press the button for the tenth floor. I sit my toiletry case down beside me to give my hand a rest for a moment. The doors close, and suddenly the air is thick as the two of them continue to ignore the fact that they are sharing an elevator with other guests. Davis and I would never…

    The elevator dings when it arrives at the eighth floor, and I'm grateful when the doors open. Walking out, it takes but a single moment for me to realize that I left my case on the floor of the elevator. I turn back around but it's too late: the doors have already started to close behind me. "Wait! Hold the elevator!" I cry out, and a deep brown hand holds it open for me. Moving forward, breathless, I'm so appreciative of the stranger within who not only kept the door open but also retrieved my case for me.

    "Thank you so much!" I exclaim, extending my hand to take the case from him. We share a smile, and I can see that he is very handsome, pretty boyish, devastatingly so. His friend has good taste, I think to myself, then glance over the see his companion huddled in the corner. It happens so quickly that I'm sure my eyes have betrayed me, but I'm horrified and dumbfounded but what I see. He's looking away from, but it's painfully obvious that my elevator hero's companion is none other than Councilman Braxton Walker. He glances at me briefly, and when he does his expression is pained and his eyes are wide with fear.

Sight confirmed, I can feel my jaw drop, completely taken aback by this development. The doors close to the elevator and I find myself alone in the hallway, still trying to process what just happened.

I find my way to my room and quickly go inside, no longer trusting my senses. It's only two months before he's scheduled to marry my best friend. What on earth is happening? It's bad enough that he's cheating on Ebony, but with a man, too? I have a sinking suspicion that Ebony would be blindsided by this development.

My heart hurts for my friend, so much so that I barely notice the beautiful surroundings of my beachfront condo. Still, I drop my bags on the bed and walk to the balcony.

Opening the doors, I am stunned by the breathtaking view. I think I'll order delivery later and sit out on the balcony to enjoy the sunset. It's so calm out there, the waves gently crashing against the coast. A few couples frolic in the sand or walk hand in hand on the beach.

I'm torn between calling Ebony to tell her about it or calling Tameka to discuss the matter with her. Although I'd love to talk to Davis about it, he still has his panties in a bunch about the whole dinner with Phillip fiasco. As much as I want him to forgive me so we can move on, I'm in no hurry to beg his forgiveness. Sure, I didn't tell him everything until after the fact, but he can't hold that against me forever. At least I hope not.

I need to get comfortable if I'm going to call someone to talk about this. I want to start with Ebony. If the shoe was on the other foot I'd want my friends to tell me. But how can I break this to her? Ebony and Braxton are set to be #BlackRoyalty in Oak City. Ebony comes from a long, storied line of affluent and influential ancestors. Braxton's folks, too. Her parents have pulled out all the stops for this wedding, the event of the year, to hear her mother tell it. How can I be the bearer of bad news? I don't even know where to begin. Sitting down at the foot of the bed, I retrieve my slippers from my bag and remove the shoes I'm wearing, replacing them with the slippers. That's better already. I also slip off my sheer, gauzy cardigan, leaving only my steel grey tank top and black yoga pants.

Finding my cell phone, I send a quick text to Tameka:

Hey Lady, you busy? Can you talk for a few minutes?

Moments later I receive her response:

Chloe's taking a nap. Call me, chick…we've got about 20 minutes before she wakes up.

I call, and Tameka answers on the first ring.

"Hey girl, did you make it to the beach?"

"Yes, I'm here. The drive down was pretty good. Uneventful. How are you guys doing?"

"We're fine. I sent Darryl on a grocery run, girl he was getting on my nerves and I had to get him out of the house. Chloe's been wide open all day, so I thanked the good Lord above when she finally took a nap. What's up?"

"I need your opinion on something, Meka." I start nonchalantly, easing into it for my benefit as much as Tameka's.

"Of course. Shoot."

"So… imagine you are on vacation and you see your friend's man here with another man. Not a friendly get together, either, but full on making out, hot and heavy two steps from a hotel room on the elevator." I'm trying to keep this casual, but I feel uncomfortable even talking about this.

"Hold up, wait a minute. Now Darryl is supposed to be at Pappo's, so what exactly are you saying? Is this your friend or our friend? Help me narrow this down a bit." See, here we go. If I say "our friend", I might as well tell Tameka outright. She can sniff out a lie better than anyone I know, too. I better tread carefully.

"We both know her." There, that narrows it down to most of Oak City.

"Girl, was it Yasmine from church? Her old nasty man is always sliding up to folks after church, hugging too hard during fellowship and watching the ushers when they walk by. Nasty self." I can't help but laugh at Tameka. I can always count on her for a laugh, and it calms my nerves a bit.

"No, girl. Not Yasmine. If it was Yasmine I would have just come out and said so."

"But you don't want to because, what? You're acting all mysterious like it was Braxton or something."

Gulp. Dead silence on my end as I am at a loss for the next words to say.

"What the what? Reese, was it Braxton?"

"Uhhhhhh, yes." I say, barely a whisper.

"Speak up, girl. Is the connection bad, I can barely hear you?"

"I said yes, Tameka. It was Braxton." My shoulders slump down now, even though Tameka can't see them. Suddenly I feel a sickening feeling in the pit of my stomach. Maybe I should have never called at all.

"Dear Lord Baby Jesus! Braxton is cheating on Ebony? And with a man! What?" Tameka practically yells into the phone. I pull my phone away, rubbing my ear a bit to lessen the pain. I figure if I soften my volume she'll lower hers, too. It's worth a shot, at least.

"Yeah, I was shocked, too. I wouldn't have believed it if I hadn't seen it with my own eyes." I say quietly.

"Well, what are you going to do, Reese? Are you going to call Ebony or do I need to?"

"I will, Tameka. No need for you to get caught up in this."

"Baby, I was caught up in it the moment you called me. Not that I want to be in it, but I'm in it now." She pauses here, and we're both quiet for a moment. I didn't want to be involved in this, either, but we're past that point now.

"I just can't believe that Braxton would do Ebony like this, and I mean, just a couple of months before their wedding, too. I never did like him, you know that. I always knew it was something about him, I just could never put my finger on it." Tameka is absolutely right. We've discussed it on many an occasion, how picture-perfect Braxton always seemed. But looks can be deceiving, and if a down-low brother isn't a perfect example of someone living a double life, than I don't know what is.

"I wasn't expecting this, though. Now I'm afraid to leave my room, I don't want to run into him again." Tameka chuckles at this, but I am dead serious.

"What's he going to do to you, Reese? He's caught now. He's the one who better stay holed up in his room, acting scared like the punk he is. If it wasn't a crying shame I would get in my car and roll down to Gulf Shores to have a word with him myself. Of course, my word would come with a slap upside the head for good measure." We're both laughing now. "Shoot, if it wasn't for Darryl and Chloe, I'd be right there with you giving him the butt whooping he deserves!"

"No, Tameka, no. Please keep Oak City sane until I find my way back. If I do run into him I'll do my best to keep it civil. Let me pray about this thang, girl. I need to get something to eat and calm down before I call Ebony. Don't you say a word, Tameka."

"Not a peep from me, you don't have to worry about it. But pictures might help, too. If you see him again, don't get scared. Pull out your phone and catch him red-handed!" I laugh in spite of. Tameka is the kind of person who takes pictures and makes videos of every single thing. She says all the time that if you can't see it then it didn't happen. She's all about the evidence, whether it's posting vacation pictures on social media or catching your best friend's boyfriend in the act. For a moment I wish she had been here instead. No doubt, Tameka would've known how to handle the situation. At least better than I do.

"Let me let you go, Meka. I'll be in touch after I talk to Ebony. It may be sometime this evening."

"Text me, boo. I'll be waiting by the phone with baited breath."

I laugh again as we hang up, but my smile quickly turns back to a frown. Like it or not, this is no laughing matter. I've never been crazy about Braxton, but I don't want to ruin their wedding, or relationship, for that matter.

There's a nervous energy about me now as I pace around the room. It's a lovely, apartment style layout, spacious with more than enough room for little old me. The kitchen features stainless steel appliances and granite countertops, plus a cute breakfast bar area that opens up to the stunning view of the gulf coast. I move my bags to the bedroom, then freshen up in the bathroom for a few minutes. I'll relax in a steamy bubble bath later on, but for now at least, a girl has got to eat.

Walking back towards the kitchen I notice a binder with menus and information about the area, standard information provided for tourists like me. Flipping through the binder aimlessly, I'm certain something delicious will catch my attention. Bored, I pick up the remote and plop down on the oversized couch in the living area. Oh my goodness, on a rainy day it could be me, a fleece throw blanket and a good book on this couch, it is just that comfortable. I channel surf but don't expect to find anything to watch, not that I came to the beach to sit in my room and watch TV, anyway. What was supposed to be a relaxing weekend has changed course, now that I know about Braxton's infidelity. Normally I would reach for the phone and call Davis, but since he needed time to "think about us" it's been radio silent between us. Does he even remember the sound of my voice?

I'm normally a news nerd when I take the time to watch television (other than bad reality TV, of course). My preferred channel is CSPAN, but I'll check out the cable networks on occasion as well. A political pundit here, a special report there, but basically I'm just flipping from channel to channel. My mind is elsewhere, so even though I eat, sleep and breathe news my thoughts are somewhere else. Ebony, Ebony, Ebony, how can I break this news to you?

 My stomach starts growling, signaling that resisting ordering dinner would be an exercise in futility. Reluctantly rising from the couch, I pick up the binder and start flipping through it again. I settle on a beachfront restaurant mere minutes away, reaching for my phone to place an order. Everything on the enclosed menu looks tempting, but tonight I think I'll try a blackened shrimp po' boy with fries, cole slaw and hush puppies. A slice of key lime pie for dessert sounds irresistible, so I might as well add it to my order. Sweet tea to drink, of course, plus a bottle of water to place in the fridge for later. Normally I would bring a small bag of refreshments with me to the beach, or plan to stop at a local store, but in my haste to get here I didn't take the time for either. Maybe I'll make a trip in the morning, if I feel like it. The food should be here in twenty minutes, but to me it can't get here soon enough.

 I consider reaching out to Davis for the heck of it, but then on second thought I change my mind. I wonder if he misses me, at least I hope he does. I miss him terribly. I miss his warm embrace, the way he looks at me, his thoughtful insight, even the way he holds my hand. I just plain miss him. I'm not going to beg him to miss me, though. I've prayed for forgiveness about the whole situation, I even apologized to him. I don't know what else I can do except honor his wishes and give him the time and space he requested. That doesn't make it easier, though.

I pick up my phone and scroll randomly through Facebook and Twitter. Twenty minutes comes and goes before I know it, and I am nearly famished by the time there is a knock at my door. Knowing what awaits, I feel a big grin spread across my face. I can almost taste the remoulade sauce as I make my way to the door. I'm greeted by a friendly delivery guy, and the bag he hands me fills the space with tantalizing smells. After paying, I carefully carry my large sweet tea and the bag over to the counter to, quite gingerly, begin to unpack the boxes inside. I place the bottled water and key lime pie in the refrigerator and then turn my attention back to the main event.

I nearly faint from the aroma that wafts from the open box, gasping with anticipation. Closing my eyes and bowing my head in a word of prayer, I open my eyes to see the beautiful sight before me: tender, succulent, perfectly grilled shrimp on a toasted baguette, glistening cole slaw and crispy seasoned fries, steam rising from the plate. I can't find my utensils quickly enough, and waste no time digging right in. I reach for the sweet tea and am pleased to find that it has just the right amount of sweetness, a perfect complement to the feast before me. Taking my food and beverage over to the living area, I retrieve a coaster and make myself comfortable on the couch yet again. This time it's better, though, because food is part of the equation.

I hear the familiar chirp of my cell phone, and, reaching for it, smiling once I realize that Davis was thinking of me after all.

I look forward to talking to you when you get home.

Be safe and enjoy the weekend.

The simple message is followed by a red heart emoji, and though there isn't much to it, my heart swells at the thought of being with Davis again. He's been checking on Mama from time to time, sending flowers to her each week, too. A "Get Well Soon" balloon bouquet one week…just sweet tokens to let her know she has his support as well. But this simple text is the first step for the two of us. I'm glad he reached out this evening; maybe the chilly attitude towards me after the Phillip debacle is starting to unthaw. And not a moment too soon.

Mood lifted, it continues to improve as I eat the rest of my food. These shrimp are simply banging! I'm so glad I made the call for fresh seafood instead of something easy like pizza. No judgment, though, because pizza will likely end up in the rotation before this getaway is done. I guess I was famished, because the meal is done in no time at all. I'll let the pie hang out in the fridge for a while, knowing that I will find my way back to it later on. Reluctantly, I pick up the phone to initiate what I have been avoiding since I arrived.

Ebony picks up on the first ring. Dang, that doesn't even give me adequate time needed to get my thoughts together.

"Hey Reese, what's up? You're supposed to have your toes in the sand, not bothering me." She says jokingly, and I can hear her smiling through the phone.

"Hey, Ebony. Are you busy?"

"Girl, just sitting here going over the wedding itinerary. I'm supposed to meet with the planner tomorrow, but I just want to make sure Sheila hasn't overlooked anything. I can talk though. Everything good? You sound sad." I wish she had told me she was doing anything except wedding stuff. But what should I have expected? This long race is nearly over, and Ebony is probably ready to break the finish line.

"Oh, I'm ok. Had a good drive down, and it is beautiful here."

"I can imagine. Reesie, you know I've already started shopping for the honeymoon. I can't wait to wear my new thong bikini in Jamaica, baby!" Might want to hold on to that receipt, Ebony.

"Yeah, I bet. So, is Braxton going with you to meet with Sheila tomorrow?"

"No, I wish. He's at a conference this weekend. I don't expect him back until Sunday."

"A conference? Down here in Gulf Shores?"

"What? No, he's in Pensacola. Why do you ask?" The jig is up, Reese. You might as well come clean. I pause a moment, sighing, dreading the next part of our conversation.

"So…I saw him on the elevator at the resort I'm staying at."

"Saw who?" Sheesh, Ebony. You are not making this easy.

"Braxton. I saw Braxton."

"You what? You saw him at your resort? He's in Florida this weekend, not Alabama. You sure you aren't mistaken, Reese?" She asks, and I hear the slightest panic as her voice rises an octave or two.

"I didn't talk to him, but I'm pretty positive it was him. He looked me directly in the eyes like he recognized me. He look scared to see me."

"That's because his trifling behind is supposed to be in Pensacola at a work conference." She says, venom in her voice. "What else? Don't tell me, he wasn't alone, was he?"

"No, E. He was in a romantic embrace on the elevator, that's why we didn't see each other at first."

"What did he look like?" I'm confused now. What did Braxton look like? He looked the same as always: shiny, suited up, too good to be true. I wish I was having this convo in person instead of by phone.

"He looked like himself, Ebony. The same as usual."

"I know that, Reese. That's not what I mean. The guy he was with, what did he look like?" My stomach forms into knots as I carefully consider what Ebony is saying. I can't help but notice that she immediately asks about a he, not a she. You mean she already knows about Braxton's secret lifestyle?

"He was handsome. Pretty, even. Well dressed. Warm brown complexion, smooth and wavy black hair. Nice eyes and a great smile."

"That sounds like Corbyn. The rat bastard. He promised he wouldn't see him again until after the wedding." I am so shocked by this admission. I cannot fathom why Ebony would choose to be in a relationship with someone she knows is cheating on her. She is intelligent, strong, attractive, and has so much going for her. There is no reason for her to settle with Braxton.

"Ebony, you've known about Braxton's behavior? How long has your relationship been like this?"

"Don't feel sorry for me, Reese. I'm a big girl and I know what I am doing. Braxton's *always* been bisexual, this is nothing new. We've had an understanding since our relationship has gotten serious. He's committed to being a good husband, the kind I want and need him to be: upstanding in the community, active in our church, a great provider and future father for our children. I've committed to being the kind of wife he wants me to be: active and relevant in the community, a bit of Michelle Obama in public with some private Cardi B just for him. He has needs, Reese, and I support that. I don't care if he gets them met on the side, just as long as he continues to be the kind of partner I'm looking for and want him to be. But he can't be running around behind my back with the guys. Let's keep this thing as safe and honest as possible. Be open with me and I will continue to love and support you. Lying about secret trips to get a little booty action a couple of months before our wedding? That's unacceptable."

I hold the phone but say nothing, completely dumbfounded by Ebony's "understanding" with her fiancé.

"So you're ok with his lifestyle? As long as you get a rock on your finger and a new last name out of the deal?"

"I didn't say that I'm ok with his lifestyle, I said that we have an understanding. Understanding your partner is part of loving them. I know he's flawed, just like he knows I'm flawed, but we love each other anyway. You've never been married Reese…"

"You've never been married, either, Ebony. Or have you conveniently forgotten that fact?"

"But I'm engaged and will be getting married in a couple of months."

"You're still going to marry him?"

"Of course I am. We'll talk about it and work through it. He won't be getting off easy, but he'll come to know how I feel about this behavior and he'll learn to act appropriately so I can continue to support our arrangement. Braxton is the real deal Reese. He could be elected mayor one day. And after that, the sky is the limit. I'm not about to screw this up because of his sexual preferences. No ma'am, I'm not letting go of this prize. I've earned Braxton."

"You've *earned* Braxton? I'm still trying to figure out what you see in the man. You deserve better than that, Ebony. I wish you could see it."

"Honey, it doesn't get any better than Braxton Walker, ok? I will make an excellent wife to him, will be a darn good mistress to our home and raise 2.5 beautiful black babies with him. Your view of love is too idealistic Reese. No relationship is ever going to be perfect. Look at Tameka and Darryl. They have a sweet little girl, they've been together for over ten years…"

"And they are absolutely miserable with one another. Is that really who you want to compare your relationship with?"

"Look, Reesie, my Mama didn't raise no fool. Braxton is not hurting me, I'm not putting up with him. We genuinely love each other and have a great rapport. He's meant to be my husband."

"And you expect God to bless your relationship? With him living a double life and you living in denial?"

"Glass houses, Reese. Glass houses. No one is perfect. Who do you think sent Braxton to me? God did. His hand has been on our relationship from day one. We're about to reach the end zone. So while I sincerely appreciate you calling to tell me what happened, I'll take it from here. No need to be concerned, you just show up to the Carlton Ballroom in December and expect to be amazed by the celebration of black excellence that will take place. Don't worry about me Reese, we're good, ok? And

I'd appreciate your discretion in not mentioning this to anyone."

"Tameka already knows." I lower my voice to nearly a whisper when I say this.

"Of course you called her first. No matter, I'll talk to her about it shortly. But don't say anything else about it, ok? I'm trying to protect his reputation for his, and our, political future. Don't mess this up for me, Reese." Ebony says, and I've had my fill of the BS she is spouting.

"I won't breathe a word. Sounds like you and Braxton have already made a mess of things for yourselves. Goodbye, Ebony." I end the call before she has time to say anything else. Heart heavy, I clean up my trash from dinner and turn off the television. This is the perfect time for the bubble bath that my body has been craving. I don't even know how to process that last phone call, either. Calgon, take me away.

CHAPTER EIGHTEEN
Starry Nights

Who's in your corner? Who's on your side? I value the relationships in my life, and try to be the type of friend that I hope to find in others. Sometimes that looks like a cheerleader, rooting for you from the sidelines. Sometimes I'm playing referee, calling out the fouls and interferences keeping you from reaching your goals. Sometimes I'm your offensive lineman, protecting your blind side. But one thing is for sure, I won't be playing games with our relationship. If I'm on your side, and you're on mine, you can count on me. I'm all in.

The Real MVP, Candy Girl

Tarsha's is my go-to for a new hairdo and a new perspective. Every turn in her chair feels like she isn't just trimming my split ends, but it also feels like she is cutting out the dead weight from my life. Sister has magic fingers, and baby, I never walk away disappointed. As I continue to prep for the BTU fundraiser, nervous butterflies flutter in my stomach. None of this would be possible without Davis. I'm still hoping he'll show up tonight. Even if he doesn't, I want to look my best. And why not treat my girls to a fun beauty session, too? Not Ebony and Tameka, no, this morning I am accompanied by none other than Sheree, Janae, and Kiara. It just so happens that their school's fall dance is on the same night as the fundraiser tonight. I thought it would be fun to help them get ready, and nothing could dim their smiles and youthful exuberance today.

Tarsha's has a full house today, each chair in her shop is full, and the waiting area is nearly at capacity. All of the stylists have multiple clients to keep up with. Carmen, her shampoo girl, is going to need a massage after today. I'm glad we had early appointments.

Margaret, one of the other stylists, and the one in closest proximity to Tarsha's chair, chats animatedly with her client. She's a hoot to be around, but will be so busy gossiping that your request for a half-inch trim will quickly become a pixie before you know it. As long as I've been coming here, I've seen it happen more than once. She can sweet talk her unsuspecting clients into approving the new cut, too, talking them into liking styles they didn't even ask for. I guess the gossip is just that good. But I only trust these precious tresses to Tarsha.

"Reese, girl, how's that fella you were seeing. Davis, was it?" Margaret asks, rat-tail comb in midair while she waits for my response. I do not want to get caught up in the web of rumors, scandal, and hearsay that is Margaret's calling card.

"I'm not seeing him anymore." I say flatly, and it's true. Not in the present, at least. But Margaret, and the rest of the salon, doesn't need more details than that.

"Mm, mm, mm, and he was a fine one. Okay? Capital F-I-N-E. So he's available?" She says, and either my eyes are betraying me or a couple of other ladies perk up in anticipation as well.

I sit up at this question, looking Margaret squarely in the eye.

"He's unavailable." I say, loudly enough for any eavesdroppers paying attention to our conversation.

"But I thought you just said that…"

"He's not available Margaret." I repeat, and she nods in response. Now you run and tell that. I hope she spreads it, too, fending off any others who might have even a passing interest in my man. Davis. I mean my friend, Davis.

"Got it, Reese. I was hoping y'all had worked out, that's all. After all that with his first wife." I get it, Iris was a saint. People don't have to keep hammering me over the head with it already.

"You knew Iris?" I ask noncommittally, knowing that Margaret probably won't let this go.

"Yeah, honey. She was a sweetheart. I remember when she got sick, too. I mean, she was so private, it seemed like we found out and she was gone soon after."

"Many people try to protect their privacy, Margaret. Especially when it comes to their health. Everybody's not nosy like you!" Tarsha exclaims, and we all laugh together, even Margaret, who is fully aware of her well deserved reputation.

"I just like to be in the know, that's all. I call it being up to date on current events. But anyway, that's not what I mean. When Iris got sick, I heard she even kept the news from Davis for a long time. He felt like if he had learned sooner he could've done more. He was devastated."

I take this in for a moment. No wonder Davis was so hurt that I kept my dinner with Phillip from him. He felt like I wasn't being completely honest with him. And now I can see that I wasn't. Over Phillip Martin. It wasn't even worth losing the trust that Davis had in us. I hope that I can earn it back.

"Thanks for sharing that, Margaret."

"No problem. Just doing my part. We all want to see Davis happy again. That's why I was asking if he was available. There's this young lady from my church..."

"He's not available." I state again, more forcefully this time.

"Oop, I guess that's that." Tarsha replies, and Margaret bats her eyes.

No, he's not available. I just need to win him back.

~

A couple of hours later, and we're a shining, shimmery, quartet of beautiful, black women. I dropped each girl off at home to get ready, and now I'm heading back home to do the same. I can't wait to slip into my new cocktail dress, an aubergine lace confection with a twirling skirt and slightly daring, cut-out back. Simple and elegant, I love the way I feel and look in it. And there are pockets. I may not want to come out of it this evening.

As I start to dress, I can't help but think about Margaret's comments earlier. Of course Davis has been in his feelings about where we are in our relationship. What to me seemed like no big deal probably brought up old wounds for him. And if I'm being real about the situation, if it had been the other way around, it would've brought up old wounds for me, too. Trust is a fragile, precarious pillar in relationships. One moment it can seem to be standing strong, and in another it can topple over. Even little movements can become momentous, causing irreparable damage and deep divides. You can trust me with your heart, Davis. You can. I can be and do better than before. Please help him trust me again, I silently pray.

~

The evening of the fundraiser is officially here. After making my way downtown (on time!), and finding suitable parking, it's time to get this party going for the kids. Months and months of planning and it is finally here. Walking into the downtown venue, I am completely amazed by its transformation. When our title sponsor pulled out before Dylan left, I knew finding another location would prove to be difficult. And it did. Countless calls and emails were unfruitful, and I began to lose hope. Reese Joseph is not a quitter, though, and I was not about to fail. Reluctantly, and after exhausting every resource I thought was available, I made the decision to finally call Davis. I'll never forget his response.

"Davis, it's Reese. I need your help, please."

"For you, Reese, anything." His simple reply was everything I needed and more.

And boy did Davis ever come through. Pulling a few strings, he was able to sweet talk a local developer into allowing us to use one of his properties for the evening. It's not on the market or available to the public yet, it's just that exclusive. And it's an amazing setting, the ballroom opening up to a gorgeous courtyard. The rooftop deck offers stunning views of Oak City as well. This will be the hottest ticket in town once it's open to the public, and Davis was able to secure it for us at a fraction of what it will likely charge for future events. We are so grateful!

Standing in the foyer, I hear the haunting refrain of Aretha's version of Nessun Dorma, tonight's DJ a happy compromise between what the larger executive board wanted versus what the junior board felt would make the event most memorable. A smattering of high-hat and round tables, along with several banquettes, are strategically placed around the ballroom. Our gorgeous centerpieces reflect the colors of the season, shades of rust, burnt orange, and shimmering golds perfect complements to the cream linens draping each table. I am so pleased that the final result is steeped in elegance and refinement. Still praying the evening goes off without a hitch.

I begin to mingle around the room, conversing with various board members, high profile attendees, and other sponsors and guests. Charmayne Wheeler, the Executive Director for BTU, is clearly delighted with the turnout, her expression one of both excitement and relief. I scan the room, searching for Davis in the sea of faces, but he's not here yet, if he's coming at all.

Disappointed, I glide over to one of the action stations to see what treats are in store. There's a carving station, a mashed potato bar, a pasta station, a salad station, and a Viennese table. Of course I'd love to start with dessert, but I'll settle for the mashed potato bar instead. I'm adding a dollop of sour cream to my potatoes when I hear my name being called.

"Reese, Reese." I turn around, excited, until I see that it's just Logan.

"Hello Logan, how are you?" I ask, crestfallen that Davis still hasn't come.

"Reese, I've been looking for you everywhere. You look fantastic!" He exclaims, his deep blue eyes wide with wonder. In this outfit, and with this new hairdo and makeup, I feel fantastic, too. The BTU event coming together certainly helps as well. Logan has cleaned up nicely himself, his dark gray suit just right for the occasion.

"Would you like to join me on the dance floor?" He asks, eyes expectant. No Logan, I wouldn't. I'd like to eat my mashed potatoes before my stomach starts growling.

"You know, I've been on the move all day long. This will be my first meal of the day. Maybe later, after I've had a little sustenance instead." I say, hopeful that he will move on and forget about asking me to dance.

"I'm famished myself, and those potatoes look delicious. Why don't I join you instead?" He says, already grabbing a martini glass to fill with potatoes and toppings. I don't even have time to protest, and Logan follows me to the nearest high hat table. If I sit down with him I run the risk of minutes turning into hours of conversation. The high hats seem much safer.

Logan fidgets for a few moments, awkwardly stepping from side to side in time with the music. I glance around his head again, still looking for Davis. No such luck.

"Reese, you really do look lovely this evening."

"Thanks, Logan. You look great, too." I say, amiable but not flirtatious in the least. I like Logan just fine, but I'm not going to pretend that we would be friends in any other setting. Glad for the connection of BTU and the junior board, but let's not make it out to be more than what it is.

"Everything looks amazing tonight. You've done an outstanding job leading the junior board."

"It was a team effort, Logan. I can't take the credit for it, I'm just happy with how everything has turned out."

"You're too modest, Reese. No one else could've pulled off what you've done here, not even Dylan." He says with utter and complete sincerity. It means a lot, especially with the whirlwind of emotions and commitments I've felt over the last several months.

"Thank you, Logan. I really appreciate that."

"You're welcome, Reese." An awkward moment or two passes, and I'm nearly done with my mashed potatoes at this point. I'm just about ready to find an excuse to exit the table.

"Reese?"

"Yes, Logan?"

"I was wondering, I mean, I was thinking, you know, I've learned a lot about you since we've been on this team together, and I think you're pretty great." Ruh-roh. I don't like where I can feel this heading.

"I was wondering if you're seeing anyone? And if not, would you like to be? Not anyone, but you know, me?" He says in such a sweet and uncomfortable manner, that I almost accept his invitation out of pity. Almost.

"Logan, I'm so flattered that you would even think of me in that way. My heart belongs elsewhere. I do look forward to growing our working friendship, though." I say, and the light in his eyes dims.

"Of course you're with someone, I don't know what I was thinking. I'm sorry, Reese. I don't want it to ever be awkward with us."

"No worries, Logan. No problem at all. I appreciate your interest."

"If the timing was different for you, I most definitely would be interested." Who knew? I take cream in my coffee but never expected this variety. Talk about your surprising turn of events.

"Whoever he is, he's a lucky guy to have you on his arm."

"I'm blessed to even know him, Logan. I truly am. And you know what? I'm glad you told me. I should probably excuse myself, though. I see a couple of board members I haven't greeted yet." I say, hopeful this awkward exchange can draw to a close.

"Of course, me too. You did great, Reese. And you look wonderful." He says with sincerity, meeting my gaze.

"Thanks, Logan. Have a great night." I say, and we give polite nods before leaving the table.

I try to be gracious in my role as chair of this event, maneuvering throughout the space to greet all of our guests, of course remembering to thank them for their support of this event. The turnout has far exceeded my greatest expectations. I'm in awe of the number of supporters in this room. BTU will not only meet their goal for the event, but it looks like there will be a hefty boost to the BTU Scholarship Fund as well. To know that I was able to contribute to this effort in this way is both humbling and gratifying. I'm so excited about what it will mean for our kids!

Time passes, and I'm so caught up with working the room that I don't even miss Davis at first. But between a few dances, and noshing on the delicious food, and refilling my glass, and talking to more people than I can remember, hours have passed, but he's still not here.

Needing to step away from the cacophony of noise in the ballroom, I discreetly exit the ballroom and enter the courtyard. The beautifully landscaped grounds, carefully spaced benches, and softly twinkling strings of lights offer just enough ambience to this space, and it's the perfect place to draw inspiration or simply clear your head. I feel like I need to do both, if but for a moment.

Tracing the manicured topiaries with my fingers, I feel a sense of calm descend over me. This is just what I needed, I can't help but think. Just a moment to thank God for his goodness, a moment to reflect on all that He has done. I close my eyes, gently swaying to the soft music playing in the background. Time stands still until I hear my name.

"Reese." Is that you, Lord? I'm listening.

"Reese." My goodness, that voice is familiar, I think as I continue to sway.

"Paging Reese Joseph." I hear his deep voice, and I open my eyes, embarrassed as I turn toward the sound of it. How long has Davis been standing there?

He's wearing a soft smile, looking utterly and completely handsome in his midnight blue, exquisitely tailored suit. How I have missed him so.

"Reese, you are so gorgeous it takes my breath away." He says, and I swear I'm the one in need of oxygen. I stand there, nervous and unsure of what to say and do. I've been anticipating this moment for so long, that now that it's here, I'm at a loss for words. I want to fix this. I want to make this right.

"Davis, I'm so glad you're here. This night wouldn't even be possible without your help."

"I was glad you reached out. Happy to help, happy to see you shine. Everything is wonderful, Reese. Everyone is saying so." He moves a little closer to me, and a tingle races down my back. I'm awash with nervous excitement to be this near to him again, and I don't retreat.

"Reese…"

"Davis." I interrupt, the words weighing heavy on my heart as I extend my hand towards his. I feel a pulse of electricity when his hand meets mine.

"Davis, I'm so sorry. I should have been completely honest with you about Phillip. I can't go back, but I want you to know that I know I made the wrong decision then. I hope you can forgive me."

"Reese, I forgive you, I do. I didn't understand why you had to see him. And if you had told me, I don't know that I would have reacted differently. I know he hurt you, Reese. I would never, ever want to hurt you." I believe these words from this man. I believe he would never hurt me.

"I've just, I just, I don't know, Davis. He was my everything at the time. I didn't know he would mean less than nothing to me now. Before God changed my heart. Before you came along."

"Before you came along, I thought that my world ended when Iris died. I didn't know if I would ever find someone special again. I didn't know God would bless me to find someone like you, Reese."

"Davis I've been perfectly fine all these years. God has blessed me with a wonderful family, great friends, a career doing work that I love, and even these kids, my girls from BTU. I've never felt like my life was missing anything. I've never felt less fulfilled just because I didn't have a man by my side."

"Your independence is one of the things I most appreciate about you. And your willingness to speak your mind. Your unapologetic faith. The way you love and support your family and friends…your kids from BTU. Even your fiery temper. Your kindness and generosity. I love these things about you."

"Oh, you love my fiery temper, do you?" I ask playfully.

"I do. I love these things about you because I love you, Reese Joseph." He says simply, moving directly in front of me. My eyes feel misty at these words.

We've been playing this silly game, at least I have, for far too long. Pretending that I didn't want this man. Pretending that I don't need him. I don't need a man to be happy, this much is true. But God wants me to be happy, and he's placed Davis in my life because he's supposed to be here. Standing here, before him, the stars above us watching, everything seems clearer. Like the heavens above, each planet placed just so, we're here together, exactly where we are supposed to be.

"I love you too, Davis. I've been so afraid of losing me that I ended up losing us."

"Reese, you haven't lost us. You've had my heart since the very beginning. You still do." His face is inches from mine now, so close that I can feel the heat emanating from his body.

"I trust you with my heart, Davis. And I want to be with you."

"You're here with me, Reese. And there is no other place I would rather be than with you." Davis moves forward, enveloping me in his arms as his lips meet my own.

The soft refrain of Nat King Cole's "The Very Thought of You" plays in the background, becoming the soundtrack to our embrace. When the song ends, I do not know, and the rest of the evening I'm grateful for gravity keeping me from floating away with Davis by my side.

Game. Set. Match. Reese Joseph is in love.

AND TROUBLES RISE

CHAPTER NINETEEN

I Believe

When I was a little girl, I believed that the Tooth Fairy was real, until my parents forgot to put a dollar under my pillow one night. I believed in the Easter Bunny until I learned that Christ's Resurrection had nothing to do with plastic eggs. And I believed in Santa Claus until I saw our mall Santa yell at a kid who peed in his lap. But when it comes to love, I've always taken it with a grain of salt. Fairy tales and fantasies are fun to hear about, they're fun to experience, but they can leave you with the bitter aftertaste of skepticism. I haven't given up on it, I'm just waiting for the Happily Never After plot twist. It's bound to come.

Once Upon a Time, Candy Girl

Oak City in December is a wonder to behold. The sights and sounds of the season are in full effect, with our quaint, historic, downtown area decorated as picturesquely as a Christmas card. I've given her a hard time about it, but a part of me gets why Ebony wanted to have her wedding at Christmastime. What I don't get, and will never understand, is why she's still going through with the wedding. Tameka and I have tried to talk sense in her, to no avail, and more stubborn than ever, she's choosing to press on.

Presently we're standing in Annabelle's Bridal Shoppe, the fateful place where Ebony said yes to the dress more than twelve months ago. Miss Annabelle is precious, a petite, soft-spoken little woman with soft, thin, sandy brown and white curls framing her pale peach, and lightly wrinkled, fair skin. Her manner and demeanor are a throwback to genteel southern traditions like mint juleps and garden parties. But don't let the twin set cardigan and tea length skirt fool you, Miss Annabelle was a Freedom Rider, and she's always been an ally to our community. She has wonderful stories to share, and we simply adore her.

"Tameka, dearie, this cut is outstanding on you. I love how the fabric drapes back here, don't you think?" Miss Annabelle asks, admiring Tameka's curvy frame. She does look good, too, the one-shouldered cut of the bridesmaid dress' bodice being tailored to perfectly fit her body.

"I love it, Miss Annabelle. It feels good, too." Tameka says, sharing a smile with the little woman.

Miss Annabelle clucks her approval before going to check on another customer.

"The bride approves. You look fabulous, Meka." Ebony says, snapping her fingers and smiling broadly. I'll give it to her. If this mess with Braxton is bothering her even a little, we'd never know. She's her usual upbeat self, with nary a sense of pre-wedding jitters. Ebony moves toward Tameka, kneeling to more closely inspect the hem of the dress.

"Perfect. It's perfect, just as it should be." She remarks, and Tameka glances over at me.

"It doesn't have to be perfect, Ebony." Tameka responds in a sing-song sort of way, and Ebony's eyes quickly narrow back at her.

"Yes, it does. And it is. And it will be." She says matter-of-factly, walking over to look at a lovely display of formal footwear.

"Daddy says that Senator Rawlings will be there after all. His assistant confirmed with Daddy's office this morning." Of course Ebony is more concerned with the number of dignitaries expected to attend that day. As long as we're focusing on what's most important.

"That's nice, Ebony." Tameka sighs, looking over at me again. I know she wants me to speak up, but what am I supposed to say? I've tried in vain to get through to this girl. Braxton is her "King" to hear her tell it; she's not giving up the crown for anything, not even her personal dignity.

"It's all coming together, Ladies. Over a year of planning in the making, and it is *all* coming together. In two weeks I'll be Mrs. Braxton Harrison Walker. Sounds good, doesn't it?" She asks, smiling brightly. Tameka nods robotically, but I just stand there, silent. I feel like I'm stuck in an episode of The Twilight Zone.

"Ladies, I'm so sorry I was away for so long. How's everything back here?" Miss Annabelle asks, looking to Ebony for reassurance.

"It's wonderful Miss Annabelle. I think Tameka is all set to go, and we're ready for Reese's fitting next." Miss Annabelle nods her head, springing to action to find my dress. She returns a moment later, my black, full-length maid of honor gown in her arms. Ebony is sticking to her Silver Bells theme, and her parents are sparing no expense when it comes to their only child's nuptials. This event will be black tie, and with Councilman Walker set to finally wed, their wedding will be the talk of the town. If folks only knew. As it stands, it seems that 400 of their nearest and dearest made the list. At least we made the cut.

Tameka and Ebony chat about wedding details while I shimmy into my gown. It's beautiful, too, gently dusting the floor. I wasn't that crazy about the one-shoulder look at first, but it's surprisingly flattering. Not that it matters. We could all wear potato sacks, or better yet, clown suits, for the shenanigans taking place in two weeks. And I hope that Ebony remembers her running shoes.

"Let's go, Reese, don't be shy. Give us a look!" Ebony calls out, and I wish my mood could match her own. Uneasy doesn't begin to describe how I'm feeling… nauseated would be more accurate. I step out from the dressing area, hesitating a bit, but Ebony squeals with delight.

"Reesie! It's gorgeous on you. So, so elegant. Don't you think so, Meka?"

"You look so pretty Reese! I love it, I love it." They ooh and ahh for a moment, making me uncomfortable in the process. Sensing my discomfort, Miss Annabelle scoots them over to the settee so that she can focus on my fit.

"Ebony, darling, your mother picked up her gown yesterday. She was stunning! You remind me so much of her." Miss Annabelle says, and Ebony smiles politely.

"Thank you, Miss Annabelle."

"Oh, of course, dearie. And she seemed so excited about the wedding. She said that Braxton is a perfect future son-in-law, too. I know they are proud of you, Ebony."

Miss Annabelle continues to work away, pinning my dress, completely unaware of Ebony's response. My dear friend is smiling so hard she is straining. She glances at me, and but for a moment, the cracks are visible. But she looks away quickly, turning her attention back to Tameka.

AND TROUBLES RISE

Something's got to give, Dear Lord. Please, Father, fix this. Give me the strength to help my friend.

~

The next evening, Davis and I are walking through downtown, enjoying the way Oak City has come alive for the holidays. Each shop's windows are gaily decorated, and brightly colored twinkling lights frame the lampposts on the streets. We saunter into a little shop on the corner, eager to pick up a few last minute gifts. They're known for their handmade ornaments, and I have my heart set on getting a special one for Mama. Just a little trinket to encourage her and commemorate the year she beat cancer again. It hasn't happened yet, but I believe by faith that it will.

Their selection of items is overwhelming: beautiful, exquisitely fragile glass ornaments, hand-carved wooden ones, even rustic, hand-painted ones. I'm not sure where to begin. Davis and I start at the back of the store, making the decision to work our way towards the front as we shop, heading to the natural exit. It seems like a good plan. A lovely glass angel catches my eye, and I stop to look at it for a moment. Davis disappears from my side, then returns with a wooden ornament featuring intertwined hearts. It can be engraved with names, dates, you name it, he says. I'm puzzled, thinking he was picking out a gift for his mother, but no, he has the bright idea to get a gift from us for Braxton and Ebony.

"Davis, I think it is one thing to go along with this, it's another altogether to celebrate it."

"Celebrating our friends getting married? Since when did that become a crime?" He asks, smiling, and I am dumbfounded by his attitude. Surely he is not cool with all of this.

"No crime in calling a spade a spade, either. It's not enough that he's cheating on Ebony, but he's also proceeding with this sham of a wedding."

"That's not fair, Reese. Ebony hasn't called it off, either. And they're both adults capable of making the decisions that are best for them. It's really not our place to interfere." He says, his gaze holding steady against my own.

"One of my best friends in the world is about to make the biggest mistake of her life, so yeah, I feel pretty strongly that's it's my place to interfere. What else am I supposed to do, stand by and do absolutely nothing? What kind of friend would that make me?" I ask, keenly aware of my increasing volume. I make a mental note to lower it when I speak again.

"The kind that knows better than to try to tell grown folks what to do. They've decided what they're willing to accept in their relationship."

"And you're ok with that?" I ask, incredulous.

"It's not that I'm ok with it, but at the end of the day, Braxton and Ebony have to come home to each other, not to me. Do I like that he's cheating on Ebony, do I cosign that behavior? No, of course not.

Do I like that he's leading a closeted lifestyle instead of living his truth, whatever that may be? No. Do I think they should be getting married, or even be together as a couple? No, I don't. But Braxton is like a brother to me. I don't have to like the choices that he makes in order to love him and offer my support. I'm in no position to judge him, and I dare not condemn him, either. I'll continue to give him my love and support, and I'll continue to pray for him, too. I suggest you do the same for Ebony."

His speech is a shock to my system. I can't find the words as I consider his own. Thanks, Ebony. Because of your stupidity, you're not only messing up your life, but now you're messing with my relationship, too.

"This is what I know, Davis. We're going to have to agree to disagree on this one, because it's not right, it's just not right. I want to be the kind of friend to my girls that they are to me. When I agreed to see Phillip, they called me out on that. They knew it wasn't in my best interest."

"But you went anyway."

"So you're going to throw it in my face now? I thought we were past that."

"You brought it up Reese, I didn't. And we *are* past that. It doesn't even cross my mind. But don't you see, Reese. They advised you against it and you did it anyway. The same has to happen with Braxton and Ebony. I can't call it off, you can't, either. They have to come to the decision that they can live with."

"But she's one of my best friends, Davis. What if I can't live with the decision she makes?"

"You love her anyway. You don't give up on a person because they don't agree with you. You can't cast her aside because her choices are different than your own. Pray that God will change their hearts; that His will is done in their lives. And then you live your life, Reese. It will work out the way that it is supposed to. Life always does." He says, reaching for my hand. I pull it back, looking up at him. The care and concern in his eyes thaws the frost around my heart, and as I feel the corners of my eyes begin to tear up, I reach back to him.

Standing here, in the middle of the ornament shop, I hold Davis' gaze. I think about Mama's cancer. I think about Tameka and Darryl. About work. My relationship with Davis. Of course I think about Braxton and Ebony. I don't understand it, Lord. I don't know why this is happening the way that it is. But I trust you, God, to work everything out in your time. I believe, Father. Please help my unbelief.

AND TROUBLES RISE

CHAPTER TWENTY
JUMPING THE BROOM

How long is forever? When it's doing something you love, or spending time with someone you love, forever never seems long enough. Conversely, when you'd rather be doing something different, when you'd rather be in the company of someone else, forever lasts a mighty long time. Make a good decision and it is soon forgotten, but make a bad one, and it feels like you have to suffer the consequences FOREVER. Relationships are that way. Some feel like for never, others seem like for maybe, but the best ones? The ones that last? The ones that are meant to be? Those feel like forever. May the love in your heart for the ones that you love last forever.

Always, Candy Girl

The sun is shining. The sky is bright blue. It's an unseasonably mild 70 degrees. If I didn't know better, I would say that it is a perfect day for a wedding. But I know better. And while it might be a perfect day for a wedding, it's not the right day for this one. No day is.

Davis and I have been on different wavelengths for the last couple of weeks. Work has been crazy, Tameka and I have been ripping and running to get through the last minute details for the wedding, and of course I've tried to help Mama as much as possible. I'm still a little miffed about our exchange in the ornament shop, but whatever. He can be the one planning their anniversary party, not me.

He's kind of been laid off as my realtor, anyway. At least for the time being. I suspended my home search when I learned that Mama's cancer had returned, but with the last round of treatment on the horizon, maybe this is the time to start thinking about looking again. We'll see. He's still my boo; just not my favorite person right now. But I believe we'll get through this bump, this hiccup. Every journey comes with a little turbulence.

I've avoided Davis all morning, choosing to ride with Meka to the wedding, knowing that he will be there to take me home. Little Chloe is a bundle of energy in the backseat, twittering with excitement until Tameka tells her to pipe down. She's going to be the cutest flower girl, and she's such a girly girl that I know she'll love primping and prepping with us today.

It's an uneventful ride to the Carlton Hotel, with Meka chattering along while my mind is elsewhere. Once we arrive at our destination downtown, we make our way to Ebony's bridal suite, which is already buzzing with activity. Poor Sheila is running around like a chicken with its head cut off, which can't be very reassuring. The wedding planner doesn't have it together? Is there even hope for the rest of us?

"Hey Queen, your ladies in waiting have arrived." Tameka announces, and Ebony turns toward us, her face breaking into a wide grin.

"Finally! Finally a sister can breathe, thank God for reinforcements. If y'all had been another minute longer I was about to go slap off on Sheila. She is working my very last nerve!" Ebony says, tying her silk "Bride" robe a little more tightly around her body as she stands.

"We're here for you, E. How can we help?" I ask, and Tameka nods in agreement.

"Nothing is going right! My makeup artist got a flat tire, the florist sent all of the flowers except my bouquet, and Braxton's niece tore the hem of her flower girl dress." She's pouting as she says this, and I wonder if she realizes that this doesn't exactly bode well for what's to come. Still wondering if it's a stupid decision to marry Braxton? Baby, here's your sign. Too soon?

"Okay, okay. We can help put fires out. Does Iesha need a ride here?"

"No, Sheila is sending someone to pick her up."

"And the florist, do I need to go get the bouquet for you?"

"No, they're sending it by messenger. It should be here within the hour."

"And the dress? Just point me in the direction of some scotch tape and a stapler." Tameka says, and we're all laughing now.

"Girl, you're so crazy. Miss Annabelle is sending her assistant over to repair it."

Wait a second, things aren't so bad after all. So what's all the fuss about?

"Sheesh, Ebony, you had us scared for a minute. Sounds like the crisis was averted." Tameka says, sighing with relief. Ebony's nostrils flare in response.

"Don't you get it? Everything is supposed to go off without a hitch today. I've planned this day, hour by hour, within an inch of my life. It has to be perfect."

"Puh-lease, Ebony. When me and Darryl got married the preacher forgot to sign the license. His mama fainted during the ceremony. The caterer ran out of food. I think you'll make it. Just get some tea or something, a place like this has to have some good bougie tea, and sit down. Let us help you. Don't stress about it."

AND TROUBLES RISE

"Easier said than done, Meka."

"But she's right, E. This is your day. Why don't you sit on the balcony and rest for a few moments. We can see if Sheila needs anything." I offer, trying my best to be helpful.

"And come in smelling like outside? Thanks, but no thanks, Reese. I'll just chill in the corner, I guess."

"Do that, girl. Prop your feet up. We've got this. Don't worry your pretty little lace front about a thing."

"Meka!"

"What? Nobody's judging you, it's your day. Do you, boo. Looks good to me." Tameka says playfully, and Ebony rolls her eyes at her. She makes her way over to the chaise lounge in the corner, and Tameka goes to check on Chloe for a moment. I begin the process of slipping into my dress and heels, and then I hear the chirp of my cell phone. Pulling it out, I see that Davis has arrived.

I'm here, Baby.

Can we talk for a few minutes before things get crazy?

I'm in the lobby.

"Hey guys, I need to step out for a moment. I'll be back in a few minutes." I say, making my departure before anyone can protest.

Arriving in the lobby, I see Davis standing there. He's already dressed for the ceremony, looking fine and dapper in his tux. Looking much too good for me to stay mad at him for long.

"Reese, Baby, hey. How are you?" He asks, smiling broadly.

"I'm good. Just trying to be helpful to Ebony right now. She's pretty stressed."

"Yeah, I figured you might get busy with that. I just wanted a chance to see you before all of the controlled chaos begins."

"Well, here I am." I say, unsure of what to say or do.

"Are you okay, Reese? Are we good? You've been distant."

"Preoccupied, that's all. My time hasn't felt like my own."

"I got that. I understand. I've just missed you, Baby. I know this isn't how you wanted things to work out, but everything is going to be ok."

"I keep telling myself that until it comes true."

His brow furrows with concern and I feel his heat as he leans forward to touch me. Leaning back, the floor seems to give way as I stumble backward in my stilettos. Instinctively, Davis reaches forward and draws me close to him. He's caught me in time. I will not fall.

"Reese, I love you. You mean more to me than you could ever know. You have been a great friend to Ebony. I know she's like a sister to you. But even this, this too, shall pass. Let's not let this break us." As his voice trembles a bit, the stubborn vise grip on my heart begins to loosen, releasing with it weeks, and months, and years of heartbreak. I sigh with relief as I feel the weight begin to shift from my body.

"I'm here for you through this, Baby. I'm here for you, Reese. If you'll let me stay, I promise I'll be here for you as long as the good Lord above allows me to be." In a flash he's ever so gently wiping the small tears that begin their descent down the side of my face.

"Just hold me, Davis." I say, pressing my finger to his lips. "Just hold me."

Davis obliges, wrapping his arms more tightly around me. Time stops as I melt into his embrace, finding safety and home in the comfort of his arms. I could stay here forever, suspended in this place, being held by my love, letting all of the troubles of our world fade away. Lest it last too long, the sound of feet stomping along the marble floors breaks our reverie.

"Reese! Reese, what are you doing? Ebony needs you. She's completely hysterical!" Tameka shrieks, ignoring Davis and grabbing me by the arm abruptly.

"Tameka, just a minute…"

"Sorry, Davis. I need to borrow my girl for a minute. Bride emergency."

His caress is tender as Tameka pulls me away, lingering only to squeeze my hand and mouth "I love you" as I begin to follow her. I pray my eyes convey my apology, and I blow a kiss to him as Tameka's grip tightens.

"C'mon, Reese. Ebony needs us. Davis can entertain himself for a minute." Tameka states more urgently, and I overlook her snide remark.

We make our way upstairs, and as we exit the elevator, it is much louder than I remember. Now the wide hall leading to the bridal suite is crowded, seemingly overrun with other members of the bridal party, not to mention a few associates of the hotel, as well. Ebony's wedding planner, Sheila, greets us at the door.

"Oh, thank God. I was hoping Tameka could find you." Sheila exhales, visibly relieved as she slowly opens the door. Her tone becomes cheerier as she notifies Ebony of our arrival.

"Ebony, our beautiful bride-to-be, look who's here to see you!" Sheila's gaiety is ironic, given the situation. Even Tameka and I are struggling to smile.

"Hey, girl, hey. Don't you look beautiful. Stunning!" I say, treading carefully as I step closer to her seat on the vanity.

"Save it, Reese. Save that crap for someone else." Ebony's eyes narrow as she looks up at me.

"Ok, now, Ebony. Don't cut the fool. You asked me to find Reese and I did." Tameka says, bracing herself against the wall. She folds her arms and clenches her jaw, waiting for Ebony's next move.

"I said thanks before you left, didn't I? Thanks, Tameka. Of course, if Reese had just answered her phone, this wouldn't have even been necessary."

"Ladies, I think I better go check on the minister." Sheila interjects, about to throw up her Baptist finger and exit the sanctuary, clearly reading the mood of the room.

"You can find me a bottle of water while you're gone. That's what I'm paying you for." Ebony hisses, and Sheila nods timidly as she scoots on out the door.

"EVERYBODY OUT NOW!" Ebony cries out, and the whole room freezes, then starts moving to and fro to quickly exit the room. I'm just about to slip out myself, but Ebony's not letting me go that easily.

"Everybody except for Reese." She says, and I purse my lips, stopping dead in my tracks. The two of us are silent until everyone else leaves the room. Tameka glances at me, but I nod to let her know we're all good here.

"By all means, please have a seat, Reese." Ebony says, extending her arm with great flourish. I find a padded seat and get comfortable, and Ebony surprises me by doing the same.

"What's going on, Ebony? What did I miss?"

"He's here." She says, and it takes me a moment to understand who she is talking about.

"He's coming to the ceremony?"

"I don't know. I guess, maybe. Braxton called to tell me he would be sitting on his side, he just didn't want it to surprise me."

"And how do you feel about that?"

"What did I do to deserve this, Reese? What have I done?" She says simply, placing her head in her hands. If only I could make the pain of this situation go away.

"He's not worthy of your love, Ebony."

"Braxton is a great guy, Reese. He just has bad judgment sometimes."

"Ebony, I…"

"Reese, we were fine until you opened your mouth. Fine."

"What are you talking about? You were everything *except* fine. If anything, I helped you."

"Helped me? I'm miserable on what should be the happiest day of my life. How is that helping me?" She says through tears.

"Ebony, if you can't see that Braxton is not worthy of your love, if you can't see that you deserve more than this "understanding", or whatever it is you want to call it, if you can't see that God has better in store for you, then I don't know what to tell you. But Braxton Walker? He's not it."

Ebony is solemn as she considers my words.

"What if this is my only chance at happiness?" She says sorrowfully, piercing my heart with her words.

"Oh, Ebony. Is that what you're worried about?"

"I know you're the 'strong, independent' one. The 'I don't need a man' one. The 'God loves me as I am' one. And that's all well and good. But even you have Davis now. What about the rest of us? I want a man in my life. I want to be a wife."

"As Ms. Bean would say, 'What you need is a man. What you have is a pair of britches'. If it's in God's will for your life, your husband will come. And you won't have to be a Sarai and try to Hagar this situation for His promises to be fulfilled in your life. God knows that you desire a husband. If He sends you one, you will know that the gift is from Him. I pray you see that sooner rather than later, E. God knows I do." I stand, preparing to exit, while Ebony remains seated, continuing to contemplate her future.

"I guess I need to talk to Braxton." She says, reaching for her phone. I take this as the perfect time to make my exit.

AND TROUBLES RISE

Slipping out the door, and closing it gently behind me, I notice a hallway full of bridal party members, their eyes wide with curiosity. Only Meka dares to ask what transpired.

"She just needs a little time, I think." I say, asking her to pray with me right then and there. We join hands and begin to pray, and while doing so I feel a hand on my shoulder. I don't open my eyes, but I continue to pray. I pray for Ebony to find peace. I pray for God's will to be done. I pray for calm. And I pray for a resolution that is best for everyone. Finally, I pray that we are able to offer the support that she needs. Saying amen, I'm amazed by the sight that I see: the entire bridal party has formed a prayer chain right here in the hallway of the Carlton Hotel. Little does she know that she has a whole army praying on her behalf.

Moments later the door opens, and our entire group is silent, waiting with baited breath, for what will happen next. Ebony walks out stoically, her expression hard to read.

"I know what I have to do." Ebony states, resolute and head held high as she walks past us. Tameka and I share a glance, her lips pursed as we follow behind quietly. Sheila reappears from wherever she had gone to in an effort to restore her dignity. Her energy is manic, eyes skittish as they dart from person to person, seeking reassurance.

"Beautiful bride, are we all set to go now?" she ventures, both a question and a plea of desperation.

"We're all set. I'll just need a cordless mic for a quick announcement first."

"Wait, what?" Sheila stammers, clearly unnerved by Ebony's unexpected request.

"I need to make an announcement to the guests. I know they've been waiting."

"And the groom...?"

"He's otherwise occupied. The mic?" Ebony asks, annoyed once again.

"Of course, one moment." Sheila is gone as quickly as she came, off to fulfill another request in her hopes of making an impossible to please bride, happy at last.

"Ebony, Suga, are you ok?" Tameka inquires, breaking the awkward silence. Ebony stands still, emotionless, her personality so restrained it's frightening.

"I'm good, Meka. I'm good. Seeing things clearly now."

"I'm back, I'm back. So sorry it took so long, Ebony. Here you are." Sheila hands the microphone to Ebony, interrupting Tameka's line of questioning. Ebony nods her appreciation, taking the mic but saying nothing. Shoulders squared, she's ready to enter the ballroom and meet her guests.

Tameka and I have no choice but to follow behind her and see how this all pans out. I continue to pray a silent prayer of strength for Ebony and peace over this situation. Peace, Lord. Peace, be still, I cry out in my spirit. Tameka steals a sideways glance from time to time, but says nothing. This long walk to Ebony's freedom seems endless, but finally, eventually, at long last we reach the massive double doors that Ebony was supposed to cross through as a single woman for the very last time.

Instinctively, I reach forward, placing a hand on her shoulder. It softens in response, lowering for a brief moment. Inhaling deeply, Ebony exhales, patting my hand and turning her head towards me. A wink and a smile from my friend, and I'm reassured that everything is going to be alright.

Ebony pulls away from me, walking forward and preparing to open the doors. Ready to start this next chapter, whatever it may look like. Certainly not meeting previous expectations.

The sunlight streaming in from the windows of the ballroom casts a hazy, warm glow around Ebony. She's not wearing her veil, but the light wafts around her in an ethereal way, and the audience gasps as she enters the room and glides down the center aisle. Still following her, Tameka and I remain silent, although the remainder of the rooms is abuzz with whispers. I catch Mama's eyes on us, and I shrug my shoulders in response. Pastor Houston, Davis, and the other groomsmen are assembled near the pulpit, but the other members of the bridal party follow close behind us, then break away to find a place to watch, all near the far aisles of the room.

I'm instantly at ease at the sight of Davis, and his eyes are warm as his gaze meets my own. Ebony reaches the altar, leaning forward to whisper in Pastor Houston's ear. Nodding in response, he steps back, giving Ebony the floor to speak. Tameka and I move out of the way, and the room suddenly grows quiet as all eyes remain on Ebony, completely transfixed in this moment.

"Thank you all for being here today. I know you all came to show your love and support to us, but Braxton and I have come to the difficult decision that we are not to be married today. We came to the realization that this union was not meant to be after all. We apologize if any of you feel disappointed by this decision." Ebony pauses, giving everyone a moment to digest this news. There are several loud gasps in response to her announcement.

"What have you done with my son?" Mama Walker stands, staring Ebony down with fire and fury.

"Mrs. Walker, Braxton has asked that I make this announcement. You can find him in his hotel room." Ebony offers, clearly over the drama of the day.

"Hmph, I didn't want him to marry your little narrow tail anyway. Not my Braxton." Grabbing her purse, Braxton's mother nearly trips over feet, and husband, too, as she exits her seat. "Let's go, Clyde!" she bellows, and Mr. Walker dutifully follows his wife.

Ebony purposely waits until they leave the ballroom before continuing her explanation.

AND TROUBLES RISE

"I'm sorry that Mrs. Walker felt that way. I'm sure many of you probably shared those feelings, but never voiced your concerns. But sitting here, as guests, and if the wedding had taken place, as witnesses, too, each of you would have been sitting before God and pledging to hold us accountable in marriage. Not everyone is willing to take that responsibility seriously, but I know of two individuals present who were. Two friends, two sisters, two who have had my back for as long as I can remember. Reese and Tameka, thank you for trusting our friendship enough to be honest with me. Thank you for valuing my happiness the way that you do. Thank you for loving me so much." Ebony's voice breaks, and my dear friend is on the verge of tears. Sheila appears again, this time wielding a box of tissues, and Ebony draws one from the box, giggling at the absurdity of it all.

"Thank you, Sheila. I'm not going to cry ya'll, I promise I'm not. I'm not messing up this beat face ok? And I don't want any of you to shed any tears, either. Braxton and I are in agreement regarding this decision. We have a lot of love and respect for one another, despite this turn of events. And in a show of solidarity, we've agreed that you can all join me at the reception today, all of the amazing food and the DJ and everything isn't going to waste. We're going to dance the night away. Daddy, we're still dancing to My Girl, you promised. Even if your bunions bother you. And Braxton is going to keep our honeymoon to Jamaica."

"You got played!" Darryl hollers out, and the whole ballroom erupts in laughter. Any remaining tension is completely broken by his unexpected and brutally honest commentary.

"Yeah, I guess I lost out on that. So ya'll better help me party tonight to make up for it. I'm going to get out of this dress, and we'll meet you downstairs after the cocktail hour. Thank you!" And with that weight lifted, Ebony skips away as light as a feather, not even the cathedral length train of her gown weighs her down.

Guests are bewildered by all that has happened; some remain seated while others begin to stand. Davis is by my side in two strides, and that familiar tingle runs down my spine. I'm better acquainted with it now, feeling it whenever he is near.

"Wonders never cease, Reese." His voice is husky in my ear.

"Davis, I'm so relieved. I'm so glad it all worked out." I say, breathless and grateful.

"Man, can y'all believe that mess? I want to know what the real deal is, ok? Give a brotha all the tea." Darryl booms, walking up to where Davis and I are standing. Tameka is right behind him.

"None of your business, with your old nosy self. You like gossip more than any woman I know. Sheesh, Darryl." Tameka says, swatting his arm away.

"I can ask, can't I? Ain't no harm in asking. No telling what goes on behind closed doors. Inquiring minds want to know."

AND TROUBLES RISE

"Well you can ask Ebony all about it at the reception, since you don't know how to leave well enough alone."

"I'm telling y'all, whatever it was, Ebony got played. Two weeks in Jamaica for some steak dinners and cocktail shrimp? Naw, man, he played her like a piano. Ain't no way."

"Shut up, Darryl. Dang, I can't take you nowhere. Hollering stuff out like we're in the club somewhere. Getting on my very last nerve."

"Tameka there you go. There you go, trying to flex in front of folks. You best simmer down."

"Simmer down or what? What you gon' do, Darryl? You can't even keep up with Chloe."

"Where is Chloe? She was standing right here a minute ago."

"Ughh, Darryl. If you have lost my baby I'm going to beat the brakes off of you."

"There she goes, down there by that other little flower girl. She's ok." Darryl says, pointing to Chloe and Ebony's cousin playing on the far end of the room. Tameka is exasperated as usual with her husband.

"Boy, you better be glad. You better. Reese, you good?"

"Oh, yes. We're good. Go get Chloe. We will see ya'll at the reception."

"Ok, cool. Let's go Darryl. Davis, Reese, we'll see ya'll in a minute."

Darryl trails Tameka as they walk away, Tameka stomping down the aisle in frustration.

~

We walk into the sumptuously decorated reception space, amazed by how wonderful and elegant everything is. Ebony definitely kept with the "Silver Bells" theme, from the draping throughout the room, to the glorious centerpieces, to the bridal party area. Sheila has been on it, too, and what was supposed to be a sweetheart table has been replaced with a throne and table for one. I know Ebony won't mind this change at all.

The reception's mood is surprisingly celebratory, buoyant with the joy of #blackcouplegoals, not in the least dampened by the reality of a relationship that was anything but.

And Ebony, my precious friend, Ebony, is practically floating across this room. Her energy is infectious, her smile signaling the joy that only comes from finding inner peace. She may not have gotten the husband she wanted, but she most certainly received the cleansing she needed. For Braxton's sake, I hope and pray he is able to find the same peace.

When Davis reaches for my hand, I don't push it away. The slightest tug lets me know he wants to dance, but he hesitates. As if realizing that we both must be invested to move forward, he doesn't pull my hand. His eyes and his demeanor are instead waiting for my consent. He has it.

I squeeze his hand, eager to let him know that I'm ready to walk beside him. Secure in my Father's love towards me, towards us, I'm ready for the adventure of knowing and loving this man. The calm I feel is nearly tangible, knowing this. I'm ready.

Hand in hand we walk, then bounce, towards the dance floor. Sensing the crowd's mood, the DJ feeds off of our energy and puts on "September" by Earth, Wind and Fire, a song that no one can sit still on. Davis is in the zone now, grooving along to the beat, his shoulders moving up and down in time to the music. I join in with his infectious energy, dancing with abandon. The whole dance floor is alive, turning, gyrating, left to right, right to left, and back again. We're determined to have a good time this evening, not letting the circumstances, or our formalwear, get in the way.

I'm transported, my body's rhythm matching his own, until suddenly the music begins to slow down, changing to John Legend's "So High". The dance floor begins to thin out, leaving a smaller number of couples out here with us. I look around, and as our bodies start swaying to the music I see we are the youngest couple out here. Holding him close, with Davis whispering words of love in my year, now it feels like we are alone in our pas de deux. I pull away briefly to look at him, and notice that his deep, dark eyes are sparkling as they smile back at me. His smile is one of pure joy. I hope we will always smile this way at one another, always feel this joy when we're together.

How is it that I know my heart is safe with this man? I just do. No longer bound by the pain of my past, I feel free. I know that Davis and I are meant to be together. I'm certain this time.

Tears spring up, blissful tears, elated tears of understanding as I consider my love for Davis. But most of all, I'm so cognizant of God's love for me, and how I understand myself a little better than before. I know this girl, this woman…I see her inside and out. I wear her flaws unabashedly, I love myself, and all of my imperfections, in ways that I never did before. It's not Davis completing me, no; I'm embracing something much different than that. It's the knowledge that in Christ I am complete, fully known and fully loved. And though no one will exchange vows today, to this feeling, and to accepting His best for my life, I will always, without guilt and without hesitation, say YES.

{THE END}

EPILOGUE

New Beginnings

You've probably noticed that I haven't written as many blog posts lately. That's a good thing, actually. The danger with the online world is that you get so busy posting about life that you forget to actually live and enjoy your life. I'm still rooted and grounded in what's most important to me: Faith, Family, Friends. Work and play and all those things are just the icing on a wonderful, sometimes a little messy, tastes better than it looks cake that I call life. But it's my life. It's the one I've been blessed with. And it doesn't have to look perfect, or be perfect. No matter what my past looked like, no matter what the future holds, as I stand here in the present, from this view, only one word can describe my feelings about it all: Grateful.

Until we meet again, Candy Girl

The last six months have been a whirlwind. With change comes the hope of something new, or different, or at least something a little better than before. Mama has completed her chemo, and her doctors are hopeful that her cancer is gone for good this time. I don't know who was more overjoyed when her last scan came back clear: me and Thad, or Daddy himself. He's been a dedicated nurse to Mama throughout this process.

  She lost her hair, as was expected, but has now opted to wear it in an easy, low-maintenance, buzz cut. It's actually quite becoming, and Aunt Cora had her hair shaved off during Mama's treatment, as a show of unity with her only sister. The two of them are closer than ever, and I'm convinced that nothing will separate their love and support for one another.

  Shelby gave birth to a beautiful, bouncing, baby boy. I don't know if it's the breastfeeding or the ways in which Dale has been so attentive, but she seems a lot more mellow now. I sent her a gift basket to welcome the baby, and I not only received a lovely, handwritten, thank you note, but she was also gracious enough to facetime me to personally express her thanks and show me her little cherub, Dale Jr. I know he'll end up being Little DJ to the family, no matter how hard she tries to get us to call him Dale as well. I'm glad to see that motherhood has seemed to change her for the better. I hope the changes are permanent, and wish her nothing but the best.

  As I sit here in my cubicle, tapping my feet with excitement, I'm struggling with containing my enthusiasm. The piece that Cam and I developed regarding the protests, and the school board's eventual decision to change their policies on student discipline and terminate teachers that had demonstrated clear bias in their punishment, was met with a tremendous community response. It was also met with critical acclaim and buzz from our field as well, and now Cam and I have been nominated for an Alabama Broadcasting Association Award for that effort! We're so excited!

Did I mention that Carol, our longtime lead anchor, was heavily recruited by our sister station in New Orleans? She's left sweet little Oak City for The Big Easy. There's been a lot of interest in the position already, which is to be expected. She was the heart and the face of WLNN for so long. But to now have learned that Wes has been advocating for me among station leadership? I honestly was not expecting to hear that. I'm still prayerful, but I know that if God desires for me to become the lead anchor, then the position is already mine, no matter who applies.

Cam steps up to my cube, stopping to closely inspect the large arrangement of periwinkle hydrangeas and white lilies delivered less than an hour ago.

"Ok now, Reese Joseph. I'll give it to Davis, the brother has good taste. Most ladies would be happy with a dozen roses and call it a day."

"He knows hydrangeas are my favorite." I reply, smiling.

It's true. He knows that about me and so much more. It was so sweet of him to send the congratulatory beauties to me. And while in the past I might have shied away from revealing too much about myself at work, it's still nice to be able to share that Davis is my man. And Cam sees it, too.

"You're glowing, Reese. This Davis is alright with me, not that you need my permission, of course." Cam says, but I know what he means. Davis is my work brother, and it's good to know that he approves of Davis. Because I sure do.

"So what time should we stop by?" He asks, and my smile widens.

Ebony and Cam. Cam and Ebony. It's all hush-hush here at work, but they're kind of a thing now, it's cute. And soon. I try to stay out of their business, trying to let the two of them figure it out for themselves. But he's a great guy, and after that mess with Braxton, Ebony could certainly use a real one to show her what real love is. And Cam is a real one. We'll see where it goes, but I'm optimistic, and even Meka approves. Braxton who, baby?

Tameka and Darryl are another story altogether. They still have their ups and downs, and a recent cloud nine season means Chloe will be a big sister in December. For better or for worse, they seem committed for the long haul.

We're all supposed to be meeting at Davis' town home later for a little award celebration. Davis asked if I would mind, and even though I don't want everyone making a fuss about it, it's nice to be recognized for our efforts. I know Cam feels the same way. Davis even invited Daddy and Mama, and his mother, too. Daphne is in town, and so is Thad, so why not, the more the merrier. I don't know where Davis will put everyone, but what the hey, we will have a good time together. It will be a full house, to say the least. Daddy and Thad welcomed Davis into the fold with open arms. Daddy did, at least. Thad still needs convincing, but that's a big brother for you. Speaking of family, I'm still not Mrs. Richards' favorite, either. We have, however, developed a level of mutual respect for one another. I can live with that.

I asked Davis what I could bring, but you know him, he's the master chef between us. So I'm going to bring myself looking cute, lol. Mama asked to ride with me, but I don't mind. She can always ride back with Thad, or maybe even Daddy, if she'll give him the time of day. She's seemed pretty generous lately. Let me just finish this last broadcast, filling in until Carol's position is filled. After I sign-off the 5PM newscast I will be ready to hit the door and head home to get dressed.

~

It's a beautiful summer evening, the mild temperatures a welcome respite from our latest heat wave. My beige, lacy sundress and nude heeled sandals are simple and elegant, and I've kept my makeup fresh and sun-kissed. Looking good and feeling good this evening. I check in with Mama, who says she is ready, which means the Joseph Ladies are ready to go.

We're riding along, making conversation about this and that, when Mama calls an audible.

"Reese, baby, I'm so sorry for the inconvenience, but we need to make a stop at a friend's house, first." Now Mama knows I don't want to be late, well, later than I would usually be. And we are already pushing it. But she knows I will do anything I can for her, so I don't see the need to deny such a simple request.

"Sure, Mama, just tell me where to go."

Mama tells me to get on Kensington instead, so I change lanes and take the next right at the traffic light. This neighborhood looks familiar, I think, as we turn onto Durham Avenue. I recognize the carefully manicured lawns and lovely rows of starter homes. Now I remember; this is where the two-bedroom I fell in love with, but didn't buy, is located. Now I'm intrigued.

We don't continue in the two-bedroom section though, no, we turn again and find ourselves in the three-bedroom section of the subdivision.

"You know Mama, I almost bought a home in this neighborhood last year."

"Oh, did? Don't say." Is her ambiguous reply.

"Mama, whose house are we going over?" I ask, curiosity getting the best of me.

"I thought I said we were going by a friend's house, Reese? And there it is, there it is right there. The white one." I look over to where she is pointing, and I gasp, taking in the farmhouse themed color, columns, and shutters. It even has a two-car garage and lovely landscaping, making for wonderful curb appeal. It's a replica of the house I wanted, just the three-bedroom version.

I place the car in park, then lean back, waiting for Mama to conduct her business quickly, and notice the music and lights already on in the place.

"Mama, I'll wait out here." I say, but Mama isn't having it.

"Reese, you will not wait out here like you are my Uber driver. No ma'am, at least come in and be cordial." She says, and reluctantly I get out of the car. Mama's not the "my daughter is on TV" type, but every now and then she still tries to show me off, and it's never a comfortable experience. I trudge behind her slowly, eyes downcast, but Mama is practically bouncing up to the door. She presses the bell, and a moment later the door is opened.

"Mrs. Joseph, I'm so glad you're here." A smooth baritone says, and I recognize the voice of my love.

"Davis?" I say, flabbergasted to see him standing here.

"Reese, hey, you look beautiful, baby." He says, showing off a wide grin.

"Ooh, Davis, the place looks wonderful." Mama says with admiration, and as I cross the threshold I see a home that looks familiar, but yet not. Clearly these are his belongings, with a few added pieces, some things that I don't recognize. But the layout of this home feels perfectly familiar. The floor plan is just like the one I passed on, and even the fixtures seem the same Similar granite, stainless steel appliances, even the large island I loved. It's all here. I look to Davis, but he's focused on arranging to food on the island. I'm still in shock as I turn to see Daddy, Thad, Ebony, Cam, Tameka, Darryl, Daphne, and even Mrs. Richards, all standing near.

The room is brightened by a sea of rose-gold, cream, and champagne colored balloons. Trays of food, mountains of it, are exquisitely laid out across the island, and a lovely two-tiered, fruit and cream covered confection is the crown jewel of the array of culinary delights that await us. Davis has really outdone himself for this occasion. Looking at him again, I see the warmth in the smile that I love so much, and his brown skin is the perfect complement to the linen shirt and tan slacks that he's wearing. Everyone is chatting happily, and the music shifts to something familiar, Ella and Louie playing in the background. Davis extends his hand towards mine, beckoning me to join him on the makeshift dance space that is his great room floor, and I oblige. We're there, the two of us at home in each other's arms, dancing cheek-to-cheek while Ella serenades with "The Nearness of You".

"Davis, I had no idea you had moved." I say, my tone more playful than accusatory. I feel his smile wide against my cheek.

"I hope you don't mind the surprise. It's been in the works for weeks now, but it was all I could do to keep from spilling the beans to you. You're not upset, are you?"

"No, not upset. Just surprised, that's all. Shocked, really. I must've worried Casey half to death checking on you. Now I understand why you've been so busy. But I'm not upset. I think it's a great home. Congratulations."

"That's a relief. All I could think about was keeping it a surprise and keeping you from being upset that I kept it from you. A home is only as good as the company you keep in it. I hope you love it here. I hope we love it here." He says, and the promise of what could be lingers between us.

"Let's go see Esperanza Spalding at the Amphitheatre this weekend." I whisper as we dance, more of a statement than an invitation.

"I'd love to take you, but her concert has been sold out for ages. I tried to get us tickets as soon as I heard about it, but it had already sold out." The disappointment in his voice is obvious, as I knew it would be. My music aficionado would like nothing better than an evening of amazing jazz, and I would gladly share that kind of evening with him.

"Then come *with* me. Accompany me for the evening."

"You have tickets? How did you pull that off?" He asks, his tone a humorous mix of excitement and incredulity.

"You're not the only one who can keep a surprise." I say, giggling with glee as he twirls me around. I notice the people we love surrounding us, many of them smiling and admiring us as we dance together. Euphoria and bliss are the only words that seem to come to mind.

And then, just when I'm getting used to this feeling, something else happens. The music shifts to Maxwell's "Whenever, Wherever, Whatever", and we both slow down. At first I hardly notice when Davis releases my hand, I'm still gently swaying to the beat and caught up in the music. When I do look at him again he's no longer standing with me, but has instead lowered himself, one leg kneeling before me. He's reaching for something in his pocket.

Eyes bright, wide and solemn, the chattering voices of the background begin to fade as I zero in on him. The laser focus of his gaze reaches the depths of my heart.

"Catherine Reese Joseph. Incomparable, amazing, exceptional Reese. My mirror's reflection. My friend and my future. The rib God has fearfully and wonderfully made, handcrafted with wonder, exquisitely fashioned just for me. I love you, Reese. I want to spend my life with you, and loving you, and being loved by you. Will you share your life with me, Reese? Will you marry me, my love?"

Eyes glistening, this beautiful man's voice envelops my body like warm honey, and to my ears he sounds just that sweet.

For the first time in, maybe, perhaps ever, I'm saying yes to love in my spirit. Yes to a forever love that can only be found in Christ Jesus. Yes to my happiness, yes to letting go of my past, to living in the present, to trusting that my future will be His very best for me. Yes to Davis, yes, but mainly yes to Reese. For I am no longer bound by who Reese was, but I am committed to who Reese is becoming. To who Reese will be. And though Davis doesn't complete me, because I was already whole in Jesus, I know that we are better together. With a hope that is anchored in God, my hope will never fail. And so, without hesitation, without question, without any doubts, I can truly say yes.

So I say "Yes", and never look back. And this time, I mean it.

AND TROUBLES RISE

AND TROUBLES RISE GROUP DISCUSSION QUESTIONS

Your reading group can use these questions to get the conversation started!

1) Which character in AND TROUBLES RISE did you most relate to? Why?
2) Which relationship (platonic, familial, or romantic) did you most relate to?
3) How does Reese seem to lean on her faith in times of struggle? In times of triumph? How do you lean on your faith in good and bad times?
4) Do you feel the friendships portrayed in this novel celebrate and uplift women? Why or why not?
5) Out of fear of disappointing her friends, Reese agrees to their matchmaking attempts despite her disinterest. How did this habit hinder or help her friendships and romantic endeavors?
6) True love is defined quite differently by Reese, Ebony, and Tameka. Which one of their views most closely models your own philosophy on love?
7) Ms. Bean opines that "Everybody needs someone. If they say they don't they are a fool and a liar." Do you agree with her opinion? Why or why not?
8) Reese struggles with her role and visibility within the community, and repeatedly disagrees with Dylan. Have you ever dealt with a "Dylan" in the workplace? How have

your professional experiences mirrored their encounters?
9) Mrs. Richards and Reese base their perception of one another through the lens of their individual relationship with Davis. Is this fair to one another? What could it mean for their future relationship?
10) Ebony was willing to sacrifice her own happiness in order to gain a husband. What are reasonable sacrifices to make in relationships?
11) Reese's refusal to let go of her past complicates her present relationships and nearly jeopardizes her future. How is letting go part of the healing process? Why is it necessary for forward progress?
12) Reese's willingness to forgive Phillip is rooted in what she witnessed between her parents. How can the examples we've seen (both healthy and unhealthy) affect our own relationships?
13) Davis is everything that Reese never knew she needed. Why is it often difficult to accept God's plan for us when it doesn't meet our expectations?
14) What were you most surprised by in the novel? Did the ending resolve your lingering questions?

Would your reading group like to host a virtual or in-person chat with the author? Morrisa would love to hear from you!

www.morrisatuckwrites.com

morrisatuckwrites@gmail.com

AND TROUBLES RISE

AND TROUBLES RISE

Exclusive Excerpt from PLAYING CHURCH, Sequel to TIMES LIKE THESE, arriving early 2022!

THE WELCOME MAT

"Reverend, I need to meet with you privately." Eight of the most dreaded words that a pastor will ever hear. It's been my experience in over twelve years of ministry that not much good seems to follow those words. It could mean that a parishioner has recently been diagnosed with, or is losing their battle with, a terminal disease. It could mean that there is infighting among the deacons' board (or just fill in the blank with any and every church auxiliary). Or, it could mean that the lonely sister in the third pew needs a little extra attention from her dearly beloved pastor. As a happily married husband to my beautiful Marianne, that third option is the one that still makes my skin crawl. There's not really a clean and easy way to reject someone without causing hurt feelings. Some of my colleagues choose to yield to temptation and suffer the consequences that inevitably will follow. I prefer to resist the devil so that he will flee.

But here I am, seated in the plush, comfortable chair reserved for the senior pastor that rests in the center of Third Day's pulpit. I have an excellent view of the entire sanctuary. I see the sister in the middle of the mezzanine who's about to feed her toddler more goldfish crackers, occasionally placing one in her mouth as well. I see the usher desperately trying to get her attention, focused on escorting her to the fellowship hall to continue the child's, and the mother's, snack. I see the young couple near the back, about college aged, I think, more interested in flirting with one another than actually participating in service. There are three, no four, different members in various stages of restfulness. Only one is actually snoring, but the drooping heads of the others confirms that they are most definitely asleep. I even see the brother on the fifth row pew who is boldly taking selfies right in the middle of service. And we haven't even made it to the general offering yet.

 Sitting here, looking out among the congregation and listening to the melodious voices of the choir, I'm reminded of the mess I inherited at Third Day. The previous pastor, the late Reverend Allen Parker, was found slain in the bedroom of his lover's home. The lover, Sister Jasmine Gilbert, was also a member of Third Day, and nearly twenty years his junior. His widow, Sister Rachel Parker, has since become one of our most faithful members. She is sitting behind my wife on the second row. Shortly after I was installed as the new pastor, the church was rocked to its core when it was revealed that someone from this congregation was responsible for their deaths. From what I have heard and pieced together from other members, Reverend Parker was just the latest victim in a long line of church administrators embroiled in scandal. Only God can help me break the chains that the enemy has held on Third Day for far too long. Only God.

 Still, I'm hopeful as I look out at the congregation. Down, but not defeated, there is only one way for Third Day to go from here. Up. Yet, I'm cautious, my BS sensors (spiritual discernment at its finest) in high gear as I recall the words from Sister Monroe, Third Day's faithful financial secretary of over 30 years. I see her bright, toothy smile replaced with a tight, forced one. There's a look of concern in her eyes and not a snow white curl moves out of place. So when she said, "Reverend, I need to meet with you privately" in my study this morning, and shortly thereafter we agreed to meet after morning worship, I know it can't be good. Whatever it is, only God can help me.

~

"Baby, what were you thinking about up there? You seemed a million miles away today." My lovely wife, Marianne, whispers in my ear as she leans forward to embrace me. It's not the greeting I would have liked to hear, but it's understandable. My mind was all over the place this morning, and I feel like I made a mess of the sermon.

"We'll talk about it later, love." I whisper back, giving her the "church appropriate" hug and kiss on the forehead that our members have come to expect from us. I never miss an opportunity to show the church that I love my wife. We try our best to model a happy, healthy relationship to the watchful eyes of others. As a pastor, it's not enough for me to love her behind closed doors. Safe from the mess of the church, our home remains a sacred place for us. Still getting to know us, Third Day doesn't yet realize the depths of my love for my wife. But they will.

After our embrace, she slides beside me, finding her place carved out to join me as we fellowship with the hundreds of members and guests attending service today. Hand after hand, smiling face after smiling face, we stand there until the last parishioner has made their way forward to greet us. It's a tradition here at Third Day that was started by Reverend Parker. We were only too happy to continue it. Preoccupied with Sister Monroe's request to meet, I meander through the final remarks and benediction. Once service is dismissed, I leave Preston in the First Lady's study with his mother, then slowly tread toward my own office. I'll have just minutes to get changed before Sister Monroe arrives. And no, I am not looking forward to it.

~

Seemingly moments later I am greeted by the sound of a gentle knock at my door. Thankfully I changed quickly, disrobing and freshening up in my suit in no time at all. I open the door to welcome the church's financial secretary in for an impromptu meeting.

"Yes, Sister Monroe?" I ask uncertainly, a hint of worry no doubt furrowing my brow. Motioning for Sister Monroe to take a seat, she offers a small smile, dusting her skirt off and gently sitting in one of the chairs facing my desk. Though the chairs are plush and stately, coordinating perfectly with the rest of the room's décor, I notice that she doesn't recline to make herself more comfortable. No, I can't help but notice that she continues to sit near the edge.

Something is amiss, and I can't quite discern if she is expecting the worst or simply hoping for the best. My guess is that it is somewhere that the two meet, squarely in the middle.

"You wanted to speak with me about a pressing matter, Sister Monroe?" I begin again, hoping this will prompt her to start.

As important as a church secretary and member as she is, I want to show her the proper level of respect. But, with Marianne and Preston waiting so we can leave for Sunday dinner, I have no desire to simply sit and stare at her. Let's get on with it, shall we?

"Well, Pastor, I'm not quite sure where to begin." She says hesitantly, her eyes fraught with worry.

Aha, she must think I'll be upset with her about something. I've passed the honeymoon phase with Third Day, but still very much getting to know the congregation, and they me. Sister Monroe has proven herself to be a loyal, dedicated financial secretary in the short time that I've known her, despite the rumblings I've already heard. Plus, she's come with stellar recommendations, which should ease anyone's misgivings. Yet something in her demeanor gives me pause, and I make the choice to proceed with caution.

"Sister Monroe, please don't feel the least bit intimidated by me or what I might say or do in response. This is a safe space for you to share whatever is on your heart with me." I say, my tone tender.

Her face starts to brighten at this expression. Shoulders relaxing a little, she releases the tight hold she had on the arms of the chair, easing back just a bit. I can almost see the gears turning in her head as she carefully contemplates her next words.

"Pastor, I'm so glad you feel that way. Lord knows I've been struggling with how to tell you this." She says, wringing her hands together.

"And…" I interject, pausing deliberately.

"And I hate to bring up another member, I really do. But it must be said that one of the deacons had conspired with Reverend Parker to use church funds to support his mistress."

"What did you say?" I exclaim, completely taken aback by this admission. I hear my volume increase considerably. "Please repeat that again."

Sister Monroe sighs heavily, placing a hand over a heart as if pledging allegiance to this confession.

"Pastor Dexter, you have to know how deeply this whole scandalous mess has troubled me. I loved Reverend Parker, and I love our deacons. But to discover that they were misusing church funds, and then attempted to cover it up, Lawd have mercy, that just really gets my goat!" She cries, her tone indignant.

I'm shocked by her words; not that this happened, but that she just confirmed everything that Sister Parker informed me about regarding this situation. Clearly Sister Monroe doesn't know that Sister Parker discussed the matter with me, and clearly she has no idea what was discussed. How could she have, unless she had a secret camera or was a fly on the wall?

The sheer audacity of this little dressed up, wrapped in hypocrisy church woman. Ma Bess used to always say that there was more hell underneath long skirts than short ones. I guess she knew what she was talking about. Sister Monroe has willfully and gleefully omitted her own role as financial secretary. I could usher her out of my office right here and now, but I believe a more tempered approach may be necessary at this time.

"I don't know what to say, Sister Monroe. I simply can't believe that church leaders were capable of such things." I say so convincingly that I believe it myself.

"Yes, Pastor, I was in denial myself." She says, her head shaking forcefully. "I'm just so disappointed by their deception. And at Third Day's expense, no less."

I know better, but despite that I continue to press on, giving her the rope that she needs to hang herself.

"Sister Monroe, Ma'am, I have to ask you to walk me through just how you discovered this. It's just so much to take in." I implore, bracing myself for what's to come.

"Well, Pastor, let me just say that I suspected something was going on for some time, but I couldn't find it in my heart to accuse anyone, I just couldn't."

She's bold in her lies but not daring enough to look me directly in the eyes as she says this: a tell-tale sign that untruths will be flowing freely from her tongue.

"So, when exactly did you come to the conclusion that this was taking place?" I press again, still waiting for the slip of the tongue that will implicate the accuser.

"Reverend, I began to look more closely at the clues being placed before me. They were just so secretive, the two of them. Always meeting in the corner somewhere."

"Discussing church business, I assume?"

"What they was discussing was anybody's guess, but I know, that if it had anything to do with this church I was going to make it my business to find out what it was."

"But Sister Monroe, wouldn't anything suspicious, like an unexpected check request, for example, have to come through you?" I ask, increasingly doubtful of her story.

"Not exactly. Clearly they went out of their way to take measures into their own hands. They circumvented our entire record-keeping system in order to carry out these crimes against the church."

"You bring up a great point, Sister Monroe. I would say that this is the perfect time to review our current procedures to make sure that something like this never, ever happens again."

"Wait, wh-what?" Sis Monroe stammers, my response clearly different than the one she expected to receive.

"Oh yes, Sister Monroe. I am certain that this is the best time to review our protocols from the top down. We need to thoroughly investigate our current processes and take the necessary steps to prevent future abuse." I'm looking at Sister Monroe squarely in the eyes, and I notice that her expression protests before the words even come out of her mouth.

"Now Pastor, I think what had happened was an unfortunate episode that is highly unlikely to be repeated. Reverend Parker isn't even with us anymore, God rest his soul."

"You're right about that, but corruption can linger. I strongly disagree that it couldn't be repeated. As a matter of fact, I think one of the only ways for us to safeguard our church is to do what we can now to make changes that will have a positive impact. It may not be easy, but the work is needed now to better prepare Third Day for the future."

"But Pastor, I…"

AND TROUBLES RISE

"And I just want to thank you for bringing this matter to my attention Sister Monroe. Now that it is on my radar, you can rest assured that I will give it the attention it deserves and keep a watchful eye on any further developments." I say, walking toward the door and smiling as Sister Monroe dejectedly moves from her seat to where I am standing. Yes, I can tell that this won't play out as she intended. I may be Third Day's newest pastor, but I refuse to be the most naïve.

"Thank you, Pastor." Sister Monroe says automatically, continuing through the doorway and into the hall.

"No, Sister Monroe. Thank you!" I say, smiling broadly until she's safely out of sight. I wait a moment before gently closing the door behind her. Wiping my brow, I take a deep breath, exhaling a prayer of relief. Being a pastor has its perks, but dealing with hellacious saints like Sister Monroe just isn't one of them.

Playing Church Arrives Early 2022!

Third Day Missionary Baptist Church has a penchant for scandal, drama, and mischief, earning the reputation of sending most pastors running for cover. Enter Paul Dexter, an unorthodox leader with just the right mix of faith, wisdom, and discernment to shepherd Third Day. His secret weapon: a loyal partner and formidable teammate in his wife, the lovely Marianne. Accustomed to working together, Third Day represents a stronger challenge than they

AND TROUBLES RISE

have ever faced before. Church politics and family interference strain the bonds of their marriage, and when a spiritual hurricane threatens their home, church, and district, Paul and Marianne come to learn whether they will only bend, or ultimately break. Grab your church fan for this sequel to

TIMES LIKE THESE!

Meet Author Morrisa Tuck

Believer. Wife. Mother. Daughter. Sister. Friend. Above all, Morrisa Tuck strives to be a Proverbs 31 Woman each day. Morrisa has always loved writing, and professional experiences in non-profit communication and development helped pave the way to her current journey as an author of faith-filled fiction. Morrisa's first novel, TIMES LIKE THESE, was published in October of 2020. As a writer of faith-filled fiction, Morrisa hopes to encourage and inspire readers by offering entertaining and engaging characters that get to the heart of the human experience. Morrisa's writing blends humor, drama, and inspiration, with a clear affection for southern culture. Her work can best be described as being a little sweet, a little sassy, and filled with a whole lot of soul. Kind of like Morrisa! Morrisa holds a Bachelor's Degree in Mass Communication and a Master's Degree in Public Administration from Auburn University Montgomery (AUM). Morrisa is currently a grant writer in the healthcare sector, and has more than twelve years of experience in this profession. Residing in Central Alabama, her greatest joy in life comes from her roles as wife to husband Jamison, and homeschooling mother to her three little kings. In her spare time, Morrisa can be found working in her church, enjoying her family, grant writing to support local non-profits and penning her next works of fiction, greatly influenced by her experiences as a pastor's daughter and wife of a deacon in the beautiful, southern United States. AND TROUBLES RISE is her second novel. Morrisa holds many Bible verses near and dear, and chooses to live out Psalm 146:2 each day. Her writing is forever a song of praise to The Lord.

Connect with Morrisa:
www.morrisatuckwrites.com

Made in the USA
Monee, IL
10 December 2021